PRAIS
THE DEBUT N

MW01042521

"A coming-of-age story without the comfort of padding . . .
A relatable and compelling character [with] a lot of wonderful snark."
— *New York Journal of Books*

"Four stars! Burstein paints a bleak picture of teenage politics and one girl's search to fit in and be loved."
— *San Francisco Book Review*

"A candid story that serves as a cautionary reminder against the power of peer pressure . . . A satisfying read."
— *SLJ*

"If you've ever felt like you didn't belong or didn't know what you wanted to do with your life, then *Pretty Amy* is a must-read for you."
— *Girl's Life* magazine

"Burstein writes this teenage misfit coming-of-age tale . . .
with a strong, assured hand and a sharp tongue. Amy has an authentic, raw teen voice, the sort that is as prematurely cynical and world-weary as Holden Caulfield."
— Alice Marvels.com

"One of the most refreshingly real YA voices I've read in years. If you're looking for a helluva trip . . . please get your hands on a copy of *Pretty Amy*—STAT!"
— E. Kristin Anderson, co-editor of
*Dear Teen Me, Authors Write Letters
to their Teen Selves*

Dear Cassie

[A NOVEL]

Lisa Burstein

Entangled Publishing, LLC
2614 South Timberline Road
Suite 109
Fort Collins, CO 80525

Visit our website at www.entangledpublishing.com.

Edited by Stacy Abrams
Cover design by Alexandra Shostak
Cover photograph by Katrina Wojcik

Library of Congress

2014   378436

Print ISBN 978-1-62061-254-5
Ebook ISBN 978-1-62061-255-2

Manufactured in the United States of America
First Edition March 2013

The author acknowledges the copyrighted or trademarked status and trademark owners of the following word marks mentioned in this work of fiction: Smokey Bear, Civic, Pepsi, Zippo, Vaseline, Styrofoam, Adderall, Rubik's Cube, *Penthouse*, Cheerios, McDonald's, *The Hunger Games*, MTV, Twitter, Ivory, *The Karate Kid*, Brillo, Pepto-Bismol, Superman, Hot Pocket, Facebook, Holiday Inn, Chuck Taylors, *Jersey Shore*

To Tim

For always knowing I could do this and
never once telling me to stop

I Don't Even Want to Say How Many Days to Go

Are you there, Smokey Bear? It's me, Cassie.

I'm in a shitty shack in the woods with nothing to start the fires you are so desperate to keep people from igniting. I also have no cigarettes to light the stuff that starts fires. I'm seriously pretending to smoke this pencil. If I find some matches I may actually end up smoking it.

I'm at a sleep-away camp for criminals—a mosquito pit that's supposed to pass as court-ordered rehab. I have no cell phone, none of my own clothes, and no jewelry. They took the dog-tags my brother gave me. They took the six silver hoops that I have worn in my ears since, like, forever. My holes will probably close up, but jewelry can be used as a weapon. The people forced to be here with me would actually consider using jewelry as a weapon.

I have been given a flashlight. Why that's not considered a weapon I don't know, but maybe it's because it's essential in a place where lights-out comes at lame-ass nine o'clock p.m. You wouldn't want to hit someone on the head with it—even though you sort of want to—because then you would have to write this mandatory "Assessment Diary" in the dark.

If you didn't see the skywriters, I was arrested with my best friends Lila and Amy on prom night with the shitload of pot we stole from the dickheads who stood us up for the dance. I was driving, Lila was being Mirror-addict Lila, and Amy was in the backseat shitting bricks. That's the short story.

I guess this will be the long one.

I'm supposed to write about why I'm here. I'm glad I have a legal reason to blame, because there is no way in hell I am going to write about why I really think I'm here.

No matter what, I can never write about that.

Like I said, it started on prom night.

I was wearing a tight red dress that Lila had picked out. Something I would never usually wear. It made me feel sexy—and normally I don't do sexy—but hell, I was already going to the prom, and honestly, that wasn't something I would normally do, either. Lila was all into it because she had a boyfriend and Amy was all into it because Lila's boyfriend was getting her a date, and, well, I guess I was all into it because it was either that or stay home with my parents. Which I didn't want to do for all sorts of reasons, reasons that will probably be another entry I will be forced to write, so I'll save it.

Lisa Burstein

The night actually started out kind of fun. The three of us dressed up: Lila in light purple, Amy in light blue, and me in red—*fucking Lila*. We were laughing and getting along, but then we got to Lila's boyfriend Brian's house and it all went to shit. He wasn't there. None of our dates was.

I had to give Lila some credit. She was so pissed off about us being stood up by our dates that she actually broke into his house and swiped his marijuana stash.

That's about all I'll give Lila credit for that night.

I'm supposed to leave the arrest behind me, but that doesn't mean I can stop thinking about that red dress hanging in my closet, like a dead body in a freezer, and wondering if my mother has hocked it yet for beer money. Oh, crap, see? Now I'm writing about my family. Moving on . . .

When I landed at the Arcata, California, airport this afternoon, after the four-hour flight from New York, the arrest wasn't even on my mind. It was occupied instead by an asshole in a tight white T-shirt and dark jeans, sitting on a metal bench in baggage claim, who kept staring at me like my hair was made of boobs.

I didn't know what else to do when I got there except sit on that bench—so cold from the air-conditioning that I could feel it through my cargo pants and on the backs of my arms. I held the strap of my duffel bag tight. It made an angry red mark on my hand.

"Waiting for someone?" he asked. He didn't turn to look at me, just talked like we were two old men sitting next to each other in the park. He had wavy brown hair, desperately in need of a cut.

"Not for you," I said. We were both sitting there looking

around—both obviously waiting for someone. Why did he care who I was waiting for?

"Who, then?" he asked, not at all understanding that I didn't want to talk to him. Maybe he was that stupid, or maybe he was that much of an asshole.

"Get lost," I said. Even without the cigarette I was dying to smoke, I needed to play it cool, at least until I saw the people in uniforms. Would they be dressed in, like, medical whites, or would it be more like policemen?

I put another stick of cinnamon gum in my mouth, but I didn't offer him any. My brother, Tim, had bought me one of those Plen-T-packs. He gave it to me that morning when he dropped me off at the airport in my Civic, which he was going to take care of while I was gone. At least my car wasn't being punished like I was for being there on prom night.

Tim had never been to rehab, but he'd been to war just like my dad, and he knew gum could be my new addiction, could be one small thing that might keep me sane. He was right. I needed all the gum I could get.

I swallowed a mouthful of cinnamon spit.

"Your mom," the asshole sitting next to me said.

"What?" I turned to him. He had that perfect skin some guys have that looks like it belongs on a girl—dewy and glowy and rosy and not all that masculine.

"You waiting for your mom?" he asked.

Did I look that young? That lame? Sure, I was still seventeen. My lawyer had said that was what saved me—made it so I could be sent to rehab. I guess it was good my parents didn't hold me back in kindergarten like my teacher had suggested.

Of course, if they had, I wouldn't have been going to the prom that night anyway.

I wouldn't have even known Amy and Lila.

"No," I growled. "Screw my mom," I added, though I'm not sure why. I didn't mean that, not really. I didn't give two shits about my mom. I had enough to deal with without thinking about her. Screw him for bringing her up.

"Poor you," he said.

Right, *poor me*; maybe it was true. I was here. Amy wasn't— she got probation for ratting me out. And Lila wasn't—she took off to God knows where. So that left me, Cassie, to deal with this bullshit all alone. Fuck them all anyway.

"What do you want?" I asked.

He shrugged, one of those infuriating shrugs that said he knew exactly what he wanted but wasn't about to tell me. He started smacking the tops of his thighs in that way guys who play drums do.

Guys who want you to know they play drums.

I watched his hands, slapping like his legs were bongos. He was wearing a thumb ring. *Um, yeah.*

"Had to leave my set at home," he said.

I rolled my eyes and sighed heavily, something I usually reserved for people I knew much better and had more time to hate. "I'm not interested," I said. I looked at the automatic doors. How much longer could I sit here without pulverizing this guy into soup?

"In what?" he asked, still slapping his knees like there was a crowd watching, cheering him on.

I continued to stare at the automatic doors and tried to

ignore him. Would the people in uniforms be holding a sign with my name, or would I hear it over the loudspeaker? Would there be more handcuffs? I touched my wrists.

"I'm Ben," he said, stopping his concert to turn to me. His eyes were wide, like sunny-side-up eggs with brown yolks.

"Good for you," I said, stuffing another piece of gum in my mouth.

He laughed and touched the back of his neck. "Not really."

"Am I supposed to tell you my name now? Is that how it works? You tell me your name and I tell you mine and then we slobber all over each other?" I spoke fast, faster than I meant to. Mostly because he made me think about Aaron, because I was always thinking about Aaron, how I wished I had told him to fuck off the first day I met him, instead of slobbering all over *him* and having everything lead where it led.

Wishing I could take it all back. Hit rewind and erase.

"What are you talking about?" Ben asked, starting to laugh, a laugh I think was supposed to let me know he would never consider slobbering all over me.

I felt my face tighten, felt my hands go into fists. I squeezed them hard, so hard that I could feel my nails stabbing into my palms, forming red, angry crescent-moon welts.

"Calm down, Hulk," Ben said, laughing harder, his mouth like a back-up singer going *o-o-o*. My breath went heavy, hot. I was going to destroy him.

I had lied to Amy. I had lied to everyone. I guess I could have told her that I had actually shared that Pepsi with Aaron when he came to see me at work at Pudgie's Pizzeria instead of throwing it in his face for being one of the guys to stand us up on prom night. That I had shared other things, too. That he

Lisa Burstein

bit my neck with his crooked front tooth and licked the inside of my ear and made me whimper; that I had actually fallen for him.

That he had fooled me.

Never again.

I looked at Ben; he was still laughing. I was ready to hit him, but instead I touched my stomach just below my belly button and put another piece of gum in my mouth.

"Too much cinnamon can kill you," Ben said.

"Good," I gurgled, practically choking on the wad. It was getting too big to chew, but there was no way I was spitting my gum out because of this guy. I pictured it growing over my tongue, my teeth, red, globular like a reptile heart.

The automatic doors swished open and a guy walked in wearing a uniform the color of a paper bag. He had one of those square heads and a brown buzz-cut so short it looked like pieces of tobacco on his scalp. I recognized the cut, army issue.

Damn, I need a cigarette.

He *was* holding a sign—two signs. One read Cassie Wick; the other read Ben Claire.

"Looks like we were waiting for the same person." Ben snickered, heaving his duffel bag over his shoulder and walking toward the door.

Fuck.

The white van we rode in smelled like puke, which didn't help what was already happening in my stomach. I'd never been

carsick before, but I was blaming my shaken-snow-globe insides on that.

Ben and I didn't talk as the city roads turned to country
roads, turned to woods on either side of us. Trees taller than
electrical poles and bark the color of brick flew past. I opened
the pop-out window next to me; the air smelled like cedar and
recently dug-up graveyard soil. We were very far away from
anyone and anything and only going farther.

I hated the woods. The bugs, the openness, the fact that
anything can come at you from anywhere, that you can be
lost and *never* find your way back. Hello? *Blair Witch Project*?

I felt anxious needles pinch the tips of my fingers—not a
feeling I was used to and not a feeling I wanted to get used
to. I gripped the seat in front of me and tried to breathe, but
it was like someone was jumping up and down on my chest.

*Where the hell are we going? What rehab joint is in the
middle of nowhere?*

The driver wasn't talking, just clearing his throat every
twenty seconds, like he needed to remind us he was there; like
at this point either of us was going to do anything, anyway.

Finally, the van moved off the country road to a gravel one.
Little rocks popped like popcorn under the tires as we pulled
in at a sign that read: Turning Pines Wilderness Camp—
Helping Teenagers, One Life at a Time.

Camp? Fucking *camp*? My parents shipped me all the way
to California to sleep in dirt? I hadn't gotten any details about
where I was going before I left. Sure, I didn't ask, but I just figured it would be rehab in a building, in a hospitalish building.
Could they have known that this was where they were sending
me? Would they have cared?

Lisa Burstein

I watched the back of the square-headed guy's square head. No explanation, no words, only his throat clearing. We passed one boarded-up shed, another, and another.

I pictured demonic kids singing, *Turning pines no turning back*. They were standing in a circle holding hands, repeating the words ring-around-the-Rosie-like, wearing dirty doll dresses and patched-up overalls.

Camp meant woods, meant bugs, everywhere, all around me, for the next twenty-nine days. I could already feel the disgusting tickle of spiders crawling on my arms—the gross daddy-long-leg ones that looked like the reflection of a regular spider in a fun-house mirror. Ticks would suction to my toes, mosquitoes would buzz as loud as helicopters in my ears.

Fuck. Fuck. Fuck.

Ben looked at me and cocked his head. I'm pretty sure my face was white and I was sweating like I was getting paid for it.

"First day is always the hardest," he said, so quietly he almost didn't say it. He thought I was having withdrawals, and I guess I was, but not from drugs—from civilization, from lack of bug spray. If I saw anything that had more legs than a dog I was going to lose it, and I couldn't lose it. Not in front of Ben, or Square Head, or anyone else I was about to meet.

I didn't *do* losing it.

The van stopped. "Wick, out," Square Head commanded.

"Seriously, here?" I asked, but I knew I was stalling. I could live in this van for twenty-nine days. At least it had doors that locked, windows that closed, a radio.

"Now," Square Head yelled, not even answering my question. And I realized whatever tactics I'd used to survive in the world outside this place were probably not going to cut it here. Ben turned to me and smiled, like he'd realized the same thing.

I climbed over him and reached for the door. "See you, Cassie," he whispered. Then he winked at me. I was too freaked out to care, which was good because if I hadn't been I might have kicked him in the groin.

A woman wearing the same brown uniform as Square Head was waiting for me in the middle of an open field. The uniform hung on her skeletal frame. She looked like a Brownie—like a very tall Brownie. The girl not the food. Her graying-black hair was in a braid and the skin on her face was so tight it was like she was in a wind tunnel.

"Welcome, Wick," she said. I was noticing a pattern: last names were first names here. I also noticed she was wearing shiny black combat boots. Her nametag read: RAWE. With a name like that she must have had a horrible experience in high school. No wonder she was here trying to make other teenagers' lives miserable.

I dropped my duffel bag on the ground and waited. It was dusk and I could already feel the mosquitoes starting to swarm, starting to jump on my arms like they were trampolines.

"You know why you're here and you know what you've done. It's my job to make sure you never do it again." She was standing so straight I thought she might tip over.

I nodded. I had learned how to nod in court. Nodding was easier because I could be sure I wouldn't say something I might regret.

I slapped at a bite on one arm then the other. A buzz got close, filling my ear, and I smacked the side of my head. This

Lisa Burstein

wasn't rehab. Rehab was supposed to be like a spa where you woke up in your nurse-made bed each morning and pretended to give a shit. This was my nightmare.

"I'd pick up your duffel if you don't want fleas," Rawe said, looking down at it.

Fleas. I pictured them crawling like ants on a giant hot dog. I picked my bag up and smacked at it like it was on fire.

"This won't be easy," Rawe said, making the words heavy with meaning. "This program is part wilderness survival skills, part personal rehabilitation."

All torture.

"We are the first group to be housed at this particular camp, so we get the unique privilege of rehabilitating it as well."

"What does that mean?" I asked.

"It means you'll be fixing up the grounds and structures for future participants."

Slave labor.

"It will be hard work. A lot of times you'll want to quit, but you know what will happen if you do, right?"

I nodded. It didn't matter what they were going to put us through—I couldn't quit. Quitting would send me right to the jail time I'd avoided. She didn't need to remind me about that—it wasn't so much that I was afraid of going to jail; I dreaded the way my brother would look at me the morning I went in.

"We have a long day ahead of us tomorrow and another long day after that and so on," she said. "Any questions?" Her diamond-hard eyes looked me up and down, seemingly wondering whether I had what it took to make it through.

I was pretty sure the answer was no.

"Is it just the two of us?" I flashed forward, this straight-laced woman with boot-eyeholes up to her chin and me for twenty-nine more days. It would be enough to turn anyone back into an addict—not that I was an addict. I knew I'd been sent *here* for a very different reason.

They say Karma is a bitch. I guess mine was turning out to be a bitch with fleas and a bony slave driver.

"Nez and Troyer are in the cabin," she said, walking toward what I thought was a storage shed.

I followed her. From behind, her hair kind of looked like a skunk tail.

The "cabin" looked like a shack built by a homicidal maniac—you know, the place he keeps his blood-splattered murder tools and rotting corpses. The door creaked as Rawe opened it—that *a room you enter and may never leave* creak. It was small, had three cots and an open door that led into a room at the back of the cabin, which I hoped was the bathroom. I hadn't peed since I'd left Collinsville.

"Nez," Rawe said, pointing to one cot. A dark-skinned girl, either Indian or Native American, was smacking out a sleeping bag. Her uniform fit her way better than Rawe's did; it was clear she was the kind of girl that everything fit better. She had dark eyes that seemed to have no pupils and hair that fell down her back like spilled black paint.

"Troyer," Rawe said, pointing to a girl sitting up on her cot with her eyes closed. She was all Barbie-doll blond bangs. Her skin was covered in goose-bump-sized acne. At least, I hoped it was acne.

Lisa Burstein

Troyer was also wearing the same uniform that Rawe wore. I looked at the empty cot, where a folded brown uniform lay—probably already crawling with fleas.

"Wick," Rawe said, pointing at me.

I guess those were our introductions. Rawe turned off the one dirty, naked light bulb that stuck out of the ceiling like a nose. Both Nez and Troyer clicked on their flashlights.

"I'd like you to diary for thirty minutes about why you are here," Rawe said, "an introduction to your leaving that part of your life behind." She handed me this notebook and a pencil, then walked to the small room at the back of the cabin and closed the door behind her. I guess it wasn't the bathroom.

"Diary?" I said. I wanted to ask where the bathroom was, but considering what the place looked like, I was also afraid to.

"Assessment Diary," Nez said. "Write whatever, they don't read it. It's for *you*." She mooed the word, then lay on her stomach and started to write.

I looked at Troyer. She was still sitting upright in the middle of her cot with her eyes closed.

"She doesn't talk," Nez said, chewing on her pencil. "Do you?"

"Usually," I said, sizing up Nez. If she was worse than me, I wanted to know it.

"Thank cheese and crackers," she said, her legs scissoring behind her. "I was going crazy. Not that we're allowed to talk, but it's nice to know you're not mute."

"She's mute?" I said, looking back at Troyer, still motionless on her cot. The way we were talking about her, I wondered if she was deaf, too.

"Hasn't said a word in the last six hours, not even to Rawe," Nez said.

"Diary and lights out in thirty," Rawe bellowed from behind her closed door.

Nez stuck out her tongue and went back to writing. I guess she wasn't worse than me, because that definitely wasn't what I would have done.

This is going to be a very fucking long twenty-nine days.

Lisa Burstein

28 Fucking Days to Go

woke up from a dream about Aaron. One of those dreams that you know is a dream while you're having it, which is good because you wouldn't be doing what you were doing if it were real.

We were parked in his father's black convertible, kissing. Actually, we were doing more than kissing. We were doing the thing that led to the thing that led me to Turning Pines. If I wasn't dreaming and he'd tried to kiss me, I probably would have pummeled his face in. But I *was* dreaming, so I kissed him and put my hands in his long auburn hair and felt that pull in my lower stomach—an ache like someone had caught it with a fish hook and was tugging me closer with each kiss. I felt the sky above us humming, the Zippo in the pocket of his jeans smacking at mine.

I woke up with my face in the pillow, Troyer snoring next to me. For someone who didn't talk, she snored like a mother. I touched the part of my stomach below my belly button. Sometimes I feathered it lightly like a scar and sometimes I punched it to make it hurt. I was punching it that morning when Nez caught me.

"Do that in the bathroom," she said from her cot. She leaned up on her elbow to look at me.

The "bathroom." There was one. But turned out it was fifteen paces behind the cabin—a pit toilet. If I hadn't been about to piss my bed, there was no way I would have gone out there alone, at night. But I had, and *awful* can't even begin to describe it.

"I'm not doing anything," I said, wondering why I cared what this girl thought. I didn't care what anybody thought— I was *Cassie Wick*. Well, not anymore. Now I guess I was just Wick.

"Whatever," she said, purring on the *r* like a cat. "I don't care, but if Rawe catches you, she'll make you do two-hundred pushups." Her black eyes flashed at me like fire coals.

What did she think I was doing? I was punching myself, *punishing* myself. Doing what I deserved because of what I had done. Maybe only Rawe was allowed to punish us.

Troyer groaned.

"Holy shish kabob, she makes noise," Nez said.

Troyer picked up her pad and scrawled on it: *Shut up, I'm trying to sleep.* She held it toward us like a surrender flag.

"Shut up yourself," Nez said.

Lisa Burstein

Nez reminded me of someone—me—but with a squeaky-clean mouth. I watched her, her hair like crow feathers against the white pillow. I already knew what I was capable of, and I wouldn't want to be in a cabin in the woods alone with me.

I guess I'd have to figure out what she was capable of.

Troyer scribbled on her pad and held it up again: *You're not supposed to talk.*

"Well, you've got that covered," I said, looking at Nez. There was no way I was letting her think she was the leader. Not that *I* was, but it definitely wasn't going to be her.

Nez laughed, pulled her sleeping bag up to her chin, and leaned forward. "You see any of the guys yet?"

"I rode in a van here with one," I said, laying back and looking at the ceiling, where urine-colored flypaper hung from it like streamers. I covered my mouth and gagged.

"How was he?" Nez asked, her head still poking out of her sleeping bag.

I put my hands behind my head and thought about it. "Annoying," I said.

She sighed. "I mean, like, how did he look?"

"Annoying," I said again. Then I reconsidered. Though *annoying* was the first thing that came to mind, he was also cute—*cutest boy in a boy-band* cute, but doing everything he could to deny it. Maybe that was why I needed to think he was annoying.

I could *never* let a boy be "cute" again.

Never again.

Troyer scribbled something on her pad, then seemed to think better of it and crossed it out.

"More for me." Nez got out of bed and stretched. Her arms and legs were lean, the color of caramel.

"Is it time to get up?" I asked. I assumed Rawe would come out blaring a trumpet or something.

Nez shrugged.

I looked at Troyer. Her head was covered with her pillow.

"So is there a shower, or what?" I asked. A shower was exactly what I needed to wash away the fantasy of Aaron's fingerprints, the illusion of his lips. The things he'd done to con me into believing he actually cared.

"There's a shower house," Nez said, "but Rawe has the key. You can use that for now." She pointed at a bucket full of water, with a washcloth hanging over the side of it, in the corner of the cabin.

"What am I, an elephant?" I said, realizing that it actually would have been better if I were. At least then I could have used my trunk to get to the hard-to-reach areas.

"Good thing there're no mirrors," Nez said, rolling up her sleeping bag.

No mirrors? Lila would have a shit fit. *Lila.* Who knew where she was now? She was smart enough to take off before she could be sentenced, before she could be sent to a shithole like this.

"So, why are you here?" Nez asked, changing into her uniform. She was wearing a hot pink bra and matching underwear. I guess bras weren't considered weapons, though the way Nez looked in hers, I was pretty sure she'd used it as one before.

I'd known this question was coming and I had been ready to answer it, but I guess I thought I'd be asked by some doctor

Lisa Burstein

in a tie, not by some girl in a custodian's uniform and porn-star underwear.

I was here because I'd been arrested for marijuana possession on prom night. We were driving around in my Civic smoking it. I was trying to stay on the road, even though I felt high enough for my car to rise up into the clouds. Lila was bitching about missing her one and only prom and Amy was sitting in the backseat feeling sorry for herself.

I just kept driving, wondering if I would ever have the guts to wear my dress again, ever have the guts to let someone who actually showed up for our date see me in it. Ever have the guts to be the kind of girl who would pick out a red dress for herself.

Then the sirens went off behind us and we got arrested and we went to court and blah, blah, blah, I'm here. There's stuff that happened in the blah, blah, blah—a lot worse than the stuff that happened on prom night—but that's not something I'm ever going to talk about.

"Pot," I said, even though part of the reason I thought I was *here* and not at some resort-style rehab was because of what happened with Aaron—*everything* that had happened with Aaron—the blah, blah, blah. I wasn't religious, but my parents were, and all I'd ever learned my whole life was that doing things like I had done got you sent to hell—and, well, this was it.

"B-o-ring," Nez said, brushing her hair.

I didn't bother asking why she was here. I didn't care. I just put on my brown uniform and made my bed. There was nothing else to do.

Rawe came out of her room a few minutes later and let us know she was giving us the day off from wilderness training to get acclimated.

Get acclimated. She sounded like Amy—that *I'm better than you* smart person way of talking, using words you would never use. Couldn't she say *get settled* or *get your shit together*? Maybe she couldn't say that because we would never feel settled, would never have our shit together.

Unfortunately *getting acclimated* meant being forced to cut up more wood than I have ever seen in my life. It was piled like a garbage-dump-size beaver dam in the middle of an old soccer field. The goals were still there but free of their hammocks, and there was a whitewashed building with a padlock on the door at the far end of the field. It looked like a mess hall. It looked like it had a bathroom with a flush toilet. I wondered if I would ever be allowed to use it.

"Grab an ax," Rawe said. She looked even more severe in the sunlight. The skin on her face was transparent blue-white, so thin it was like I could see her skull underneath.

There were seven stumps lined up with an ax stuck in each one like a sandwich toothpick. I didn't want to grab an ax. I'd never grabbed an ax before. I'd never even *seen* one in real life.

"Company coming?" Nez asked.

"The boy's camp is going to help," Rawe said.

Great, so that would probably include Ben. I wondered if he would turn chopping wood into some kind of drum solo or, even worse, a way to make me start thinking about Aaron again.

"Rawrrrr," Nez growled, clutching her chest like a black-and-white-movie star. She was like Lila on steroids—steroids laced with Ecstasy.

Lisa Burstein

Troyer walked over to one of the stumps, pulled out an ax, and held it. I wasn't sure if she'd left her pad in the cabin or if she just had nothing to say.

"You guys ever cut wood before?" Rawe asked. I felt like she probably should have asked that question *before* she ordered us to *grab an ax*.

"Yeah, all the time back at the ranch," I said, and then I wondered why. There was no one here I wanted to make laugh. No one like Amy who laughed at everything or Lila who laughed as long as the joke wasn't about her; no one like my brother, who I could make laugh with a look.

"Excellent, Wick," Rawe said, clapping her hands together like cymbals. "You can start."

I stood there and stared at my ax, speared diagonally out of the stump like a penguin butt sticking out of the water, and realized words were probably going to mean little in a place where you had to live up to them.

"Any time," Rawe said, her shiny left boot tapping.

"I've used an ax," Nez said, saving me. "Lots."

"Good," Rawe said. "Teach them."

Nez's face melted into a smile. "Can I teach the guys?"

"Nez," Rawe said, in the kind of voice it seemed that Nez had heard already, because she walked toward the stumps without protest. "All of you," Rawe said, looking at me.

I followed Nez and waited.

"Put a log in the center of the stump," Nez said, picking one up and balancing it like a baby block. Her eyes shot to something across the field.

The boys' camp was marching out in a line. They walked with high knees behind Square Head, wearing the same paper-bag-brown uniforms we wore. It was Ben, a skinny kid with braces, a heavy-set kid with curly hair, and a guy with tattoo sleeves down his arms.

"Sweet odds," Nez said, whistling under her breath.

"They're all yours," I said. "Just watch your lips on the one with the chain-link fence on his face."

Troyer seemed to pull her neck into her chest like a turtle.

"Nez, more teaching," Rawe said, standing behind us. She sounded angry enough for fire to be coming out of her nose.

Nez held the ax high and wiggled her butt.

"Nez," Rawe spat. "One more and it's three-hundred push-ups."

"What? It's my technique," Nez said, rearing the ax back and splitting in two the wood in front of her. It sounded like the crack of a bat at a baseball game.

I waited while Troyer lifted her ax. She closed her eyes when she swung, but she hit. When the log cracked down the middle, she opened her eyes with the surprise of a little kid seeing her birthday cake all lit up in front of her.

"Wick," Rawe shouted, "your wood is going to start growing again. Let's go."

I heard the boys march up behind us. I heard Square Head tell them to *halt*. He seemed a lot more army-like than Rawe did. I hated to think it, but he kind of reminded me of my father.

I lifted the ax; it was heavier than I thought it would be. I reared back like you might at one of those carnival games with a bell and smacked. The ax bounced off the wood and forced me back, splaying me right on my ass.

Lisa Burstein

I could hear the guys laughing, could hear *Ben* laughing. The skin on my face seared.

"Silent," Square Head bellowed. But they were still snickering.

"Again, Wick," Rawe yelled.

I sat there for a moment, my tailbone throbbing. What was I doing? I didn't belong here. This seriously sucked. Even Troyer could chop wood, and she couldn't even talk.

"Wick," Rawe said, in the same voice she'd used on Nez.

I got back up, but my legs felt shaky. My ass burned. I stood in front of my stump.

The boys lined up beside us. Ben was directly next to me; he'd pulled his hair back in a red bandana. He held his ax high. I didn't want to watch him, but I couldn't help it.

I wanted to see him fail.

I watched his arms go up and then down, splitting the wood like he was wielding a karate chop.

"Hot," Nez whispered, her eyebrows wiggling.

Ben saw me watching him and winked. I looked down at my uncut log.

"Want some help?" he asked, then stuck his ax into the stump in front of him. He moved it so fluidly, so not like how I moved mine.

"Not from you," I snarked.

"You don't seem like the kind of girl who would take help from anyone," he said, his brown eyes as sharp as his ax blade as he picked it up again.

"Then why the hell did you ask?"

"Because I'm not just anyone," he said, picking up a log and splitting it so hard I felt the ground shake.

I tried to remember to breathe.

I tried to remember that this might be how things started, but it wasn't how they ended.

"He likes you," Nez said.

"Who cares?" I said. I felt my stomach cinch up like a drawstring waistband. I didn't care what any guy thought of me — guys could like me or hate me, but they were never touching me again.

Never again.

"What's his name?" Nez whispered.

"Asshole," I whispered back.

"Wick," Rawe said, her voice exploding out of her like a volcano, "if I say your name one more time . . ."

"Jeez Louise," Nez whispered. "You better make this one."

I lifted the ax, looking at the log like a bull's-eye. I could do this. I *had* to do this. I closed my eyes and thought about Aaron, put his face in the center of the log. I would smash it. I would destroy it. I would annihilate it. Do everything I never had the chance to do.

I swung and hit right in the middle. The log cracked in two.

"I did it," I said, feeling weirdly relieved. No one else could hear me. They were all chopping, too, the sound around me like homerun after homerun after homerun. I turned back to Rawe. I wanted to make sure she had seen.

"Great," she said with a sarcastic thumbs-up. "Only four hundred more logs to go."

Aw, fuck.

Lisa Burstein

Hours later, in bed and diarying, all I can feel is searing, burning pain in my shoulders and hands, splinters I can't even see, and calluses the size of almonds on my fingers. This was supposedly our day off, and it was pretty much the worst day of my life so far.

Well, the worst day I'm willing to write about.

Not that I have to. I'm supposed to be writing about my family.

Rawe said that if we knew where we came from, it would be easier to see how we'd ended up where we'd ended up.

The crap not falling far from the butthole and all that. Or maybe that was just my family.

I can't help thinking about when I was a kid and we had this same assignment in class. Back then I always said, *I have a mom and a dad and a brother and I love them all. And they all love me.*

It was a lie then and it's more of a lie now.

I have a mom, but she's an alcoholic. I have a dad, but he's in the army like my brother and he isn't home a lot. He's deployed most of the year. When he comes home, my mother tolerates us and he tries to figure out everything that has happened while he was gone. When he leaves, my mother gets drunk.

She couldn't even wake up to say good-bye to me the morning I left for this camp. My father had gone on his deployment right after I was sentenced and when I went into my mother's bedroom to tell her I was leaving, she was passed out, unconscious, her empty bottle of vodka sleeping in my father's spot.

Not that I was surprised. She was too drunk to say good-bye to me most mornings, but most mornings I wasn't leaving for thirty days.

When I was little I used to be embarrassed for her. I didn't understand.

But now I do. I know my mother would say she drank because she missed my father, because she didn't know what else to do. It makes me sick that I know this, that I understand what it really feels like to not know what else to do.

That I punish myself, make myself remember, because I don't know what else to do.

Lisa Burstein

27 Fucking Days
to Go

t was still dark in the cabin when I woke up. Troyer was sitting in her bed, a flashlight on in her lap. Even from the side, I could tell that her eyes were closed. I guess she was meditating, but I wondered why someone who didn't talk needed to meditate. Wasn't she able to keep the noise of the world out by keeping her mouth shut?

"What are you doing?" I whispered into the dark cabin.

She turned to look at me, her eyes opening slowly like a bullfrog sunning itself. She blinked once, twice, then turned back and closed them again. Forget Nez—I was beginning to wonder what *Troyer* was capable of.

I could see Nez, a lump in her sleeping bag, could hear her even, long breaths from across the cabin. I tried to fall back to sleep, back into one of the ways I used to turn my thoughts off, but I couldn't. I tossed and turned, seeing Aaron, seeing Ben, seeing the flashing lights of a cop car. I rubbed my eyes and knew that sleep, along with the cinnamon gum that had been confiscated, was another thing that could no longer keep me sane.

After morning chores and a shower (!), we stood around the bonfire pit waiting for Rawe to speak. The pit looked like it had been used in the past for the kind of singing, marsh-mallow-roasting fires we were sure never to have. Our fire was all about survival—staying warm and cooking food and, ap-parently, scaring away the bears that lived in this neck of the woods. I did also consider that Rawe might use a bonfire as a way to get us to open up, the way she was doing with our diaries. Even I knew there was something about being in the dark with a fire going that allowed you to talk like you'd had a couple beers—well, at least when the people sitting around it were normal. It was becoming obvious that *we* were not.

"Okay, get on your knees," Rawe said, not getting on her knees. We were going to learn how to build a fire without matches or a lighter—as if my hands weren't already fists of tenderized meat on the end of my arms. As if they weren't already raw, Rawe.

"There is no way I am getting on my knees," I said, kind of surprised that I did, but maybe like Rawe appeared to be testing us, I was testing her. What would she do if I said no?

"Wick," Rawe said.

"Here," I said, still pushing. It was hard to be afraid of her, she was so thin. Honestly, if it came down to it, I was pretty sure I could take her.

Lisa Burstein

"I'm not going to ask again," Rawe said.

Troyer nudged me, her eyes screaming, *Can we please just get this over with?*

I looked at Nez. I could see she was trying to stifle a giggle.

"Only because I'm tired of standing," I said, kneeling down. Troyer was right—there *was* something to just getting this over with.

"No boys today?" Nez asked.

Rawe shook her head and held two sticks in front of her. They kind of looked like drumsticks, which made me think of Ben and made me glad he wasn't here. At least I wouldn't have to expend the energy I was supposed to put toward building a fire toward failed attempts to ignore him.

"Awesome," Nez said, her body in full mope.

Rawe placed one stick between both hands and threw the other on the pile of kindling below her. I tried to picture her at the kind of bonfires this pit was meant for, telling ghost stories and tales about her grandmother who used to make her apple pie that she would eat with whole milk. It wasn't easy to picture, yet I knew she had to have a life before this one, like we all did.

Rawe started rubbing her hands together—the stick in the middle as if she were warming her hands to give someone a massage. "Like this," she said. "All of you, let's go."

"But won't we have you to start our fires?" I asked, buying time. I might have gotten on my knees, but I didn't want to pick up my stick. I didn't want to do anything with my hands other than bathe them in ice water and lather them with Vaseline. My hands and arms and shoulders ached, felt like they had been jackhammered all night as I slept.

"Not always," Rawe said. She didn't elaborate. She didn't have to. I knew that meant there would be times we would be alone in the woods and would have to start our own fires, so we didn't starve to death, freeze to death, or get mauled by a bear.

I was beyond not looking forward to those times.

I rolled the stick in my hands like Rawe did and tried to ignore the pain.

Troyer wrote something on her pad and held it up. *My hands hurt.*

I was kind of surprised she had the guts to say it—well, write it—because I was pretty sure that was exactly what Rawe wanted. I was pretty sure that was the whole point. As the days went on, there probably wouldn't be a part of our body that didn't feel like it had been through a pasta maker.

"Tough," Rawe said, her lips thin white dashes. "This isn't a hospital. Get building, or it's four hundred push-ups *then* building, which will hurt a lot worse."

I looked at Troyer. She dropped her pad and picked up her stick. The only one of us who had done any push-ups so far was Nez, and considering how badly she seemed to be craving male company, she appeared to enjoy the pelvis-thrusting part of it.

"This would be a lot easier with a guy in front of me to get me in the mood," Nez whispered.

I couldn't help it; I laughed.

Nez played it up, pretending to kiss her stick. She may have been as boy-crazy as Lila, but she was a hell of a lot funnier.

"Wick, you think starvation is a joke?" Rawe asked, spinning her neck as fast as a top to look at me. "If you want to eat, you build a fire." She sounded like she had repeated this a million times before. I was pretty sure she had. We certainly weren't the first set of girls to hear it, and knowing kids my age, we certainly wouldn't be the last.

Our fires were supposed to heat up something that would help us make breakfast—not like that was any kind of incentive for me. It was hard to be hungry when there was a pit toilet waiting for you on the other side. It was hard to be hungry when, for my sanity, I needed to keep my stomach a painful, hollow cavern.

I continued to roll my stick between my fingers in the center of my kindling pile. I wanted to be finished with this before my hands fell off.

"This is lame," Nez whispered.

"Whatever," I said, which was how I was going to have to deal with all of this. I couldn't care either way or I would lose it.

And like I said, I didn't *do* losing it.

I looked at Troyer, tears pricking her eyes as she tried to start her fire. She really was in pain. Pain enough to cry— unless something else was making her cry. Not that she would ever tell anyone what it was. It made me wonder for a moment if she was actually writing everything Rawe was telling her to write in her Assessment Diary, like I am in mine. Well, everything I'm willing to write.

"Keep working," Rawe said, her voice booming. "I'll go get breakfast supplies." I watched her walk away, her braid swishing.

Nez dropped her stick the minute Rawe left us. "What's up with Zipper Lips?" she asked, jutting her chin at Troyer.

"Leave her alone," I said, still rolling my stick. I could feel heat starting to come from my hands. Hot enough to start a fire? Probably not, but I wasn't stopping until I started one. I needed to stare at the flames and try to lose myself in them.

Part of the reason I liked smoking so much was fire—that you could hold something so uncontrollable and deadly in your hand. That you could bend it to your will with simply a flick . . . well, when you were allowed to use a damn lighter.

"Fine," Nez said, looking at me. "Then what's with you?"

"Nothing," I said, still rolling my stick, harder, faster, trying to drown her out.

"Maybe not now," she said, slithering closer to me, "but there was something. I can see it following you around like a shadow."

She could *see* it? Could she see what I was desperate to forget but felt the need to make myself remember? No way. No one but my brother knew the truth and no one ever would. "Why don't you go tongue your stick," I said, not looking at her.

"I'm just saying you're not fooling anyone," she added, her hands on her hips, her arms sticking out like butterfly wings.

"You're not fooling anyone, either," I said, dropping my stick and meeting her gaze. The thing is, I'm not sure why I said it. She was. She was fooling me. She seemed unaffected by everything, by all of this.

"You know the woods can sense if you're uncomfortable," Nez said.

"Nez, please spare me your Native American mumbo jumbo," I said, thinking I could smell smoke, but it might have been the skin on my hands burning off.

Lisa Burstein

"Listen," Nez said, and I could feel her stare tighten. "One of us understands all this"—she gestured, her hands going up—"and one of us is terrified by it. I'm trying to help you. I'm just saying that it can tell, and your feelings breed more fear."

Troyer turned to look at me. She put her stick down and wrote something on her pad. Then she ripped off the sheet of paper, folded it up, and put it in my pocket.

"What, are you passing notes now?" Nez cackled.

"If you want I can write my own note and pass it to you, but it would require surgery to remove," I said. My palms felt hot, as hot as the sun on my face. I was starting to sweat. I could feel it rolling from my forehead to my lips.

"You wouldn't." She laughed. She was joking; she wasn't angry with me. This was all a big joke to her. Ha, ha, ha.

I felt my hand drop and go into a fist almost by memory. This was how I got people to stop. By hitting them and hitting them and hitting them until I saw black.

I hit people because . . . well, I guess that's another entry.

"Are you serious right now?" Nez indicated my hand.

I looked at my fist, calluses on it still shiny bumps not even hardened yet, as squishy as tapioca pearls. If I hit her, they would turn to open sores. How badly did I want to hit her? How much more did I want to hurt?

"Nez, Wick," Rawe yelled, walking back into the circle. She kicked a rock in our direction to wake us from our trance. It fell in between us with a *thud*. "Just because I'm not here doesn't mean you can stop."

I kneeled again, picked up my stick, and went back to it— any excuse to spare Nez for now. She picked up her stick, too.

She pretended to play it like a flute, like a snake charmer might. She seriously was beyond anything I had ever experienced.

"Nez," Rawe yelled, her voice like a gun shot, "if you don't start a fire in five minutes . . ."

I looked at Troyer, her note still in my pocket. She was rolling her stick and trying not to cry, but I could see the pain on her face. She wasn't fooling anyone, either. The difference was that I'm not sure if she was trying to.

I stared at my kindling pile as I worked and wondered why I wasn't crying. Was it because I never cried anymore? When I was a kid and still used to cry, my mother would put me in my room and close the door. She never reacted to it the way mothers on TV did, by hugging me or telling me everything would be okay. She just ignored it. After you're ignored for so long, you start to do other things to get noticed. Not that I want to go into that again, but if you need a refresher it's *Assessment Diary Entry #2*.

In front of each of us, Rawe threw a canteen that hit with a *clang* and a freeze-dried food pack that read MOUNTAIN STEW. "Start you fires or eat it raw, but I can tell you raw tastes like Styrofoam ass." She smiled, her teeth huge against her thin face.

I reached into my pocket while Rawe wasn't looking to read Troyer's note. It said, *Nez is a bitch*.

Maybe Nez isn't fooling anyone, either.

Lisa Burstein

26 Fucking Days
to Go

N ez shook me awake, put her hand on my mouth so I
wouldn't scream. I could taste wood smoke and dirt.
Her other hand went to her lips in a shush. This was it:
I was about to find out what she was capable of. I guess Troyer
was right: Nez was a bitch—a sneaky-ass bitch who was going
to come at me while I was sleeping.

I should have flattened her at the bonfire pit when I had
the chance.

We'd spent the day hiking and hacking out brush from the
trail—*the whole day* from sunrise to sunset walking in a line
and carrying packs as big as sea lions on our backs. Rawe had
warned us about not "touching" any animals we came across
on the trail.

"Animals?" I'd asked.

She started counting off on her fingers. "Mole, raccoon, deer, skunk, weasel, fox, bear, rabbit, chipmunk, wood rat." Luckily she stopped once both hands were full, even though it was obvious she could keep going.

We were surrounded by living, rabid things with teeth and claws. I wondered why she had to warn us. There was no way in hell I was touching anything. Of course, there was always the chance Nez might if it was male.

When we got back that night, Rawe told us to "free-write" in our Assessment Diaries. I was tired of falling for her crap, so I spent the time filling a page with: *there is nothing free about being tricked to feel.*

Maybe I should have been writing my will.

"Put on your uniform; we're getting out of here," Nez whispered, letting go of my mouth.

"Out of here?" I asked, with my sleeping bag still up to my chin.

Did she mean like escaping? I was too tired to escape. My legs felt like cement, my feet like they were on fire. They definitely didn't want me to move. I rolled over.

Nez pulled my sleeping bag so I faced her.

"What gives?" I asked. Maybe she *did* want to fight.

"There's a boys' cabin somewhere at this camp and I'm finding it," she hissed into the darkness.

"So find it," I said, my voice sounding like a shrug.

"Please," Nez begged. I could see her latch her hands together and push them at the center of her chest like she was praying. "Come with me."

"What do you need me for?" I asked.

Lisa Burstein

"I don't want to go alone," she whined. "I'll owe you one," she added, which was enough to make me consider. It would be good to have a favor on reserve. Of course, getting caught would beyond suck.

"But that square-headed guy is in there with them," I said, sitting up.

"He sleeps, doesn't he?" she said. Her eyes shone like the surface of a lake in the moonlight.

"What about Troyer?" I asked, looking at her cot. She was still asleep, or at least pretending to be.

"What *about* Troyer?" Nez sneered.

"She should come, too," I said. There was no way I was going out into the night alone with Nez. It was a sure way for one of us to get killed.

Probably her.

"Ugh." Nez sighed. "Fine, wake her up."

I got out of bed and shook Troyer awake. Her face looked like a baby's—her lips pouted in confusion, her eyes wide with fear.

"It's okay, it's just me," I said, thinking it was most definitely the first time I had ever said that. Usually if I was approaching someone in the dark, it was *not okay*.

She looked at me, at Nez, silently asking, *What?*

"Come on," I said, beckoning her in the darkness.

Troyer sat up and watched as I put on my uniform. "You, too," I said, pointing at hers. It was folded in a tight brown package on the trunk in front of her cot.

"Hurry up," Nez said. I could hear her boot tapping on the floor.

After Troyer and I got dressed, we each grabbed our

flashlights and followed Nez out of the cabin. Troyer closed the door quietly behind her, our flashlights still off.

"What if Rawe wakes up?" I asked. I looked at Troyer. She nodded.

"We tell her we all had to use the ladies," Nez said.

There was no way Rawe would believe that. It was bad enough going out to the bathroom on your own—you did not want to stand next to it waiting for someone else.

We walked down the path to the soccer field, huge cedar trees on either side of us, our flashlights three small spotlights on the ground.

"Do you know where we're going?" I asked.

"I can smell boys," Nez said, sniffing the air, "like meat cooking."

"Any chance you can smell us up some smokes?" I asked. "They smell like tobacco cooking." Being outside at night made me crave a cigarette. Well, to be truthful, *everything* made me crave a cigarette.

Nez ignored me and kept walking. It was definitely the middle of the night. The air had that feeling, like even it was asleep.

"What are we going to do when we find their cabin?" I asked the back of Nez's head. We walked like we had that day when we were hiking, in a straight line, army style.

"I haven't figured that out yet," Nez said.

"If we get caught, I'm going to punch you so hard you're going to need to make out through a straw," I muttered, though I had to admit it felt pretty good being bad again. Other than my break time escapes with Aaron from Pudgie's Pizzeria, I hadn't been out at night doing something I wasn't supposed

Lisa Burstein

to do in a *very* long time. I felt the familiar adrenaline rush, the buzz in my ears.

We stood at the edge of the soccer field, the sky above us filled with stars, like someone flung a football stadium full of glitter into the sky.

"Maybe we should skip the boys' cabin and check out that locked building over there," I said, pointing to the white mess hall. There had to be something inside we weren't supposed to get to, since it was locked. I liked getting to what I wasn't supposed to get to.

"Does that locked building have four boys inside?" Nez asked.

Troyer shook her head.

"Very good, Troyer," Nez said, like she was a puppy.

"We can head to their cabin after," I said.

"There's nothing for me in there," Nez said, waving it away.

I looked at her.

"I am not spending another night alone," Nez said, not bothering to explain more.

I was glad.

Nez turned and started across the field. There was nothing else to do, so I followed her. I could hear Troyer running to keep up behind me. I hadn't noticed it when we were chopping wood, but there was a flagpole standing flagless at the far side of the field. There were also bleachers and beyond that, a baseball diamond complete with dugouts.

"I guess this place really used to be a summer camp," I said.

"Wow," Nez said, not turning around. "You're a fudging genius." She was walking so fast, I was out of breath trying to keep up with her.

"Well, you're a *fudging* bitch," I said. Then I turned to look at Troyer. "You okay?"

She shrugged.

We kept walking, our boots swishing in the grass and our breath sighing. The night air felt sharp in my lungs.

"There it is," Nez said, pointing.

It's not like they were hiding it. The boys' cabin was only a few paces past the far edge of the soccer field and looked exactly like our cabin—as small and as shitty.

"So what are you going to do now?" I asked, putting my hands in my pockets. I felt myself sneer. Now we would see what size balls Nez actually had.

"Duh," she said with her own sneer. "Get one of them to come out, or one of them to let me in." She walked to the side of the cabin. She was about to be totally fucked, and not in the way she wanted to be.

If it was built like ours, there were windows along both sides. That was probably where she was headed. Was she going to climb in? Lila had climbed into Brian's house on prom night after he and his friends had stood us up. When she swiped the pot that eventually got us arrested. This probably wouldn't end any better.

I remember sitting with Amy on Brian's front lawn while we waited for Lila, smoking cigarettes and trying to figure out why the hell I was so pissed off about being stood up by a boy I didn't even know. I knew why Amy was upset and that made sense to me—she had a lot of girlie notions about what prom night was supposed to mean. What didn't make sense was how angry I felt. Maybe because I had allowed myself to be fooled. That was how I felt, like a gullible idiot in a skanky red dress.

Lisa Burstein

I guess that was why I hated thinking about what had happened with Aaron, because he'd made me feel the same way . . . minus the dress.

I could hear Nez heave herself inside the cabin with a grunt. I guess I couldn't blame her. If there were cigarettes waiting for me in there, I would surely be doing the same thing. I would probably be kicking the door down with the boots that felt like anchors on my feet. I guess Nez saw boys like I saw cigarettes.

"Come on," I said, leading Troyer over to the bleachers. "We'll wait over here for her to get busted."

Troyer and I sat on the cold metal. The outdoors made its outdoorsy sounds around us: crickets and mosquitoes and whatever the hell else was out there that I didn't want to think about.

"Nez is pretty fucked up," I said, looking at Troyer.

She nodded.

"Like you said . . ." I put my hands on my thighs. "A bitch."

Troyer smiled, and I wondered if she'd ever talked. If something had happened to her like what had happened to me that had made her stop talking. Was there anything that I had stopped doing because of what had happened with Aaron? Other than letting myself fall for another guy's bullshit?

"Hello, Cassie."

Ben.

Speak of the fucking devil.

I turned. Brace Face and Curly Blond Hair Dude were standing next to him. I guess that meant Nez was in the cabin with Arm Sleeve Tattoo Guy doing *golly knows what.*

Brace Face and Curly Blond Hair Dude ran past Troyer and me onto the soccer field. They sprinted around like they had both drank a ton of coffee and were trying to work off their energy. Ben sat down next to me.

"Why don't you go play with your friends?" I asked, sliding closer to Troyer.

"No thanks," he said, looking at me. I could feel Troyer on the other side of me trying not to giggle.

"You look good in brown," he said, biting his bottom lip.

Ha, ha, funny, like I don't already know I look like shit. Fuck off, Ben.

"You don't," I said, staring at the guys on the field. In the dark, I could only see their skin, their heads and hands floating.

"I thought I looked pretty good," he said, pulling the top of his uniform out so he could see it.

"Go away," I said, turning on and off my flashlight—*click, click, click*. Maybe Troyer knew Morse code. Maybe she could teach it to me. What was Morse code for *Die, you asshole*?

"That's Eagan with the braces," Ben said, pointing to him running by. "Well, Patrick Eagan, and the other one is Leisner, or Kurt."

"Who cares?" I said.

"You're as pleasant as ever," Ben replied, tapping his foot. His boot clanged on the bleacher below. I could tell he was doing it like a drummer would, like he had a bass drum sitting in front of him. He was such an ass.

Troyer wrote something on her pad and passed it to me. It said, *He's cute*. I crumpled the note and stuffed it in my pocket.

Never again.

"Who's that?" Ben asked, stopping his concert.

"Troyer," I said.

Lisa Burstein

"What's her first name?" he asked, looking over at her.

"Why would I ask?"

"Why *wouldn't* you?" he said, and his face went screwy. "I mean, you've been here long enough." He turned to me with those wide brown eyes again. In the dark I could only see the whites.

"She doesn't talk," I said, looking at my hands. They were in fists on my thighs.

"You could still ask her name," he said. He looked over at Troyer. "What's your name?"

Troyer wrote something down on her pad and passed it to him.

"Laura," he said, showing me the paper in his flashlight beam. "Her name's Laura."

"I might not know how to make you disappear," I said, rolling my eyes, "but I do know how to read."

"So Patrick is here for Adderall addiction and Kurt got caught breaking into a competing high school to steal their athletic equipment," he said, ignoring me.

"What are you, a game show host?" I asked. I didn't care why anyone else was here. All I cared about was making it through the next twenty-five days without killing someone.

I guess he knew how to make *me* disappear, because he continued. "That's what the running is about, is all. They have a lot of energy to expel."

"I guess Nez does, too," I said. I turned and looked at the cabin, but it was quiet.

"Stravalaci, Andre—he's the one inside with your friend," Ben said.

"I doubt she cares what his name is," I said. I didn't bother adding, *And she's not my friend*, because I still wasn't quite sure what Nez was.

"You should probably tell her to stay away from him," Ben said.

"Nez can take care of herself." I paused and looked at Troyer. "Well, tonight I guess she needed some assistance, but usually she can."

Troyer's hand went to her mouth and she giggled.

Ben ignored my joke. "Stravalaci brought a gun to school," he said, his skin looking pale. "Said the only thing that stopped him from using it was that a teacher saw it in his pants pocket. That's about as fucked up as it gets."

"He probably said that to scare you," I replied.

"I'm not scared," Ben said. "I might not have done something that fucked up, but I'm not scared."

I realized maybe that was what was driving me so crazy about Ben. He wasn't scared. Not of Stravalaci, not of asking Troyer her stupid name, not even of me.

I needed him to be scared, so he stayed the hell away.

"You gonna tell me about Square Head now?" I asked. "I mean, since you feel like it's your job to narrate this bullshit."

"Oh, you mean Nerone?" Ben asked, pointing at the cabin behind him with his thumb.

"Yeah, the charmer who drove us here." I looked at him, could feel my lips smirk. "What's *his* first name?"

"He never told us." Ben shrugged. "He's kind of a dick."

"Shocker," I said.

Troyer wrote something on her pad and held it up. *Why are you here, Ben?*

Lisa Burstein

"I'll tell Cassie if she asks," Ben said.

"Cassie doesn't care," I said, even though I kind of did. Whatever Ben had done, it didn't appear to have broken him. Not like Troyer was broken. Not like I was. I could feel him looking at me, but I didn't turn, just watched the boys running around the field. How were they not tired? Hadn't they hiked ten miles that day like we had?

"Laura," Ben said, leaning over me, so close that I could feel my heart in my ears, "you like it here so far?"

"Are you fucking kidding me?" I asked.

Troyer snorted.

"Lucky you," Ben said, tilting back. "You have an audience now."

Troyer got up and walked to the center of the field. She sat cross-legged like she did on her bed, but the boys kept running around her.

"So, you wanna know why I'm here?" Ben asked.

"How many other ways can I say no?"

"I want to know why *you're* here."

"Why?" I flashed my flashlight in his face like a cop might, wanting to piss him off because he was pissing me off. "Seriously, what is your deal?"

"I'm trying to figure out what makes you tick," he said, knocking his knee into mine, slowly, carefully like he wanted me to know he was touching me. There was no way I couldn't know it. I felt my chest tighten; my skin pulsed.

"Good luck with that," I said. I knocked his knee back, but not playfully. Hard. I hoped I left a bruise.

"I also think you're hot," Ben said.

I could feel him staring at me, like he wanted to watch the words hit my heart. My face felt smothered. My throat went dry; my neck and chest burned.

"Yes, Cassie, I just called you pretty," he said, still staring.

"Go to hell," I said, my hand to my stomach, ready to hit, but it was shaking. *I* was shaking.

"Usually people say 'thank you' when someone gives them a compliment." He ran a hand through his hair, a move that had probably worked on a lot of other girls. It would not work on me.

None of this would work on me.

"It's not a compliment; it's a line," I said.

"It's not a line if it's true." He smirked, his lips open like they were waiting for something. "You're welcome." He touched my knee as he got up, so gently it made me sigh. I coughed, attempting to hide it.

At least he left before I had to respond, because for once in my life, I was fucking speechless.

He joined Patrick and Kurt on the field. They played a weird kind of tag, two of them chasing the other, and then once the two caught the one, they broke off and chased the other one. Troyer sat in the middle of the field, not even noticing them, her eyes closed, her palms facing up on her legs.

I punched my stomach again and again, because Ben had touched me twice, and I had let him. Because his touch made my body react, even though my mind was telling me not to. I kept punching because I wanted to make myself remember that letting a boy in only ended in pain.

Lisa Burstein

25 Fucking Days to Go

Rawe spent the morning giving us a big long lecture about how we should use our Assessment Diaries like road maps for our lives. Look at each choice and every decision that led us here and attempt to see where we could have veered another way.

A better way.

What's weird is I wouldn't change what happened on prom night. I know people would say, *But if you hadn't gotten arrested then none of this would have happened,* and while that's true, I'd pick another night to go back and erase until the paper ripped.

The night I met Aaron and fell for his stupid crooked-toothed smile and *I'm hot shit* swagger. The night I let myself get sappy and fooled because I was so lonely, because I had nothing but a pizza-shop shit job and jail to look forward to.

Because his blue eyes were so blue and his Zippo was so silver and shiny.

I was working at Pudgie's Pizzeria and was on dough that night. Covered in flour, I probably looked like a clown, white faced and silly. I also had that sharp, rancid smell of yeast in my hair and under my fingernails. And even though I was covered in flour, I still had to manage the counter because everyone else I worked with was in the back room drinking stolen beer from the cooler.

I could hear them laughing while I rolled out the dough for a sheet pizza, a big white rectangle that I poked tiny pinholes in with a fork. I would have liked to be drinking stolen beer from the cooler, but after the arrest, my mother did a sobriety check every time I came home. Which was beyond ironic, considering my mother's breath could have gotten me drunk.

Before I was allowed to enter the house, I had to stand in the middle of our front yard and touch my finger to my nose. Then I had to say the alphabet backward and walk in a straight line like I was on a tight rope and stand on one foot. I must have looked like a human yard flamingo.

When Aaron walked in, I remember it being hard not to look at him. He had long, sunset-orange-colored hair, wore a pair of jeans that were down to strings on his knees and fit him like he slept in them. He was extreme-sports cute. That kind of guy who doesn't care if he breaks his cute face, who if he knew he was cute would try to break his own cute face.

When he walked up to the counter all I could think was, *Why the hell am I wearing a bakery?* But then I wondered why

Lisa Burstein

I even cared I was wearing a bakery. I wiped the flour from my cheeks and the front of my shirt.

"Welcome to Pudgie's. Can I take your order?" I automated.

"You can try." He smiled. He had a crooked tooth. It poked out over his bottom lip like a fang.

I stared at him. He probably wanted me to laugh and I might have, if it had been two months ago—before prom night. I might have if I were drinking one of those stolen beers in the cooler.

"Large Pepsi and a slice of four-cheese with onions and peppers," he said.

I cut him a slice and filled a large cup and handed it to him, the ice clinking inside. He put his hand around mine as he grabbed it, left his fingers there long enough for me to know he wasn't doing it by accident. Long enough for me to pull away, but for some reason I didn't. Maybe it was because he was the first teenage boy besides my brother I'd talked to in weeks, or maybe it was because his eyes stayed right on mine like targets. Like blue, blue lasers.

"You're Cassie, right?" he asked.

"That's what my name tag says." His hand was still on mine. I finally pulled my hand away like I had burned it, and I almost spilled his drink.

"Cassie Wick?" he asked, bringing the cup to his mouth and taking a squeaky sip from the straw.

"How the hell do you know my last name?" I asked, folding my arms over the pizza-sauce-stained apron that covered my chest.

Instead of answering, he said, "I'm Aaron Chambers."

"Who the fuck cares," I said. "How do you know my name?"

Maybe one of the assholes I worked with was playing a trick on me. They always made fun of me for not being able to get wrecked with them, because I was stupid enough to get arrested for what they weren't afraid to do in the break room every night while they were supposed to be working.

"You don't know who I am?" he asked, putting his drink down and leaning on the counter like he was planning to stay a while.

"Should I?" I was going to kill those assholes in the back room. Maybe even call the police on them one night when I wasn't at work, so *they* could be stupid enough to get arrested. So they would realize it wasn't about being stupid, it was about being doomed.

"I'm one of the guys who stood you up for prom," he said, taking another sip of his soda. It was good I wasn't taking a sip of it, because I probably would have spit it out, right in his face.

"Well, fuck you, then," I said.

He smiled.

I didn't.

"I came to apologize," he said.

"Not to me," I said. "You were Amy's date." I picked up a rag and started wiping the counter. I was afraid if I didn't do something with my hands I would strangle him. "Go apologize to her."

"I want to apologize to you," he said, smiling again, his crooked tooth coming down over his bottom lip.

"I don't need your apology," I said, still cleaning the counter. My cheeks started to burn.

He put his hand on the wrist that held the rag and squeezed.

Lisa Burstein

"You probably want to let me go before I make you," I hissed.

He didn't move. "I know everything that happened that night," he said.

"Wait," I said, my head starting to spin with fear. "Did Brian send you here to kick my ass or something? Because you can tell him Lila's the one who stole his shit."

"I know," he said. "Brian knows."

"So now we're back to how I don't need your apology," I said, my anxiety turning to anger again, the heartbeat in my ears changing from the pounding of running feet to machine-gun fire. I pulled my wrist free, left the counter, and went back to my bucket of dough. I grabbed a baseball-sized glob and started rolling it out on a pastry board, smacking the middle of the dough harder than I had to, to get it started.

"Who says?" Aaron asked, leaning even farther over the counter, grabbing onto the shelf on the other side to hold himself up.

"You're not supposed to be back here," I said, still pounding on my dough.

"Who says I was Amy's date?" he asked, hanging halfway into the kitchen like a kid on a jungle gym.

I rolled my eyes but didn't turn to look at him. "Lila. Lila said you were Amy's date."

"Oh, *Lila*," he said, making his voice sound fake haughty. "Well, I guess she knows everything."

"Lila sucks," I said. We hadn't talked since prom night and I doubted we were going to, unless *she* apologized to me, which she would never do.

"I've met her," Aaron said. "I agree."

I turned to look at him. His eyes were still on me. Boys didn't say Lila sucked—most boys, anyway.

"When's your break?" he asked, letting go of the counter and standing back up.

"Why?"

"I want to take you somewhere so we can talk more," he said. He folded his slice in half and ate the whole thing in three bites.

"Forget it," I said, pretending my dough was really interesting.

"Come on, you got something better to do?" he mumbled through his full mouth.

I turned and looked at the closed door of the back room. I could still hear my coworkers laughing behind it.

Assholes.

"I'll give you twenty dollars," he said, taking it out and shaking it in front of me. His blue eyes were big.

"What, do you think I'm a fucking prostitute?" I asked.

"I just really want to talk to you," he said.

"We're talking now," I said.

"No," he said, "not here." He walked up to the counter and traced a circle on it, waiting.

"You've got to do better than that," I said.

"This is the best I can do with the lights on," he said.

I fought back a smile, even though I knew it was a line. This boy was something. "Fine," I said, wiping my hands on a rag. "Meet me outside. And I still want that twenty." I walked to the back room and kicked the door, once, twice, three times. "Going on break, fuckers," I said, throwing off my apron and grabbing my cigarettes.

Lisa Burstein

Aaron waited for me in a black convertible, so clean that it shined in the streetlights like an oil slick. I walked over to the driver's side and put a cigarette in my mouth. He pulled out a Zippo and leaned over to light it before I could even grab my lighter.

"Wanna take a ride?" he asked.

Fuck yeah, I wanted to take a ride.

I walked around the back of the car, opened the door, and sat in the passenger seat—leather, bucket. The dashboard had so many lights and buttons it reminded me of the Batmobile.

Aaron lit his own cigarette, moving his Zippo through his fingers like a baton, pinkie to thumb and back again, as he put the top down. We started to drive, the wind blowing the flour out of my hair so that it flew behind me like snow.

It made me think about my own car. My poor impounded Civic, which I might be able to get back if I stayed out of trouble. Sitting next to Aaron in his car, staying out of trouble was looking doubtful.

He pulled into the entry lot of the park down the street and turned off the car.

"I thought you wanted to take a ride," I said, throwing my spent cigarette on the ground. I watched it fly through the air like a miniature rocket.

"We just did," he said, taking the last drag of his cigarette and doing the same.

I stared at the windshield. The headlights were still on and were spotlighting two empty benches, a garbage can, and a sad little aluminum slide.

"How much longer do you have?" Aaron asked, his hands circling the steering wheel.

I looked at the clock on the dash, the same bright green as a glow stick. "Forty-five minutes."

"Well I'd better hurry up, then," he said, taking off his seat belt and leaning in to kiss me.

I pushed him, hard, in the center of his chest. "No fucking way, Aaron Chambers."

"You don't want to kiss me?" he asked. He seemed surprised. I guess people didn't usually push him away.

I pointed at my forehead. "Does it look like I'm wearing a sign that says *chump*?"

He stared at the steering wheel like he didn't know what to do.

"You said you came to apologize, so apologize," I said. I caught my reflection in the side mirror. I still had flour on my nose. I rubbed at it.

"I'm sorry," Aaron said, turning to me, making his face go soft.

"On your knees," I said. If this boy wanted to apologize, he was going to do it right. I mean, he wanted to kiss me, so who knew what I would be able to get him to agree to?

"Seriously?" he asked.

"Um, you stood me up for my prom," I said. "I got arrested that night. My life is a world of shit because of you. Get on your fucking knees."

"You're pretty cute when you're angry," he said, reaching for my hair.

I whipped my head away. "Apology," I said.

"Okay, Miss Cassie," Aaron said, getting out of the car and

Lisa Burstein

coming over to my side. He opened the door and held out his hand.

I looked at it, waiting.

"You're supposed to take it," he said.

"Ugh," I said, "fine." He led me to the front of the car. The headlights were still on, shining out for miles into the darkness. He kneeled in front of me and held both my hands. It was very marriage-proposal and I felt my cheeks light up.

"I'm sorry about prom night and I would like to make it up to you," Aaron said, his eyes never leaving mine.

"How?" I asked. It felt pretty good to have someone on his knees in front of me begging for my forgiveness. After the shit luck I'd had, it felt better than good.

He kissed one hand then the other. I felt static electricity travel up from them, to my shoulders, neck, and the base of my skull.

Who was this boy? Why wasn't he afraid of me? Why wasn't I afraid of him?

"I don't think you can make it up to me," I said, but I didn't pull my hands away.

"I'd like to try," he said, looking up at me, his eyes very puppy-dog.

"How?" I asked again.

He stood and took my chin in his hands. "Like this," he said, kissing me. I reared up to knee him in the balls, but his lips made me stop. They were persuasive and warm and doing all the right things. The kind of lips that make you forget you're even kissing. I guess I did, because I stood there kissing him for minutes upon minutes, my leg cocked and loaded but never making contact.

He stopped and looked at me. "Am I forgiven?"

"Not even close," I said. I could still taste his pizza and Pepsi, onions and sugar, on my lips.

We made out for the rest of my break standing like that, his hands grabbing the back of my head, the car's headlights reaching out on each side of us and into the night, like the arms of a star.

That is what I would take back. Not because of what happened that night, but because of everything that came after.

Because of everything I can never take back.

Lisa Burstein

24 Fucking Days
to Go

This morning, we followed Rawe down to the water-
front—Nez in front, me in the middle, Troyer in the
back. Nez kept turning around and whispering to me
about Arm Sleeve Tattoo Guy, making X-rated facial expressions and tongue movements like she was having some kind
of porno stroke.

I didn't want to hear about it and tried to ignore her, but
that just made her keep going.

"Then he put both hands on my butt," Nez said, holding
her hands up and squeezing.

Rawe twisted around to bust her, but it was like Nez could
sense it and she turned away from me, staring straight ahead
and marching like she was a model prisoner, before Rawe

could say anything. I looked down at my boots, clomping on the dirt path. Even with our short escape the other night, that was still how I felt. Like a prisoner.

Maybe I would have felt that way even if I wasn't here.

The four of us finally hit the rocky beach. Murky green lake water gurgled with seaweed and foam like a cappuccino. The boys were already there, standing in front of three canoes. Weathered Adirondack chairs were piled up with a bike lock. The door of a boat house, no bigger than our cabin, banged open and closed in the wind.

"It smells like I'm in a goldfish cemetery," I said, covering my face.

"You can handle the pit toilets, you can handle this," Rawe said, spinning her head around, *Exorcist*-style, to look at me.

I didn't want to get into the fact that *any* toilet was really a goldfish cemetery.

"Sweet," Nez whispered. "Maybe Andre and I can slip away for some afternoon delight." She licked her lips.

"If it will finally shut your mouth, I hope so," I murmured.

"How do you make out with your mouth closed?" Nez asked.

"Once I staple yours shut you can figure it out," I said, not wanting to let Nez get the last word. It was about all I had left.

"Ladies, line up," Rawe commanded.

We were in a line already, so we all looked at one another. Maybe Rawe was showing off for Square Head—Nerone or whatever. The boys were already in a line, too. Ben turned and waved to Troyer. He mouthed, *Hi Laura*, before he glued his eyes back on Nerone.

Lisa Burstein

Nez looked at me, her mouth hanging open practically down to her knees.

"We had our own fun while Andre was squeezing your butt," I said, making the same hand motions Nez had. I bet Ben was probably only being nice to Troyer to piss me off, but if I could piss off Nez in the process, all the better.

"We're splitting up three-two-two, co-ed," Nerone yelled. Then he went through some canoe safety tips. Like Rawe or Nerone really gave a crap about our safety.

I looked at the canoes, laying diagonally like huge green bananas on the lakeshore.

"I hope I get three—boy sandwich," Nez whispered, practically drooling.

"Seriously, Nez, shut the fuck up," I said.

She turned and stuck her tongue out at me, as opposite a facial expression as any of the ones she made on the walk over here. I was learning that Nez viewed sticking her tongue out like I might view giving someone the finger. And like me, she did it a lot.

"All right, Nez, Wick, Troyer, pick a boat," Rawe said. She stood next to Nerone, breathing heavily through her nose. She was shorter than he was, skinnier, paler, and unlike him, her head didn't look like a Rubik's Cube.

We each walked over to a canoe. I looked inside. Three sandy, wet life jackets lay in the bow. How long had those been in there?

Nerone sent the boys over next. He put Ben with Nez, Troyer with Arm Sleeve Tattoo Guy, and me with Brace Face and Curly.

"Looks like I'm with your boyfriend," Nez said to me, shaking her ass as she bent over and picked up a life jacket.

"Looks like Troyer's with yours," I sneered. I could have told her that I got the boy sandwich, but thinking of those two in a boy sandwich would put anyone on a hunger strike. I also could have told her Ben wasn't my boyfriend, and I wondered why that hadn't been the first thing to come out of my mouth. *Fucking Ben.*

Nez snapped her fingers to get Troyer's attention and mouthed, *Touch him and die*, making a slicing-open-her-neck motion. I wondered why everyone thought they had to mouth words to Troyer. Even if she didn't talk, it was obvious she could hear, and it was even more obvious that she'd looked scared even before Nez's warning. Stravalaci's hair was as dark as the black tribal tattoos that snaked up his arms. Troyer had heard from Ben why he was here and I was pretty sure she didn't want to be alone with him on the water or anywhere else. I mean, I could probably handle him, but Troyer was afraid of *words*.

I waited while Eagan and Leisner walked over to our canoe. At least Leisner had some muscle on him, flabby as it was, but Eagan had arms like pipe cleaners. Unless his braces gave him superpowers, it looked like it was going to be Leisner and me carrying most of the weight.

I put on a life jacket. I could smell mildew. It had that disgusting, cold, wet feeling that only lake water can give.

"Do we get helmets?" Eagan yelled over to Nerone. "There are two million traumatic brain accidents each year." He slurped on the saliva that got stuck on the metal attached to his teeth.

Lisa Burstein

This was going to be one long fucking boat ride.

Nerone sighed. "You're not fighting the rapids, Eagan. It's a simple trip to the dock at the middle of the lake and back."

"I'd still prefer a helmet," Eagan said.

"What you prefer doesn't matter," Nerone yelled, his square head turning red, like someone had solved that side of the Rubik's Cube. "Get in the goddamn boat."

"You girls got anything you want to whine about?" Rawe yelled. I guess she wanted to make sure Nerone knew that she could be an asshole, too.

None of us spoke. I looked out at the dock we were supposed to paddle out to—it didn't look simple. The lake was huge. To make it to the middle would probably take an hour at least.

With Eagan in my boat, probably longer.

"Hi Cassie," Leisner said, sidling up next to me, his curly blond afro shining around his head like a pubic hair halo.

"How the hell do you know my name?" I hissed.

Leisner looked at me and smirked. He didn't need to answer. Ben had told him my name. What the hell else had Ben told him? I watched Nez and Ben take off in their canoe, Ben in back, Nez in front, each paddling on opposite sides, their paddles splashing water.

"Eagan should probably sit in front in case we need his brace-face for radar," I said, throwing each of them a wet life jacket.

Leisner caught his, but Eagan winced as his hit his chest and fell on the sand.

"Nice catch," I said.

"Nice throw," Leisner said. I didn't think it was possible,

but he was worse than Ben. It could have been because he didn't look anything like Ben.

I glanced over at Troyer, who was sitting at the back of her canoe with Stravalaci in the front. Her mouth was closed so tight it looked like it was glued.

"You get in the middle, Cassie," Leisner said. "Let the guns run the stern." He made a muscle.

"Your guns look like they're out of ammo." I laughed. There was no way I was letting one of them be in charge of steering this thing. If I was forced to go out into the middle of the lake with these two idiots, at least I wanted to know I would be able to steer my way back.

Leisner's face screwed up as he stepped closer to me. "Maybe I should test them, Cassie."

Was he starting something? I hoped so. I wanted to punch the curls right out of his hair. "Call me Cassie one more time and it will be your last."

"Wick," Rawe yelled.

"Leisner," Nerone yelled.

I got into the back of the boat before Rawe could say anything else. There was no way I was doing push-ups on sand covered with dead fish guts.

"Sorry, Cassie," Leisner taunted as he got into the middle seat.

I picked up the paddle and ignored him. I knew how to steer a boat. My brother and I used to go fishing on Lake Erie when I was a kid. During the summer we would stay for a week with my dad's sister who had a beach house that she lived in all year round. It was filled with seashells and too many cats. Every morning, before anyone woke up, my

Lisa Burstein

brother and I would sneak out and down the path to the row-boat rocking in the water at the dock. We would row into the middle of the lake to fish while the sun rose, talking about how we could survive on a desert island without anyone in our stupid family.

So yeah, I knew how to steer a fucking boat.

I also knew that once the 'roids were out of Leisner's system, I could probably lay him out with one punch.

Eagan got his life jacket on and sat in front of the canoe. With everyone in place, we finally pushed off, gliding on the water, our paddles thrusting us forward.

"You know drowning is the fifth highest cause of accidental death," Eagan said.

"So is talking too fucking much," I yelled up to the front of the boat. My voice echoed off the metal of the canoe and the water below us.

"Ben said you were feisty." Leisner said. I could hear the smirk in his voice.

Feisty? I'd been called a lot of things in my time, but feisty was not one of them.

"Ben's an asshole," I said, staring at the back of Leisner's curly blond head and picturing myself drop-kicking it.

"He said you'd say that," Leisner added.

"Can we please stop talking about Ben?" I kept paddling. My arms already ached, water splashing underneath us as the canoe moved forward.

"Who's talking about Ben?" Leisner joked.

I pulled my paddle out of the water and soaked him with it.

"You're lucky you're a girl," he said.

"You're lucky you're not," I said.

"Be careful, you guys," Eagan said. "I'm fairly sure this boat is at least twenty years old. Do you know what happens to metal as it ages?"

"Maybe Ben will come save you, Cassie." Leisner laughed.

I felt fear splash up from my stomach to my chest. Leisner bothered me in a way I recognized, which meant I was screwed. As much as I wanted to deny it, annoyance was not at all what I felt for Ben.

I looked out at the lake. Ben and Nez were in the lead, the sun making them seem like shadows of themselves. I needed to stay the hell away from him.

"It's a long row to the dock," Leisner said. "What do you want to talk about, Cassie?"

"I don't," I said, paddling so hard my hands burned.

"We could sing," Eagan said. I could hear the saliva flying out of his mouth as he said it.

"Start singing and I drown you," I said.

"You don't have it in you," Leisner said.

"Well, maybe not when it comes to him," I said, flicking my chin up at Eagan, "but you're a different story."

"I'm right here," he said, stopping mid-row to turn to me.

I allowed the anger to build—fire starting in my chest, flames licking out to my arms and hands. I wanted to take my paddle and whack his knowing smile so hard that it landed in Ben and Nez's boat.

I had managed to keep myself in check the whole time I'd been here, but Leisner was different. I deserved my fist in my stomach as a painful and constant tattoo needle, but he deserved my fist in his face because he was an ass-clown.

"I knew it." Leisner laughed and turned back around.

Lisa Burstein

I paddled harder, picturing the water as his stupid jock face. I was annihilating it in my mind, splitting his skull, breaking his nose, cracking his teeth.

"Let's sing the name song, Eagan," Leisner cooed. "I'll start. *Cassie, Cassie bo-bassie, banana-fana-fo-fassie, all talk no action-assie, Cassie.* One more time . . ."

"Shut your blow-hole, or I'll shut it for you." The fire moved into my eyes. That's how it feels. I think it's why people call anger *blind.* You can't see anything but red covering your target. You can't feel anything but searing force pushing you.

"I think we all know, including Ben," Leisner said, indicating him out in his boat with Nez, "that you won't do anything."

I stood up. Leisner didn't notice; he started singing again — still mocking me — his blond-curled head bobbing up and down like someone juggling a soccer ball on his knees.

The canoe teetered as I edged toward him. He was so high on himself, he didn't even notice me standing behind him, breathing, waiting, trying to decide what to do. I tapped him on the shoulder, still unsure. I waited. It would all depend on what he said when he turned around.

"Look, Eagan, I caught a Cassie with my song," Leisner said, his smile greasy. "I figured she was easy, but — "

"I asked you to shut up," I said quietly. That's another thing about anger; it makes you calm when you let yourself do something about it.

"Sit down! You're going to capsize the boat!" Eagan screamed.

"She'll sit," Leisner said. "She wouldn't want to do anything she'd regret."

I already had too much I regretted to let this one go.

I don't feel anything when I grab for someone, just a rush of relief, like when you are desert-thirsty and take that initial drink. So at first I didn't even notice that I'd pushed Leisner—that I'd launched him airborne—until he reached out to steady himself and we both fell into the water.

It was so cold when I hit, it felt like twenty thousand self-induced punches to my stomach with an icicle.

"Boy and girl overboard," Eagan yelled.

I was in the water, bobbing, trying to keep it out of my mouth.

"You are so dead," Leisner said, water bubbling up around his head.

I treaded as best I could. I was so angry, I'd forgotten I couldn't swim very well—that I should not have been pushing people around on a canoe. That without my brother, there was no one to be sure I made it back to shore safely. My life jacket was holding me up okay, but it was clear that it had a shelf life and mine was expiring. I reached for Leisner. I didn't know what else to do.

"You look like a wet dog," he said, his smile bobbing on the water. "A wet bitch."

"You look like a naked, upside-down female synchro-nized swimmer in need of a wax," I spit through the water. "Desperately."

"You're on your own now, tough girl," Leisner said, swim-ming past me and pulling himself back into the canoe.

Eagan was reaching his paddle out to me, but I was too far away to grab it. I looked at the shore—the water fishy, muddy

Lisa Burstein

in my mouth, starting to fill my ears. Rawe and Nerone stood there. They hadn't moved, hadn't even yelled. I was surprised one of them hadn't jumped in.

Of course, I hadn't yelled *help* yet, either. I didn't know if I could. Was I really stubborn enough to let myself drown rather than admit I needed it?

I felt arms surround me, pulling me up, my mouth free of the water.

Ben.

"What the hell are you doing?" I asked, but I didn't fight him even though he was touching me again, all of me, and was still technically male.

"Saving you," he said, droplets of water sticking to his eyelashes. "You looked like you were drowning."

"I'm wearing a life jacket, moron," I said, but I still didn't struggle away from him. It was just like Leisner said: Ben *had* come to save me. Could everyone see something between us? Something I was trying so hard to contain?

Never again.

I heard another splash—Nez jumping in. She flailed, but it was clear she was faking, at least to me.

"Looks like you have a real damsel in distress," I said.

"She told me she was on her school swim team," Ben said, squinting in the sunlight.

"She's probably just trying to get your attention," I said, watching her swim closer to us even as she pretended to struggle, her black hair whipping and splashing like a fish flipping on a line.

"You weren't?" he asked, his arms still tight around me, the kind of tight that makes it hard to breathe but has nothing to do with being held and everything to do with who you are being held by.

"I fell in," I said. His body still stuck to mine in the way only bodies can stick.

"Do you want me to let you go?" he asked.

I wanted to say, *Yes*, say, *Never touch me again*, say, *Why do you have to be the kind of guy who jumps into Port-O-Potty–colored lake water to save me*? but I couldn't. I leaned into him, letting his strength keep us afloat, letting myself stop fighting him for just that second, knowing that once I was out of the water, I could pretend I hadn't wanted any of it.

"First you, then Nez," he said, pulling me over to the boat. He secured me with one arm, swam with the other, my mouth on his shoulder, on his wet hair.

"I think you lost something," Ben said to Leisner, treading on the side of our canoe, one of his arms still around me.

"Nope, we're all set on skanks," Leisner said.

"Fuck you," I spit, the red filling my vision again.

"Are you okay?" Eagan asked.

"I will be when I get back in this fucking boat," I said, pulling myself up, the water splashing behind me.

"Next time you try to drown someone you should probably make sure you can swim first." Leisner laughed.

"I'd be scared for next time," I said, picturing it: my fist, his face, the brittle crunch of cartilage.

I sat in my seat, wet and cold, Ben's eyes on me.

Nez started to scream for him, to flail more forcefully, but Ben didn't move.

"She's going to forget she's supposed to be drowning if you

Lisa Burstein

don't get her soon," I said, anything so he would stop staring, *anything* so he would go away and I wouldn't be tempted to jump back in.

"I guess I'll get my thank-you later," Ben said, swimming toward Nez, to someone who could definitely admit she wanted his arms around her.

I shivered and looked out at the water. The sun sparkled on it like millions of paparazzi snapping flashbulbs. Taking pictures of me, the outside of me. The part I couldn't hide.

The only part I know I can ever let Ben see, no matter how he makes me feel.

23 Fucking Days to Go

W aking up in the morning is different here. I don't have coffee to revive me. I don't have my brother hocking up loogies in the bathroom next door and forcing me to go bang on the wall to tell him to *stop being so fucking disgusting*. I don't have my open pack of smokes waiting on my nightstand, luring me with their exposed brown butts.

I only had Rawe kicking the side of my metal cot so hard it rattled and grunting, *Ten minutes till morning calisthenics. Try not to fall into the lake between now and then*, then leaving the cabin to do whatever it was she did for the ten minutes we got ready for morning calisthenics.

Nez and I had already done our punishment push-ups, three hundred apiece on the shore when we got back, the fishy sand sticking to our wet uniforms, to our mouths and noses; I still had sand in my teeth.

I stared at the ceiling and thought about Rawe. Maybe she left every morning so she didn't have to watch us. Watch our eyes open, blink once, twice, and realize it wasn't a nightmare. Deny our zombie movements as we put one leg in our brown jumpsuits then the other, while we tried to forget that we had another long day ahead of us doing things we were bound to hate, things that were supposed to make us better, even though no one ever told us how.

Or maybe Rawe left the cabin to get a break, because Nez was so fucking annoying.

Nez got out of bed and stretched. She reminded me of a cat, would probably lick herself clean if she could reach. I put my hands into the water bucket and tried to ignore her, splashing my face wet but not clean. I wiped my skin with the washcloth, scrubbing the smell of dead fish and lake water from my eyelashes, from under my fingernails. Unfortunately the water in the bucket didn't smell much better.

I heard Nez yawn, one of those long, drawn-out yawns that sound like you're saying *yahhh*, making a big deal about how tired she was. Then she yawned again, louder, longer, prob-ably because no one said anything about her first yawn—not that Troyer could have and not that I would have.

I knew Nez was yawning because she wanted an audience. She wanted to tell us why she was so tired, but she didn't have to. She'd gone to the boys' cabin again last night. She'd made a big deal about telling us while we wrote in our Assessment Diaries before lights out that *Ben* had asked her to come. We were supposed to be writing about what scared us, but considering what I had realized about Ben the day before, I didn't write anything because I was having trouble topping it.

Luckily my head was still in the water bucket when she started talking.

"Wow, last night with Ben was amazing," Nez said.

The rotten swell of jealousy came up from my stomach and I tried desperately to ignore it. Ben had saved me yesterday, but clearly he wanted more, and since he wasn't getting it from me, I guess he got it from Nez.

I guess *she* gave him his *thank-you.*

I felt sick.

I forced myself to look at Troyer. She was brushing her hair and ignoring us. I wanted her to turn to me, to mouth that *Nez is a fucking liar.*

"Did you hear me?" Nez asked as she put on a lime green bra and matching underwear. We hadn't done laundry yet and I had no idea how this girl could still have clean underwear, especially considering how much time she spent making it dirty.

Troyer stopped brushing and pretended to launch her hair-brush at Nez. Maybe she *wasn't* ignoring us.

"Nez, we don't care," I said. I wiped my face one more time and dropped the washcloth in the bucket with a splash, only thinking afterward that Nez might have used it to clean up when she snuck back in last night.

I felt myself involuntarily shudder.

"Well, I don't care if you care," Nez said, turning around and fixing her black eyes on me. "I need to talk about it. It was very, very special and also," she whispered, "super hot."

"How did you not wake up Nerone?" I said with a lilt in

Lisa Burstein

my voice that I hoped let her know I sort of didn't believe her.

"He sleeps like he's been dead fifty years," she said, explaining my skepticism away. "I mean, I was definitely screaming and he didn't wake up."

I looked over at Troyer. She was writing furiously on her pad and not looking up. I guess you had a lot of feelings to get out when you didn't talk all day. Of course, she could have been writing *Nez is a bitch* over and over, filling each line on the page, like a kid being punished in school.

"Thanks for the fucking update," I said, trying to act like I didn't care, but I did. I shouldn't have, though. If Nez were with him maybe he would leave me alone. And isn't that what I want?

I walked back over to my cot to get dressed. It was good I had no plans to be with Ben or any of the other boys stuck at this camp—any other boys ever—because they were all bound to have whatever diseases Nez did. It was clear she probably had enough that Troyer would wear out her pencil writing them all down.

"Please don't swear," Nez said. "I'm talking about beautiful, magical things here." She took a deep breath, sounding very swoony.

"The only magical thing about you and any of those boys knocking boots is that it shuts your mouth for five minutes," I spit. I was tired of hearing the way Nez threw sex around like it didn't matter.

It did matter. I knew what it could do, what it could make you do.

I felt my hand go to my stomach involuntarily and punch, once, twice, three times.

"B-T-Dubs," Nez said, completely oblivious, "Ben is so not annoying. He's actually super cute."

"He's all yours," I said, the punches to my stomach making me nauseous. I turned away from her and continued to get dressed. I didn't know Ben well, but he didn't seem like he would fall for Nez's bullshit. I guess when you're in a place like this you'll do anything you can to forget you're here.

Even Nez.

"My only complaint is that he smells like an ashtray," Nez said, sounding like she was critiquing a restaurant.

I turned around mid-dress and looked at her, my jumpsuit half on, the arms hanging at my sides. The fabric was still damp with lake water, still covered with sand. This was interesting information. "How can he smell like an ashtray if we're not allowed to smoke?" It had been seven days since my last cigarette and while I didn't crave them in the same anxious, needling way, it didn't mean I wouldn't take one if it were offered, especially if someone here had them.

"We're not allowed to do a lot of things, but that didn't stop me." Nez paused and pursed her lips. "Or Ben."

"I don't think a fifty-foot wall of nuns could stop you," I said.

I left Nez bragging to Troyer. I had to use the bathroom, and it was the kind of day where peeing on the side of the cabin wasn't going to do it. Not that I ever liked using the pit toilet. Basically, I felt like I was in a metal coffin filled with shit—and the last time I was in there I saw a spider on the ceiling with a body as big as an avocado. The whole time I was trying not to sit, I was also trying not to stand. But it's not like I had a choice.

Lisa Burstein

The way I didn't have a choice about most things at Turning Pines.

I found Rawe in front of the cabin on her knees, facing toward the sun. Her eyes were closed and her hands were palm to palm at her chest like she was praying. Her mouth was moving but not making sound. She *was* praying. What was she praying for? Who was she praying for?

Hopefully not Nez.

Or me.

I still hadn't figured out why Rawe was here beyond her paycheck. Why would anyone choose to be in a shitty cabin with three fucked-up girls for thirty days? Three fucked-up girls who totally didn't want to be here. Three fucked-up girls who hated her because of who she was, who hated themselves, who hated so much, there was no room for anything else.

I tried to walk by without her noticing, but the boots they gave us were not made for sneaking around, probably by design. It made me wonder how Nez hadn't been caught yet. Maybe she was paying Rawe in sexual favors.

"Morning, Wick," Rawe said, not turning around. Her black braid was as tight as ever, the hair in it probably suffocating from lack of air.

I wasn't sure what I was supposed to say back, because she was kind of being nice and I wasn't used to it. Not from Rawe. If she used my name, it was in command, not in greeting.

"Morning," I said. What people say when they see someone on the street that they don't know but who is nice enough to say, *Morning*, like an old man with a hat that he tips.

I was surprised Rawe was even talking to me. Not that I wanted to talk to her, but when I heard I was going to rehab,

I was kind of expecting to be forced to confide my feelings to someone. So far I had only been confiding to myself.

"Care to join me?" Rawe asked, patting the ground next to her, calling me like a dog.

"I came out to use the bathroom," I said. Was she asking me to join her or telling me to join her? I wasn't sure. If I didn't, would there be more push-ups? I had to use the bathroom too badly to do push-ups. I had to use the bathroom too badly to do anything.

"Maybe on your way back," Rawe said, still not turning around. She was kind of spooking me out. I could take seeing her as a soulless, angry bitch or the prescriptive voice pushing us to write in our Assessment Diaries, but I didn't know what this was.

"Um, maybe," I said, even though I was positive if I kneeled down to pray, the sky would open up and lightning would fly out like octopus arms and burn me to a crisp. I didn't deserve to pray. Not that anyone but my brother knew it, but I didn't deserve anything except to go take a crap in a pit toilet.

"It's about changing patterns," Rawe said, like she could read my mind.

"I don't have a pattern," I said. I did before I came here. I did before Aaron, but now I was surviving. Waking up every day and struggling like a sapling against the wind.

"Sure you do," Rawe said, finally turning around. She squinted. "You weren't sent here because you're special. You were sent here to change."

"Into what?" I asked. I was fine with changing. If changing meant I didn't have to feel the way I felt anymore, then I was more than fine with it. But it certainly didn't seem like that was what this place was about. How are you supposed to change

Lisa Burstein

when your body is so tired you can barely see? How are you supposed to change when you're forced to rehash your life nightly by flashlight?

"That's what you need to decide," Rawe said. "The goal here is to prepare you for your future."

"Some future," I said. I thought of everything I'd done since I arrived. The only life this was going to prepare me for was one as a lumberjack.

A very poorly paid lumberjack.

"Come pray with me," Rawe said.

"I can't," I said, instead of just saying *no*.

"You don't have to be religious to pray," she said.

"But you have to be good." I paused, looking at the orange pinecones that covered the ground. "Deserving," I continued, "and I'm not." I was surprised I'd admitted it out loud. It was one thing to punch myself until I couldn't breathe and keep everyone away like I had porcupine needles coming from my skin.

It was another thing to say it, especially when I couldn't even write what that really meant yet.

"You'll feel better," she said.

It was tempting, but pretending to pray was probably not the best idea. I was already on a slippery slope with whatever was looking down on us.

Rawe was naïve enough to think I was someone who deserved a second chance.

But as I walked toward the pit toilet, I couldn't help thinking that it didn't matter where I was. I would still feel this.

I would still be me.

I will still have done what I had done.

22 Fucking Days
to Go

After a day spent repainting the lines on the tennis courts without the boys, we are back in our cabin being forced to write about what we want to do when we leave here. Considering the day we had, which involved enough masking tape and white paint to turn the three of us to mummies, "painter" is definitely not on the list.

But honestly, until Rawe gave us the directive, adding that we needed to start planning our lives beyond this place, I really hadn't considered it.

As much as I wanted to leave, I certainly didn't want to think about what my life would be like when all the choices were mine. It was obvious I was pretty shitty when it came to making choices: look at everything that happened to me before I got here. Or, more specifically, everything I let happen to me.

Cue stomach punch.

Once I was done here, I would have to make real choices — life choices. Even though I hadn't had a chance to experience much of it, I had graduated from high school. I was "out on my own," or would be once I was allowed to leave here. Would I move back in with my parents like my brother had? Would I even be allowed to? It's not like college was ever a choice for me. Community college maybe, but not anywhere with kids like the ones who used to go to this camp.

I stared at the flypaper on the ceiling and the names carved under the shelf above my bed, people who'd written they "wuz here" and the year. My guess was none of them ever had to wonder whether it would only be them and their duffel bag when they left this place, waiting at the bus station or airport for someone to pick them up and having no idea if anyone would.

That sucked to think about, so instead I started counting the flies stuck like dead raisins to the flypaper, which looked like sickly stained glass when I aimed my flashlight at it. Maybe I couldn't think about what I wanted to do when I left here until I thought about where I was supposed to be instead of here — where I was supposed to be with Lila and Amy instead of here.

Fuck Rawe for opening that can of worm crap.

It had all been set until three weeks before prom. As usual we had spent the night at Lila's and as usual when I woke up bleary eyed on Lila's floor, Amy's sleeping bag was empty. It didn't matter how early in the morning it was or what time of year it was, she was always out on Lila's fire escape.

Sometimes I would go out there with her and have a cigarette and we would sit together without talking, just sharing inhales and exhales, breathing in a rhythm until Lila woke up. I would watch the sun rise around Amy's head while I wondered what she was thinking about. While I wondered if she was wondering what I thought about. While I wondered why sitting with her like this and not saying anything made me feel so calm. I figured it was partly because for once I didn't have to talk.

The morning everything went to shit, I woke up to find Amy's sleeping bag empty as usual. She was out on the fire escape, thinking about the things she thought about.

I was ready to go out there and join her when I saw she wasn't alone. She was talking, *whispering* with Lila. They were both still in their pajamas, and Lila had a comforter wrapped around her. The sun was coming up, big and bright, turning them into silhouettes. The window was open. I lifted my head slightly and tried to hear them.

"We'll be okay," Lila said. "It will be okay."

It was the first time I think I'd ever heard Lila try to comfort anyone.

Even though I was straining to listen, I stayed low to the ground and pretended to be asleep. What were they talking about? Were they talking about me? I'm not sure why I thought that—it's not like when Amy and I were out there we talked about Lila nonstop—but I guess I *always* thought they were talking about me, that lingering feeling when I entered Lila's room after they had both been together for

Lisa Burstein

hours, when I would find them having just said something and stopping.

"But what will you do without me next year?" Amy asked.

"What will you do without me?" Lila mimicked. I couldn't help thinking about Amy's stupid pet parrot. Lila was repeating her words the same way, empty of meaning.

What the hell? Last I'd heard we were going away together, the three of us. Traveling the country, driving in my car to wherever we felt like.

"But I don't want to go," Amy said. "Not without you guys."

I got up and crawled out onto the balcony.

"What are you bitches talking about?" I asked, like I couldn't care either way.

"Good morning to you, too," Lila said.

I looked at Amy. She looked down.

"What the fuck?" I asked, unable to hide that I did care.

"Amy's leaving us," Lila said, letting the words settle.

"I didn't say that," Amy said.

"Don't be stupid," Lila said. "You're going."

"Where?" I asked, looking at Amy. "Where are you going?"

"College," Amy said, in the voice she had that always sounded like someone had turned the volume down on just her. It was the voice she used with us a lot. "My mom sent in my acceptance for me, but I didn't say I was going to go."

"So you're not coming with us?" I asked, still trying to act like I didn't care, like I wasn't pissed, but really I felt like when something gets taken that you don't know you'll miss until it's gone.

"I'm not going to decide anything today," Amy said, her voice trembling, tears filling her eyes. "I still have time."

"Don't worry," Lila said. "Cassie and me still have each other."

"Lucky us," I said, even though my head felt like a cavern being whipped through with wind. Aside from my brother, Amy and Lila were all I had.

"At least you won't have to sit in the backseat of Cassie's turdmobile for three thousand miles," Lila said.

"Yeah, there's that, I guess," Amy said, turning to me and wiping her face. "Cassie, you okay?"

It was only then I realized I was shaking. "Yeah, I'm fucking fine." I pulled out a cigarette. "Just having a nic fit," I said, barely able to light it.

"I'm okay, too," Lila said. "Thanks for asking."

"Sorry, Cassie just seemed upset," Amy said, but I could see she immediately regretted it. I didn't get upset.

I didn't *do* getting upset.

"One of us is crying like a little bitch and two of us are not. Who's upset?"

"Sorry," Amy said again.

"You will be if you keep whining like your diaper is too tight," I said, finally getting my cigarette lit. I looked at Lila, wondering how many miles we would be able to drive without killing each other. Without Amy to balance us out, I doubted we'd make it past the state line.

I don't know if Amy ended up deciding to go to college, but Lila left town before we were even sentenced—took off on both of us before Amy even could. I wonder now, if I had been honest that day, not covered up my feelings with angry words, whether Lila wouldn't have left me, too.

Lisa Burstein

Whether Amy wouldn't have ratted me out to the cops.

But I know eventually everything goes to shit.

Eventually everything falls apart.

What happened on prom night and after is more than evidence of that.

21 Fucking Days
to Go

oday was hiking again. Hiking was important because apparently we were going to do a lot of it when we stopped training.

If we ever stop training.

I'm still not sure what we were training for. Not like we could ask, but Rawe never told us. Maybe she knew we wouldn't train very hard if she did.

Our hike started early—butt crack of dawn early. I never truly understood what that meant until I got here. The never-ending horizon of the wilderness was the butt crack of a giant, the sun peeking through like a wink from one of his big white cheeks. We had a long, tiring day ahead of us. That would have been bad enough, more than bad enough, but of course, the boys were waiting at attention for us at the trailhead. They stood in a line: Nerone, the guys next to him in order of height. Ben was in the middle, grinning at me like someone behind him was pulling back his skin.

"Claire, what's with the smile?" Rawe asked.

"Just ready to hike with my fellow hikers," Ben said.

"You look deranged," I said.

"You look like you'd be into deranged." He smirked, daring me.

"No more talking," Nerone yelled.

I smirked back, thinking Ben was lucky that Nerone had told us to be quiet. Not that I had any idea how to respond. I *was* into deranged.

Nez was clearly drooling. She was like a vampire, but instead of blood she craved boys, needed them in the same sick, singular way. If she wasn't starting to piss me off so much, I might have actually felt bad for her.

"I hope Ben can still walk after the other night," Nez said.

Well, actually, probably not.

"Move out," Nerone said, leading the way.

We walked boy, girl, boy, girl, Nerone's square head the front of the gangly brown animal we made and Rawe's tight braid like our tail all the way in the back. Nez made a big deal about wanting to walk behind Andre so she could stare at his ass.

Whatever. It was fine if she wanted to drool all over Andre, because I didn't have to fight with her about walking behind Ben. I would have to try to ignore his ass, because I wanted some cigarettes.

I needed some cigarettes.

I didn't say anything at first. I guess I was still trying to figure out if Ben had really been with Nez. Watching him march in front of me and play air drums against the sunrise, it didn't seem possible. Watching his arms, as thick and strong as the branches on the trees around us, it was hard to believe. Sure, Nez said they did, but it's not like I trusted her.

I watched her walking behind Andre. She moved like a boa constrictor, surveying Andre's ass like it was prey. She would probably swallow it whole if she could. She would probably grab him from behind and throw him into the ferns that grew waist-high on the sides of the trail.

I listened to the crunch of sticks and shuffle of leaves below me. The birds in the trees above me were singing bird songs to each other and talking their bird way of talking. I couldn't help thinking about Amy and that stupid parrot she had.

I was in her pink bedroom only once. Apparently her mother hated me, hated me so much that I wasn't allowed back after I was invited to Amy's house once for a dinner that her mother hadn't even bothered to cook. I can remember that bird squawking and talking the whole time we were in Amy's room. It repeated the things Amy said, the things I said—as annoyingly as a little brother mimicking you—and the cage made her whole room smell like bird ass.

I remember saying, "How can you fucking think with that thing in here?"

And she said, "I can't; that's the point," her face sad.

I didn't understand it then. Thought it was another of her weird Amy-isms. But I totally got it now. I would keep anything near me if it were loud enough to make me not think, even if it shit on my shoulder sometimes.

Even if it made *me* smell like bird ass.

Lisa Burstein

I looked up. A flock of them flew from one tree to another. They moved again to the next tree and the next, like they were following us as we hiked.

I looked at Ben still walking in front of me. It was now or never. Well, it was now or two miles from now.

"What's with those birds?" I asked—not that I really cared, but I needed to say *something* to him.

"We're scaring them, so they keep moving," he said.

"Why should they be scared when we're way down here?" I asked.

"I don't know, Cassie," he said. "Why are you scared?"

I felt my legs stop. My chest go cold. What the hell was this? "I'm not," I said, forcing myself to walk again. "I'm not scared of anything," I lied.

"Okay, whatever." Ben didn't turn to look at me, but I could hear a smile in his voice.

Was this what Aaron had done to me? Could boys now sense that I would cringe at their touch? At even the thought of their touch?

Fuck.

"Did you and Nez have a good time?" I asked, trying to show how *not scared* I was. I figured I should get that out of the way before I asked about the cigarettes. I guess I also thought he would be more likely to give me one if I brought up his beautiful Nez first.

"What are you talking about?" he asked.

"N-nothing," I sputtered. "Nez said—"

As if she knew we were talking about her, she started skipping down the trail, like there were fucking gumdrops and lollipops on either side of her.

"Nez is fun," Ben said. I could hear the smile in his voice.

"Spare me," I said.

"What?" He shrugged. "She doesn't let things get to her."

"That's because there's always a boy on top of her. 'Things' can't get through," I said.

"I thought you didn't want to talk." He spoke with his back to me. His hair moved up and down like a mustache when he talked. "Or maybe you really do," he cooed.

I considered launching him into a blackberry briar but looked behind me instead. Leisner was there, his feet pounding the trail like two sledgehammers, his curly blond hair as puberific as ever. He wagged his tongue out like he was trying to make his beard grow by adding saliva.

"You wish," I said.

"I think Ben wishes," Leisner guffawed.

"Tell it to Nez," I said.

"Oh, I will," he said, his tongue still hanging out of his mouth. I looked up, wishing that one of those birds following us would take a crap right then.

I guess Nez's reputation was getting around. "Have fun getting herpes," I said.

Behind Leisner, Troyer was making a gun out of her hand and shooting him repeatedly in the head with it. I smiled at her. She smiled back and pretended to blow on the hot gun barrel before sticking it in her pocket. She didn't even talk and she was probably the most entertaining person here. Well, besides me, of course.

Eagan hiked behind her, his braces shining in the sun and probably catching gnats like the grill of a car on a road trip. I could hear him talking about how many poisonous species

Lisa Burstein

of plants existed on this hiking trail, then pointing out each one by its scientific name. I was surprised Troyer wasn't pretending to shoot herself. I was surprised Rawe wasn't telling him to zip it and making him do push-ups with his mouth open on top of those poisonous plants, but maybe she was glad someone was doing something other than talking about boys and bitching.

I turned back to Ben. I was so tired and I so wanted a cigarette. Maybe that was the thing I could use to not make me think, like Amy and her stupid, smelly bird. Maybe I could smoke a ton of cigarettes and suffocate myself into oblivion, feel the feeling of holding my breath for so long that the area in between my ears whirs like a blender, spins up my brain like one. It was either that or suffocate myself in the pit toilet.

"Hey," I whispered. "I hear you got smokes."

"Who told you that, Cassie?" Ben asked, adding my name to piss me off.

I ignored it. He was going to make me ask, make me beg. Maybe I deserved that, but it wasn't like he knew it. For all he knew I was just some girl who didn't like being called Cassie.

"I want one," I said.

"No 'please'?" he asked, his voice almost purring.

I looked all the way to the front of the line at Nerone. Luckily, he was too far ahead to hear us and was reciting some marching call that no one was responding to.

"You're not serious," I said.

"I think 'please' is the least you could say, Cassie," Ben added, lingering on my name.

"What does that mean?" I asked, even though I figured he

meant that I hadn't thanked him for saving me, at least not like Nez supposedly had.

"Your choice is between 'please' or what I really want to know," he said.

Super. It was worse than that—we were back to him pestering me about why I was here. Ben was nothing if not insanely fixated.

"Fine, please," I said, so fast it was like I barely said the word at all.

"Hmmmm . . ." he said, acting like he was thinking about it. "No."

I felt my stomach roll. He wouldn't have said yes, no matter what I did. He'd just wanted to make me say please.

Asshole.

He started to smack his thighs and whistle like those fucking birds.

"Why do you want to know why I'm here so badly?" I asked, even though it would have been simple: pot, arrest, the whole long prom night story. But I didn't want to tell him that. Because I knew it was a lie, knew there was more to why I was here. The reason that I carried, so massive it felt like it could bend me in two, pummel me to dust.

The reason why no matter how much I denied it, I *was* scared of Ben.

I couldn't deny that after what had happened with Aaron, boys scared me a little. Not because of what they could do, but because of the out-of-control things they made me do.

"You're not telling me your secrets," he said. "Why should I tell you mine?" He stopped and turned around to look at me. Maybe he wanted to see my face, or maybe he wanted

Lisa Burstein

me to see his. I tried to walk around him and he blocked me. I turned. Leisner and the rest of them were at least a quarter of a mile behind us. There was no escape except to talk.

"Move," I said. I tried to walk around him, but he was as unmovable as the tree trunks that lined the trail.

"Say please," he teased, leaning toward me.

"One more step and you'll be begging *me*," I said, starting to form a fist. I couldn't stop looking at his lips. My skin burned like the sun above us was in my blood. I needed to stay the hell away from him, even though he had something I wanted so desperately. Even though I couldn't stop thinking about how his arms had held me tighter than they needed to in the lake.

"You really think you could beat me up, don't you?" he asked.

"Of course," I said, my hand still a tight fist.

"Tough and beautiful, a lethal combination," he said.

"You've got the lethal part right," I said.

"Less talking more hiking," Nerone yelled, only noticing us when we stopped and our voices rose. "Each word I hear will be an extra half mile."

"If you want the cigarettes, come and get them," Ben whispered. "They are under my mattress waiting for you."

"I take that as a challenge," I said.

"Take it however you want. It will still mean you're coming to *my* cabin at night." Ben shrugged, a *sucks to be you* move, and started walking again.

I am getting those cigarettes if I have to kill him to get them.

It is clear that killing him is becoming my only safe option.

20 Fucking Days
to Go

've been sparing this journal some of the crap we have to do. I mean, I am bored out of my gourd as it is, so I'm doing my best not to have to relive all of it. There is very little of what I'd expected rehab to be—which is good; it's not like I wanted people talking to me about my feelings.

Each night Rawe just gives us a lecture on some aspect of our fucked-up lives and tells us to write about it, which, *Screw me*, I just realized is actually sort of working.

There is a lot of hiking, marching, waiting in line. There is a lot of trying to forget. There is a lot of watching Nez talk and watching Troyer not talk. There is a lot of walking past locked buildings that I know have flush-toilets and running water inside and not being allowed to enter them. There is a lot of smelling my armpits on days Rawe doesn't let us shower and then wishing I hadn't. There is a lot of pretending that Ben isn't getting to me even though he is.

But mostly, there is a lot of wondering if I'll ever feel better even after I leave this place.

If this is what I am now—a girl who used to know who she was, who used to be able to make people afraid of her, but is now only scared of herself.

Of what she will do if she lets one more boy in.

Rawe led us up the hill to the stables. Even though the horses were long gone, it still had that stable smell. Like fresh dirt and sweet hay right up your nose. Like dirty hair. I wished the horses were still there. I hated a lot of things, but I loved horses. How big, beautiful, graceful, and calm they were.

How unlike me they were.

My brother loved riding and would take me sometimes when I was a kid, boosting me up into the saddle. I would hold onto the horn in front of me and the horse would start walking under me like magic.

Like a magic earthquake.

My brother and I would ride trails, him in front, the clomp of horse hooves on the ground. His horse would swish its tail every so often at a fly, one side of its butt moving up while the other moved down like a seesaw. Back then it was easy to pretend we were in a fairy tale, in another time. And it was easy to believe while we were riding those horses, as magnificent as dinosaurs.

Now, I was just in an abandoned stable, waiting to get the hell out of this place.

We walked from the dirt-covered ring to the stables and

Rawe turned on the lights. They made that humming noise that lights that haven't been turned on in a while make. They were bright and made me squint with the realization that the empty, smelly stable had better lights than our own cabin did.

We were being treated worse than horse shit. Fossilized horse shit.

Rawe handed us each a rake and pointed us to a stall. Mine had a burnished wood sign hanging on it that read PEANUT.

"I don't do horses," Nez said, her lips tight.

"I thought you did everything," I said.

Nez stuck her tongue out at me.

"The horses are long gone, Queen Nez," Rawe said, doing a fake bow. "Rake out the hay."

Troyer lowered her head and entered her stall.

"Why are we doing this?" Nez asked, holding her rake upright next to her.

I guess I was glad she asked and I kinda wondered why I hadn't. It was just the kind of question I ordinarily would have snarked out, either loud enough for Rawe to hear or under my breath. But I hadn't even thought to say anything. I just took my rake and entered Peanut's sad old stall. Was I changing without even realizing it, like Rawe had said? Or was I tired, so incredibly tired in my body and in my mind that I couldn't even be baseline normal Cassie?

Or had I lost her before I even got here?

"I'll be back in twenty minutes, so you better hope you're done," Rawe said, slamming the stable door behind her.

"What's her problem?" Nez asked.

"Who knows?" I said. Rawe was acting like a completely different person than she had been the day I found her

Lisa Burstein

praying. Maybe she wasn't that person. Or maybe for some reason, she was only that person with me.

I started raking. The hay was high, as high as grass that hadn't been mowed in weeks. It crunched under my feet as I thought about Peanut. He was probably a pony, a light brown pony that all the campers must have loved and fed apples and carrots to.

When I was a kid and my brother and I would ride, that was what we would do: watch as the orange carrots we fed our trail horses were crunched and crunched and disappeared into their big, spongy mouths. We would pat them as they chewed, their fur as soft as a dog's ear. I might not have missed being home, but I guess I missed my brother.

I heard Nez and Troyer in the stalls on either side of me, also raking. Nez was grunting, like she was hooking up with the hay, and it made me wonder why she hadn't complained yet that the boys weren't there. She hadn't even snuck out since the night she was with Ben, or had claimed to be.

As I raked, I couldn't help thinking about the kids who'd gone to this camp, whose parents came to watch them ride on visiting weekend. They probably had the kind of parents who would always tell them they were awesome, even when they sucked. I had the kind who told me I sucked when I sucked. I couldn't even remember a time they told me I was awesome, but maybe that's because I never was. Maybe that was because my mom was too busy drinking instead of talking and my dad was too busy killing other people's children with army-issue weapons.

"This stinks," Nez said over the stall, in her typical Nez way.

"You stink," I said, in my typical Cassie way.

Troyer said nothing. I was beginning to wonder if part of

the reason she didn't talk was because she didn't want people to figure her out, didn't want to have a guy like Ben make it his daily mission to.

"I'd much rather be rolling in the hay than raking it," Nez joked.

"How about we work for a change?" I said. I actually liked raking and thinking about Peanut. How I would have liked to ride Peanut and brush her blond mane. I probably would have liked going to this camp. I might have turned into a completely different person if I had.

"If I don't talk, who's going to?" Nez said over her heavy breaths. "All you do is swear and all Troyer does is drool." I knew Troyer could hear Nez from her stall, but she didn't stop working, didn't even act like she could hear her. I listened to Troyer's rake move along the floor of the stall, scratching at dirt and hay.

I ignored Nez, matched Troyer's movements.

"I'm trying to stay sane," Nez said. "What are you trying to do?"

"Get the hell out of here," I said, still raking. My shoulders burned like they had the day we split all that wood. The hay was as heavy as the snow I had to shovel from our driveway when my brother conned me into doing it for him.

"Just make sure you don't lose it before then," Nez said.

"Just make sure you don't trip over your vagina before then," I said.

"At least I know how to use mine," Nez said.

There was no way she could have known what had happened before I came here, but when she said things like that, it was like she did.

Lisa Burstein

"This sucks," I said, slamming my rake against the hay below me. "Fuck," I spit.

"Why do you swear so much?" Nez asked.

"Because I like it," I said, not turning to look at her. "Why do you sleep around so much?"

"Because *I* like it," she replied.

"It's fucking disgusting," I said.

"So is swearing," she said. "It's like swallowing the whole pit toilet and then spewing it out again." Her words were like tea—calm, warm.

God, I hated Nez in a way that I never hated Lila. Nez was definitely as vain as Lila, but there was something else about her, something where just hearing her voice could make my skin crawl.

I heard the stable door open: a heavy, dusty creak. "Troyer, Wick, tack room," Rawe yelled. "Nez, you finish the stalls."

"All of them?" Nez wailed.

"You have other plans?" Rawe asked.

"You have to be flicking kidding me," Nez said, huffing.

Maybe Rawe did actually care.

Troyer and I followed her into the tack room. Saddles and bridles hung from the wall. A desk, empty except for a shiny cowboy belt buckle paperweight, sat in the center.

"Dust," Rawe said, handing us two rags. "Don't move anything, don't touch anything. Don't take anything. Understand?"

"Yeah," I said. I wanted to ask her how we were supposed to dust without touching anything, but Rawe had been nice enough to remove Nez from our lives for a short time. That had to be worth me keeping my mouth closed. I also wondered what there was to take. I wasn't really in need of a saddle. But maybe I could use the bridle to shut Nez the hell up.

"Troyer?" Rawe asked.

She nodded, just once, fast and sharp like the blade of a guillotine going down.

"Okay," Rawe said, leaving us to work. "You have ten minutes."

I started on the saddles. They hung on wooden dowels adorned with golden labels, a girl's name on each of them.

A girl's *first* name.

Troyer started dusting the top of the desk. "At least this is better than hiking," I said, realizing that even in a room with someone who didn't talk, I felt the need to make conversation. I hated to think it, but maybe Nez was right. Maybe we did have to do whatever we had to do to stay sane.

Not that anything I had tried yet appeared to be working.

Troyer looked at me, then back down at the desk. She picked up the belt buckle paperweight and held it in her hand.

"My brother and I used to horseback ride," I said as I shined one of the labels. *Rachel.* A girl with a saddle. A girl who probably didn't smoke pot, who probably didn't get arrested and then fall for stupid boys who made her feel more stupid, who made her do stupid things she could never forget.

Troyer looked up but didn't write on her pad. Maybe she didn't have it with her and maybe she didn't care that my brother and I used to horseback ride. I mean, why would she? It was the first time I'd even bothered to think of it in years.

Troyer wasn't listening anyway, so I stopped talking and dusted. The smooth leather of the saddles started to shine like caramel under my rag. They were English saddles, the

Lisa Burstein

kind that rich kids used. This was probably a rich kids' camp. A rich kids' camp that some poor messed-up kids were now cleaning. Rachel was probably at an Ivy League college right now. One like maybe Amy would have gone to if she hadn't started hanging out with Lila and me. Even before all this, I knew an Ivy League school was the kind of place I would never see.

Rawe stuck her head in the tack room door, her white skin stark against the worn, dirty wood. She spoke like her words were a snare drum. "Troyer, come help Nez load up this hay. Wick, finish up, grab the rags, and turn off the light when you're done."

I watched Troyer leave. From behind, her blond hair reminded me of what Peanut's mane might have looked like.

All alone, I took the chance to sit in the desk chair. I wiped my forehead—it was covered in sweat. My hands were dusty. Dirt crusted in my nails. Without a shower in two days, this was clean now. Without a cigarette, this was relaxing now. I looked in the desk drawers, opened each one slowly and quietly so Rawe wouldn't hear, but they were all empty.

I don't know what I was hoping for, maybe that the equestrian counselor was a smoker and left her smokes behind on the last day of camp.

I got up, pushed the chair back in, and noticed the belt buckle paperweight was missing. I looked on the floor, thinking that Troyer must have knocked it over while she was cleaning, but it wasn't there. Had she swiped it? Maybe that was why she was here. Maybe that was why she was afraid to talk.

I might not be able to figure her out, but I know who I am taking with me to steal those cigarettes from Ben.

19 Fucking Days
to Go

We were crunching on our allotted afternoon snack of trail mix—the shitty kind without chocolate chips, because, *hey, we are being punished*—when the letters came. In plain white envelopes like we really were in prison. Rawe gave Troyer and me one each, and then handed Nez a stack as thick as a deck of cards. Maybe all her sexual partners had written her specially to thank her for giving them gonorrhea.

"I didn't even know we were allowed to get mail," I said, looking at my envelope. I recognized the handwriting; it was from my brother. Nez got letters from hot boys. I got a letter from my brother.

Aaron truly had ruined me.

"Well, someone in your family read the manual," Rawe said, "even if you didn't."

"I read it," I said, because I was feeling argumentative. Really, I had figured I could learn the rules when I got here, that I would have more than enough time to learn them when I got here. I should have read it. Then I would have known I was coming to the Nazis' idea of a relaxing vacay.

"Great," Rawe said. "I guess you missed the section on approved mail, and also the one on approved language."

Nez laughed.

I shrugged.

"Twenty minutes to read," Rawe said. "Then we start the dinner fire."

She went into her room at the back of the cabin with her own envelope, maybe from someone who knew her by her first name, like the people who had written our letters knew us. In that moment I realized that I didn't even know Rawe's first name. I probably never would.

The dinner fire sucked. If we couldn't start it, and by *we* I mean Nez, Troyer, and me, then we didn't eat. There had been several nights we didn't eat. I considered leaving the rest of my trail mix for later just in case.

"I'm definitely going to need longer than twenty minutes," Nez said, rifling through her letters.

"You better get started then," I said. I considered adding "shut the fuck up and" before "get," but I wasn't in the mood to fight with Nez. I had my own letter to read.

"What the hell do you know? You got one letter and it's probably from your mommy and daddy," Nez said. "Like Troyer's."

Troyer looked up from her envelope and gave Nez the finger.

"Say it or I can't hear you," Nez said.

Screw you, Troyer's lips said, but no words came out.

"It's from my brother," I said.

Nez bounced on her cot and looked at me excitedly. "Is he hot?"

"Do you ever turn off?" I asked.

"So that means he's not," she said, frowning.

"It means you make the cast of *Jersey Shore* look like prudes," I said.

"Jealous," Nez smiled, fanning herself with her letters.

I ignored her, picked up the envelope, and looked at my hands. The areas around my nails and on my palms were cracked and bleeding from rock climbing that day. They looked like they were made out of bloody wax paper. I wiped them on my uniform; it was dirty anyway.

Troyer was already reading, her face hidden behind a stack of stationary pages. I wondered who her letter was from. Maybe she had a boyfriend at home. What a catch, a girl who couldn't bitch at you.

I looked over at Nez. She had turned away from us and was lying on her stomach reading one letter at a time.

I opened my letter. Inside were two envelopes: one from my brother and one from someone else. The only someone else it could have been was my mom or my dad.

Crap, what the hell did they have to say to me?

Rather than find out, I opened my brother's first.

I unfolded the letter. In the middle of the page were three lines:

Lisa Burstein

You can do this.
You will do this.
I love you.

Sometimes I wished I could meet a boy like my brother and sometimes I wondered if my brother was the only boy I would ever meet like him.

I sniffed the paper, hoping to catch a whiff of cigarette smoke, wanting to do anything other than read the letter that I knew had to be from one of my parents. What the hell were they going to say? It certainly wouldn't be as nice as the letter from my brother. It probably wouldn't even have the word *love* in it.

I pushed the paper against my nose but couldn't smell anything. My brother smoked, always had a cigarette dangling out of his mouth, but the paper smelled of nothing. It was sad to realize that it had traveled so far that his smell had worn off.

Troyer turned to me, my nose still to the paper.

"What?" I asked.

She stared at me. I knew her look asked, *You know you're smelling paper right?*

"I miss my brother," I said as explanation, but I'm sure that didn't really make sense, even though it might have been the first true thing I'd said since I'd been there.

She blinked slowly and went back to reading her own letter, which was many pages, written on both front and back. It was like whoever had written to her was so used to doing all the talking when she was around that he or she felt the need to still do all the talking even when she wasn't, even when it was in writing.

I braced myself and opened the other envelope. Whatever my parents had to say, at least they weren't here. I unfolded the letter. Loopy girlish cursive covered the page. Not my mom's writing, certainly not my dad's. I recognized it, but not enough to make the connection without looking at the bottom of the page to see who had signed it.

Amy.

It was from Amy.

Snitch-rat Amy.

The last time I talked to her was the day I was sentenced. The first time since the arraignment that my mother, father, and I had gone anywhere together. The last time we had gone anywhere together.

We were waiting in the judge's chambers. His crimson-haired assistant had already come in and told us he was stuck in a meeting and would be with us momentarily. Right, I knew that meant he would be with us whenever he damn well felt like it. I knew that meant, *Your future can wait.* None of us was talking. My mother was rolling an unlit cigarette between her fingers and my father was cracking his knuckles, one by one, like they were walnuts.

I had to get out of there.

"I'll be back," I said, leaving before I could hear either of my parents respond.

I went out into the hall and lunged for the nearest bathroom. I went into the stall and sat without even taking off my pants. I breathed, in and out, in and out, trying the technique my brother had shared with me for keeping myself calm. The one he used when he and his fellow soldiers were, as he put it, *in the shit.* It didn't work. I flushed out of habit and when I

Lisa Burstein

came out I saw Amy at the sink drinking water like she had a camel in her stomach.

Without even thinking about it I pushed her, hard—hard enough that she screamed. I held her against the wall. She squirmed under my grip and I watched her, as helpless as a potato bug that had been turned over. I was going to punch her. I was going to kill her. I wanted to take her big, fat, snitch mouth and break every pretty tooth in it.

She was the reason I was even meeting with the judge. The reason I was here with my parents wondering where the hell I would spend the next month of my life. My lawyer had told me that she had signed some confession that made the fault "rest" on Lila and me. When my mother asked him *what the fuck that means*, he said, "It means we need to make a deal."

Rehab was going to be my deal.

Amy's face was priceless, her mouth open wide, her eyes darting, like I was holding a knife instead of a fist. I was ready to hit her, but then she brought up Ruthie Jensen spreading around that shit about me and I let her go.

Mostly because I couldn't breathe; her words were like the punch I hadn't gotten off.

To change the subject, to *kill* the subject, I'd told Amy the lie about throwing a Pepsi in Aaron's face and telling him to get lost.

I put my hand to my stomach and read her letter.

Cassie,

I hope you're doing well. (Yeah right.) *I am trying to move past prom night and the arrest but there is something I feel like I need to tell you in order to do that.* (What the fuck is this?) *Remember when we were in the bathroom the day we were sentenced and you talked about that guy Aaron?* (Oh fuck.) *Well, I lied to you. I did know him. I was sort of his girlfriend, I guess.* (No fucking way.)

I felt my hands fist on the paper, squeezing so hard, so angry, so tight.

He tried to get me to turn myself in. He tried to get me to do a lot of things. I guess he made me do a lot of things. (Oh don't I fucking know all about that. Fuck me, that fucking bastard.)

Anyway, I'm sorry. I probably should have told you that day, but I was embarrassed that I fell for it. That I believed anything he said. I want you to know that most of the reason I signed that confession was because of what he did to me, was because I was tired of being used by everyone. I know it didn't turn out the best for you and so I'm sorry. If I could go back I would have done things differently, probably a lot of things.

Amy

My teeth were clenched so hard that my jaw felt like it might dislodge. I ripped the letter once, then again and again smaller and smaller. I guess I was grunting because Nez turned from her *Penthouse* letters and sat up.

"Who spit in your Cheerios?" she asked, cocking her head to the side like someone had put her in a cubist painting.

Lisa Burstein

I couldn't even respond. I ran from the cabin, slammed the door so hard behind me that it screamed on its hinges. I sat on the ground. I felt like I might cry, but I wasn't going to. I had allowed myself to handle what had happened with Aaron, allowed myself to deal with it as a mistake, as something that was out of my control. But now, I realized that it was something completely in *his* control. That he knew exactly what he was doing—and he did the same thing to Amy.

I felt sick. I threw up the trail mix, punched my stomach again and again and again until I couldn't breathe. Aaron hadn't just fooled me, he had fucking fooled me and I had fallen for it.

Fuck.

I heard the door to the cabin open. Rawe walked out. I wiped my mouth and turned away from her.

"You okay, Wick?"

I wanted to say, *I'm fucking fine,* but I wasn't. I wasn't. "Don't worry, I have my Assessment Diary for times like this," I snarked. That was what it was for, right? Pouring our shit ton of feelings into it so Turning Pines could claim it was doing *something* to make us better.

"You can talk to me if you want," she said, coming up beside me and touching my shoulder. Part of me wanted to fall into her and part of me wanted to break her hand. I couldn't decide which to do, so I didn't move.

"Right," I said, my eyes on my boots. I couldn't talk. I couldn't see.

"When it's the three of you," she said, her hand digging into my shoulder trying to get me to look at her, "I'm on script, but when we're one on one, I'm here to listen."

My eyes were still on my boots.

"I get it," she said. "There are all these things inside you. Being here you feel them starting to come out and you don't know how to deal with them. It's like someone is pouring you a glass of water and it's full, full, full and then it's overflowing and you just keep screaming, 'Stop, stop, stop.'"

I looked at her. She was right and I hated it. I hated her for finally being nice to me when I most needed it. For all the people before her who never were.

I left her there and went back to the cabin. I didn't know what else to do but write. I put my pad on my lap and carved into it—*fuck, fuck, fuck*, over and over and over—the word I used as a shield and a bullet.

The word I used as a mantra.

Fucking fine, fucking okay, since nothing else is working, I'll fucking write the thing that led to the thing that brought me here. I'll finally burden this journal with the words that are true, even if I can't say them.

Weeks before the day with Amy in the bathroom, the rumor Ruthie had been spreading about me came true. When I found out, I couldn't admit it right away. For two weeks, I told myself I must have counted wrong. But when a whole month went by, I knew my period wasn't just late, it was ridiculous.

Aaron was supposed to come and see me at Pudgie's that night, like he always did during my break, so we could do the thing that did the thing I was now dreading was true. I knew I couldn't see him, so I told him I was staying home sick. I

Lisa Burstein

needed to know before I could see him again. I needed to know *if* I could see him again.

That night, instead of meeting Aaron in his black convertible and driving to the park and moving into his warm leather backseat, I went to the drugstore across the street from Pudgie's and bought a pregnancy test. I'd never thought about it until that night, but I guess it wasn't a coincidence they were in the same row as the condoms. Maybe that was their way of warning you.

Apparently, I didn't get the message.

I paid for the test with my head down and carried it in a lunch-size paper bag to the McDonald's next door. I walked in to that familiar McDonald's smell, fries and ammonia. I fought back the nausea that was high in my throat.

I went into the bathroom, locked myself in one of the stalls, and tried not to think how pathetic *that* was while I peed on a stick. I stood on the toilet for ten minutes while the test percolated—so no one could see me—while I waited to see if my shitty life was about to get exponentially shittier.

I had some time to think during those minutes. Some time to read the things written on the stall. Things about girls to call for a good time, about being sweet and wiping the seat. I thought about how my mother must have felt when she found out she was pregnant with me. She couldn't have had any idea that one day, the baby she'd be having would be standing in a McDonald's bathroom waiting to see if she was going to have a baby. Wishing she was not going to have a baby.

A baby she couldn't have.

A baby I knew now was made with a boy's lies.

The alarm on my cell beeped. It echoed in the stall as I

got down off the toilet and picked up the test. It wobbled in my hand like it was one of those old thermometers that people were meant to shake. Like my mother standing over me as a child, while she told me I better not be sick because her bus route wasn't going to drive itself so she could stay home with me.

I looked at the test. It had a blue plus sign and a circle on it. I didn't even have to look at the box to know I was totally fucked. My head buzzed like there was a jet engine between my ears. I couldn't think. I couldn't see and I had to be back at work.

Soon.

Now.

I wrapped the test up in a tissue and threw it in the trash. It had done its job—tell me I was royally screwed—so what did I need it for anymore?

That night after work my mother picked me up like she always did. Her car was running while she waited in Pudgie's parking lot, the headlights on, like she didn't even want to waste the time to turn them off. I knew it was because she couldn't wait to get out of there, so she could get home and drink.

I got in the car and tried not to think that there were three of us in there instead of the usual two, that there had been three of us in there for a whole month and I didn't know it.

"I'm out of smokes," my mother said, staring out the windshield. She didn't usually say hello, so this was not surprising.

I didn't respond. The only thing in my head was, *Holy fuck, I'm pregnant. Fuck me. Fuck me for letting Aaron fuck me.*

I'm sure I looked white, whiter than I usually did, even with

Lisa Burstein

Pudgie's dough flour all over me. I'm also sure I was shaking, not that my mother would notice anyway because she was out of cigarettes. She didn't notice anything when she was out of cigarettes.

"I hope you don't have to piss or anything, because I'm stopping on the way home," she said, pulling out of the lot.

I still didn't respond. I guess I was afraid to. Anything I could say would seem stupid considering what I was dealing with at that moment. How could I ask her why she didn't stop off on the way to pick me up instead, now that there was something growing in my belly? I put on my seat belt. When I clicked it shut, I couldn't help feeling my stomach. What was in there? A little me, a little Aaron. I looked at my mom. A little my mom?

God, I hoped not.

My mother turned out of the parking lot, her face as taut as a pulled-back rubber band. She was chewing on her lip, which meant she had been out of cigarettes for a while. I thought about having a cigarette when I got home, about being alone in my room and smoking as many cigarettes as I had left in my pack out my bedroom window, maybe even burning the insides of my wrists with them so I could *feel* something, but then I remembered the warning about smoking during pregnancy being harmful to your baby.

I was pregnant. I had a baby.

"I'm stopping here," my mother said, pulling into Gas-N-Go. She didn't really need to tell me, but maybe she'd noticed how silent the car was and felt like she had to say something. At least I didn't have to.

I'd been to Gas-N-Go before. The place was a hole, but it was pretty lenient when it came to carding. Of course, no one was going to card my mom. On her best days her skin looked like a rotten potato.

She didn't ask me if I wanted anything, simply slammed the car door and left me in the parking lot. Not like she usually asked me, but I guess it seemed weird because I was pregnant now. Not that she knew it, but pregnant women needed things, didn't they?

She took her keys with her, leaving me sitting in the dark, quiet car. No music or A/C for me, but maybe she was afraid I would drive away. That night I might have considered it. I could just go. Drive far away and never look back. Maybe my baby and I could make a life for ourselves in North Dakota or some other state with two words besides New York.

Aaron, that fucking bastard. Of course, this wasn't entirely his fault. We used protection, but obviously it didn't protect me. I felt myself start to cry, hot, fast, and furious, like the steam coming from a whistling teapot. I never cried. I didn't even cry on the night I was arrested. Lila cried like a fucking drama queen and Amy seemed too scared to do anything but stare at her nails.

But I was crying now, and that scared me more than anything because it let me know how scared I must truly have been.

I needed to get home, to lock myself in my room and get under my covers and suck on my unlit cigarettes.

What was taking my mom so long? I tried to look through the front window and into the store.

I saw my mother up at the counter. There was no one in front of her, she was already holding her cigarettes, so why didn't she pay for them and get outside so we could go? I looked closer. She was talking to someone, *yelling* at someone.

Lisa Burstein

Amy.

I went for my seat belt. Amy. I hadn't seen her since our arraignment. I missed her. Missed how I knew she saw me, like someone strong. Like someone who could defend herself. Like someone who didn't fucking cry. Then I stopped.

What was I going to tell her? And what would she say back? Considering she was working at Gas-N-Go, she had her own shit to deal with. Considering she was talking to my mother right now, she had more than her own shit to deal with.

And looking back, what I hated to realize was that Aaron had been part of it.

He probably used her, just like he used me. Or maybe he'd liked her and I was the one getting used. Either way, knowing what I know about them now, I am glad I didn't go in to see her.

I watched as my mother continued to yell, and I couldn't help wondering why she never yelled at me. Why was she picking Amy to yell at? I looked down at my lap. I didn't want Amy to see me. All I needed was for her to look out there. For her to look at me and know something was wrong. Know something was very wrong.

Know that something happened to me that I could never take back, no matter what I did.

Know that she had been this close to being me, but was somehow stronger.

18 Fucking Days
to Go

waited to wake Troyer until I could hear Nez snoozing. Luckily, Nez was very tired. I was very tired, too, but Nez was even more so. That day we'd learned how to pitch a tent and while Nez claimed she could easily make a boy pitch a tent in his pants, actual tent-pitching was beyond her. While trying to put hers up she had looked like someone dressed as a ghost on Halloween, with the tent as the bed sheet. She flailed around underneath it, like she couldn't find the eyeholes.

As much as I would have liked it to be because Nez was an idiot, it wasn't her fault. We weren't allowed to use those easy pup tents that even someone without hands can put together.

Our tents had lots of metal pole pieces and parts and stakes that looked like giant nails. By the end of the day Nez had almost said a real, actual swear word.

When we'd gotten back to the cabin, Rawe sat us on our beds and asked us if we wanted to talk, like the way she had seen me the day before had jogged her memory that she was supposed to be "helping" us in more ways than just Assessment Diary word count.

None of us had spoken. Not like Troyer would have anyway, but even Nez kept her mouth shut. It was clear that the more Rawe tried to get us to talk, the more we burrowed into ourselves. But it was impossible to burrow into yourself without thinking about why you didn't want to talk in the first place.

I was starting to wonder if that was the whole point.

I stood above Troyer's bed and shook her. Fortunately, I didn't have to worry about her making noise, so I could be sure she wouldn't scream and wake Nez up. Nez could not be a part of this mission. I needed Ben to myself. It would have made sense to bring her so she could have kept Ben busy while I snatched his cigarettes, but his cigarettes were hidden under his mattress. So I would have to be right there watching Nez keep him busy while I tried to snatch the smokes.

I definitely wanted his cigarettes, but I didn't want them that badly.

When Troyer's eyes opened, like white saucers in the dark, I said, "Come on, I need you."

She didn't move right away, just looked at me, her sleeping bag pulled up to her chin, her face peeking out like a pea from a pod.

"Troyer, seriously," I said, showing her my flashlight. I swept it over me so she could see I was totally dressed, complete with my boots.

She grabbed her pad and scribbled, *Why? Where?*

"Please, Troyer," I said. I didn't want to get into why and where because the more time we spent in the cabin, the better chance Nez would wake up.

Troyer sat and indicated Nez across the room.

"Screw Nez," I said.

She took out her pad and scribbled on it again. *If she finds out we went without her she'll kill us.*

"I'll take care of her," I said, even though I had no idea what that meant.

Troyer bit her bottom lip and got dressed.

We closed the cabin door quietly behind us and once we were far enough so our flashlights couldn't be seen when we turned them on, Troyer held my arm.

"What?" I asked.

She looked at me. She didn't have to write her question down. I was starting to understand her facial expressions. She was asking me why we were doing this.

"I need a smoke," I said.

She continued to look at me, her eyes hooded.

"Yes, that badly," I said, trudging in front of her. I heard her follow behind me.

We were going to get Ben's cigarettes. I sure as hell didn't know how, but we were going. If Nez could shimmy in that cabin twice and hook up with two different boys and not get caught, I was definitely going to be able to get in there and find the cigarettes hidden under Ben's mattress. I didn't even

Lisa Burstein

bother telling Troyer that I was bringing her with me because I knew what she had done at the stable. I was saving that in case I ever needed it.

"You'll go in first and check things out," I said. "You're so quiet they probably won't even notice you."

I heard Troyer stop walking behind me. I turned and saw her arms smack at her sides.

"What?" I asked.

She tilted her head.

"Yes, I know this is for me," I said.

Her head stayed tilted.

"Fine," I said, "I'll go in first."

She nodded and we kept walking past the dining hall. I considered forgetting the cigarettes and breaking in there so I could sit on a real toilet. Flush a real toilet. Turn on a faucet with clean, cold water, not pump water. It was weird the things I'd started to miss. You would think it would be my cell phone, the Internet, music, even TV, but no, it was the feel of my ass on cold porcelain. It was a shower without a time limit. It was a bed I didn't have to check for fleas.

It was froofy-smelling soap.

We hit the soccer field. The grass was high and wet with dew; I could feel the dampness coming through the legs of my uniform. I looked behind me—Troyer was still following. I could hear her breath, steady like the chug, chug, chug of a locomotive.

"Do you need a break?" I asked.

She shook her head, like she was saying, *Let's get this over with.*

I could feel the stars above me, so many of them that they

were fighting for space in the sky. So many that it seemed like some of them might fall out—overflow like a cup of soda fizzing over.

Overflow like the cup of feelings Rawe had described.

Obviously the feelings had always been there. The venom-like sickness that I felt—fear and repulsion, instead of the joy and excitement I should have felt if I were someone who wanted to have a baby, who could have a baby.

It had been there, was *still* there, but I'd managed until reading Amy's letter to keep it inside. Now it was out and my whole body felt exposed, like I had bathed in acid.

I felt my face burn, the shame and anger of what happened with Aaron slapping me in a new and even more embarrassing way.

Searching out stale cigarettes was all I had to combat that now. With the words of Amy's letter affixed to my brain, I felt like anything I had even sort of believed about Aaron and me was a total sham. Sure, it had turned into shit before all this, but I had believed he really liked me, had real feelings for me. But now I knew I was just another girl he'd tried to fool—and I had fallen for it.

I had ruined myself for it.

I saw the boys' cabin in the distance and stopped. It was dark, so quiet, so much the place I should not be breaking into. But I *had* walked all the way here.

"I'll go in the side window like Nez," I said. "Since you don't want to go in, you wait here and be a lookout."

Troyer took her pad and scribbled, *How will I warn you?*

It was a good question. It's not like she was going to yell,

Lisa Burstein

or make a hawk call, or any call for that matter. I doubted she could write loud enough for me to hear.

"Throw something," I said.

I walked to the side of the cabin. The window was open. Easy.

I took my boots off and only then wondered how I would be able to figure out which bed was Ben's without waking up the whole cabin. Well, except of course Nerone. I definitely should have listened to Nez instead of ignoring her when she discussed her and Ben's sexcapades. At least to hear which bed they had been on.

I heaved myself up and into the dark cabin. Luckily, there was enough space for me to get in without hitting either of the beds against the wall. I turned and looked at my boots on the ground outside. Hopefully a bear wouldn't come and eat them. Of course, if there was a bear around, it would probably eat Troyer, too.

My eyes were already adjusted to the dark and I could tell Eagan's bed right away, could see his braces shining in the moonlight as he snoozed with his mouth open. I didn't know what the boys had done that day but they were surely as tired as we were, if not more so. Nerone was a total hard ass, even if he did sleep like he was in a coffin.

I looked at the next bed. Stravalaci was snoring like he was saying *achoo*, over and over again. He didn't look so scary while he was sleeping. He kind of looked like a little boy. His hair was mussed and his mouth was open slightly — certainly not the face of someone who dreamed about guns and Nez's ass.

Across the cabin I saw Leisner's and Ben's beds. Leisner was clutching his pillow to his chest like it was trying to float away. I considered sucker punching him, but his wailing would probably wake the whole cabin. Ben was sleeping on his side, his body moving up and down in his red sleeping bag, like a beating heart.

I would have to make one quick move, grab the cigarettes from under Ben's mattress and get the hell out of there before he or anyone else heard me. I stood above Ben's bed and watched him breathe, watched his lips, realizing I could just as easily suffocate him or kiss him as take his smokes. People were so vulnerable when they were sleeping.

People were so vulnerable all the time.

I reached under his mattress, trying to keep the springs from creaking, trying to slow my heart even though I was so close to him, to his bed. I rooted around, flying blind, my hand going deeper and deeper but coming up empty.

I almost screamed when Ben grabbed my forearm. He didn't say anything, kept holding it tight, his skin on mine. So tight it kind of hurt. So tight I kind of liked it.

"Cassie," he whispered. "I knew you'd come."

"Not for you, for smokes," I hissed. I was trying to talk as little as possible. I was in a minefield of sleeping teenage boys.

"Nice excuse," he said, still holding my arm. I could see his eyes shining in the dark, dancing over my face.

"What stinks in here?" I asked. I'd smelled it when I first entered the cabin, but it was stronger now, noxious and rancid.

"Someone left a skunk in the pit toilet with Leisner the last time he took a leak," Ben said.

Lisa Burstein

"Someone?" I asked.

He shrugged.

I felt my arm go limp. Ben had defended my honor. Or maybe he just thought Leisner was as big a tool as I did. Either way, he was doing whatever he could to be my knight in shining armor.

Unfortunately, I was no princess.

"Can you please let go?" I said, trying to pull away, but his hands were strong. All that drumming practice turned his fingers to vices.

"You sure you want me to?" he said, starting to move his thumb back and forth on the soft underside of my wrist.

I hated that he'd asked, because for the old Cassie, Cassie pre-Aaron, pre-everything-that-happened-with-Aaron, the answer would have been no. But things were different now. I was different now.

I wished that I could just lie down next to him, put my head on his shoulder and hold on like I had that day in the lake. Stop fighting him. Stop fighting everything.

"Don't make me ask again," I said, trying to ignore his thumb, the pulses it sent up my arm as it played with the bottom of my palm.

He let go. "I'm not going to force you."

"So where are they?" I asked, rubbing his touch away from my wrist. It was hard to breathe, hard to think. Even in the dark Ben could see right through me. Even in the dark I couldn't help staring at him.

"Not here," he said, sitting up. His bed squeaked under his weight.

"Why do you have to make everything so difficult?" I asked. I would never have admitted it, but I meant *everything*, including that overflowing cup of feelings I was trying to keep safely in my head.

"Because it's the only way I can get you to talk to me," he said.

"Why do you want to talk to me?" I asked.

"You actually listen," he said.

"Fuck you," I said, trying to deny that I could feel my stomach lift, that familiar weightless feeling.

"Not exactly the response I was hoping for." He shrugged. "But you did respond."

"So you're never going to stop giving me crap," I said.

"I think we both know that's not what I meant," he said, leaning toward me, so close. "But it does seem like pissing you off has become my new addiction."

"Does that mean you had an old addiction?" I asked, wondering if he had been sent here for the same stupid reason I had. The reason that I now knew covered up something much more fucked up.

At least for me, and considering what Ben had done to Leisner, probably for him, too.

"You really think I'm going to tell you," he said.

"Good luck with your new addiction. The withdrawals are a bitch," I said, knowing I had to get out of there before I allowed him to become mine.

I snuck back to the other side of the cabin. Ben was dangerous. Whatever wall I'd built up after Aaron, he was attempting to sledgehammer it down. I needed to stay away from him, or *his* new addiction could be my downfall.

Lisa Burstein

I grabbed the bottom of the window frame and heaved myself back out. My boots were still there, which I hoped meant Troyer was still alive, too.

Fucking Ben.

The problem is, I like dangerous.

17 Fucking Days
to Go

had another dream about Aaron, but in this one we weren't
making out or doing the thing that did the thing that
brought me all the way here. This one was about prom night.
Not what really happened on prom night, but what my out-of-
control sleeping mind made happen on prom night. What my
anxiety-filled brain turned the already horrible night that was
prom night into.

I was still in the short, tight red dress I wore. The skin-to-
fabric ratio was very high on the slut scale, so I felt as uncomfortable in it as I did in real life. But my shoes didn't hurt, so
I was wearing them when I parked the car. I didn't have to
take the time to put them on in Brian's driveway. Leave it to
dreams to make impossible shoes comfortable.

Amy was in her light blue strapless prom dress and Lila in her spaghetti-strapped light purple one—just like prom night—but in my dream, Amy had her stupid yellow and green parrot with her. It was riding on her shoulder, digging its black nails into her skin.

After I shut off the car in Brian's driveway, the fucking bird kept repeating, *Turn around, turn around, turn around,* in that annoying squawk that he had.

"Shut that bird up," I said, "or I'm going to shut him up for you."

"He can't help it," Amy said, feeding him seed from her hand, trying to quiet him. The bird ignored the food, kept saying, *Turn around, around, around,* like a record that was skipping.

"I thought you trained him and stuff," I said. "Train him to shut up."

"Are you guys going to fight all night, or is Brian going to get to see me looking spectacular in this dress?" Lila asked.

I turned to Lila. She *did* look spectacular—her dark brown hair was curled, her bee-stung lips were shiny with lip gloss. She always looked spectacular, even in my fucked-up dream.

"AJ is usually right about things. We should probably listen to him," Amy said. I could hear him finally nuzzle into the food in her hand.

"There is no way I am missing my prom because of a bird," Lila said.

"If AJ's right, we're going to miss it anyway," Amy said.

AJ's right, AJ's right, AJ's right, AJ repeated.

"Enough. Let's get this over with," I said, like I didn't already know what happened. Like I didn't already know that our dates stood us up and we ended the night in jail, but this was a dream, so maybe I didn't already know what was going to happen. Maybe this would end better, unless it was a nightmare. Even as a nightmare it had the possibility of ending better.

Our heels clicked up the walk and we stood behind Lila as she rang the doorbell. AJ was still on Amy's shoulder, like she was a pirate, a prom pirate. He tweeted a repeat of the doorbell sound right in my ear.

"Damn," I said, rubbing it. "I would rather he was still saying we should turn around."

"I'm telling you, we should listen," Amy said, perching him on her finger and turning to look back at my car.

"Why did you even bring him with you?" I asked.

"I need AJ," Amy said, rubbing him under his chin. "You'll see why."

"Be quiet, you guys, someone's coming," Lila said. "And if you can, Amy, hide your bird. He's weird."

"He's right," Amy said, her voice as robotic as her bird's.

I saw someone behind the obscured glass of the door, a blurry movement of skin and black. I guess this time instead of us ringing the bell over and over, waiting for someone to answer the door and free us, the door was going to be answered.

So far, Dream prom: 1. Real life prom: 0.

It was Brian, Lila's boyfriend, who opened the door, a smile as big as a cantaloupe slice on his face. Aaron stood next to him, his auburn hair slicked back into a ponytail. Both of them were in tuxedos.

Maybe this prom was going to turn out better. I couldn't

Lisa Burstein

stop looking at Aaron. It was hard to deny that, even considering how much I wished his penis would wither like a raisin and fall off, he looked really hot in a tuxedo.

"We're ready," Lila said. "Let's go."

"Not yet," Brian said.

I looked at him and looked at Aaron and realized there was no third guy. This mythical third date did not exist. Not in my dream and in all probability, not in real life. It was only the two of them filling the doorway to Brian's house.

Brian pointed at me and then at Amy. "One of you can't come," he said.

AJ squawked, *I told you, I told you, I told you,* while Amy looked down at her shoes.

I kind of wanted to look down at my shoes, too, but instead I asked, "What the fuck does that mean?"

"We should have listened," Amy whispered into her chest. It was covered in glitter like tiny lights. So much possibility in those lights, about to be snuffed out.

"This isn't our fault," I said.

Lila broke free from us and walked over the threshold, joining Brian and Aaron inside. She held Brian around the neck and kissed him — deep, long, making us all watch.

Then the three of them looked down at Amy and me. The doorway seemed to have turned into an elevator that had gone up five flights.

"What now?" I asked.

"Aaron gets to pick," Brian said, wiping Lila's lip gloss from his mouth, as shiny as the glitter on Amy's chest. He looked at her. He looked at me. He looked at her. He looked at me.

"He shouldn't get to pick," I said. "He shouldn't get to do

anything." I could feel anger, feel my stomach burn hot, my hands turn to fists, my teeth start to clench.

"There are two of you and one of him." Brian shrugged.

"Don't worry," Amy whispered, "he'll pick you." I could see her starting to cry, her tears shiny, too.

"I don't want him to pick me!" I screamed. "I don't want him to pick me!" I screamed again. I could feel myself scream it, the way in a dream it feels like you are trying so hard to be heard, but no one can hear you.

I woke up in the cabin, slick with sweat, before Aaron gave his decision, even though I already knew what it was. He had picked both of us and done as much as each of us would let him get away with.

What I let him get away with had been my choice, not his. Otherwise Amy would have had her own rumors circulated by Ruthie Jensen about being pregnant and wanting so badly to believe it was a rumor.

Wanting so badly to take back every kiss and touch and sigh.

"You were screaming in your sleep," Nez said.

I sat up and watched her brush her black hair so that it shone like a wet rock. We hadn't showered in days and her hair still looked beautiful. Girls like her and Lila needed to be killed.

"Thanks, Nez," I said. "'Cause I don't have ears."

"Well, you woke me up and not that I asked Troyer, but I'm going to guess you woke her up, too."

I looked at Troyer. She shrugged. It was the most she could do to defend me against Nez.

"We had to wake up anyway," I said, rubbing my face and trying to force out the stare of Aaron's blue, blue eyes. My

Lisa Burstein

stomach felt empty. As empty as Aaron's eyes. I put my hand into my sleeping bag and punched it over and over, until I could barely breathe, until Rawe came out and told us to get dressed.

Putting on my uniform, I stared at the welts that were starting to form, as red as the skin of a screaming newborn.

I could see it, just pulled out—so alive, so raw, so feral.

Maybe it was mine, maybe it was someone else's, but I knew it was crying for the mother I knew I could never be. Wanting anyone to hold it, to love it, to make the pain and fear that was flooding it now that it was out in the world go away.

Just like me—a lump of crying skin and bones, an open wound grasping at anything except the people around it who want to help.

*16 Fucking Days
to Go*

My body hurt so much it was hard to fall asleep. That day we dug a new pit toilet. When Nez complained about it, Rawe told her it was either that or we dug out what was in the current one. Well, that was only after Rawe had given us the choice of digging out a toilet or sitting in a circle with her and talking about our feelings. Digging a hole all the way to China that would eventually be filled with our shit was definitely a better deal.

The work was hard, backbreaking. Never before I came to this place could I use the term *backbreaking* to describe anything. Here, it was pretty much an everyday occurrence. The boys did not join us that day. Probably digging out their own new pit toilet. Or maybe Nerone was sadistic enough to make them dig out their current one.

I was dirty, sweaty, and I couldn't help thinking that like everything else I had been forced to do since I'd been here, that I deserved this. Actually I probably deserved worse. I deserved to attempt to dig through a sidewalk with a child's beach shovel.

I saw it, the one I would have bought for my little boy or girl—yellow, plastic, small enough to fit in the hands that had been inside me, that had touched parts of me I would never see.

Even in the dark, I stared at the ceiling of the cabin, trying desperately to doze off, trying to ignore the searing pain in my back and shoulders, the fresh coat of dirt that once had been the ground and now covered my body.

I must have eventually fallen asleep, because later that night I could feel someone watching me. I figured it was Nez, so I reached out into the darkness to smack her. But it wasn't Nez. My reaching hand hit a boy and boy parts.

A boy part.

I opened my eyes, ready to scream like I was getting paid for it, when Ben covered my mouth.

"What the hell are you doing here?" I hissed through his fingers. He tasted like dirt. I suddenly wished a very big wish that the boys had spent their day like we had, digging a *new* pit toilet.

"Be quiet. You want to get us busted?" he whispered.

I jerked my head.

"Can I let go of your mouth now?" he asked.

I nodded, but angrily. I guess he could tell.

"You sure?" he teased.

"Fuck yes," I hissed.

"See?" he said, his hand still tight to my mouth. "That's why I can't let go."

"I will bite you," I said, starting to growl.

"Promise," he said, finally letting go.

I sat up and wiped my mouth. "What the fuck?" I whisper-yelled. Of course, I didn't really have the right to, considering I had been standing above his bed, doing the same to him, minus the soft bondage, a day before.

"Come on, I want to show you something," he said.

"If it involves taking off your uniform, I'm not interested," I said.

"You haven't even bought me dinner yet," he retorted. "Of course, I'm not really hungry."

I felt my face burn. How could he embarrass me so easily? Make me feel everything so easily?

He didn't move.

I looked over at Troyer. I could tell she was awake but trying to act like she wasn't. "I'm not going anywhere with you," I said.

"You sure?" he asked, still smiling.

"Take Nez," I said.

We both looked over at her. She was sleeping, snoring like a fucking lawnmower. Like a fucking lawnmower with asthma.

"Sexy," I said, looking at Ben.

"I want to take you. That's why I'm standing above your bed and not hers," he said.

I didn't respond. I couldn't. All I could do was feel him saying that in the bottom part of my stomach, like I had when he'd said I was pretty, not just once but twice, making sure I'd

Lisa Burstein

heard it. When had I become such a sap? *Again* the boy had rendered me speechless. I did not like this pattern.

"I have cigarettes." He took out the pack with a flourish.

I could see the plastic wrapper that covered it glint in the darkness, like it was winking at me. "Where are we going?"

"It's a secret," he said.

"I hate secrets," I said, looking down and realizing that my boobs were totally showing through my shirt. I pulled the sleeping bag up over my chest.

"Do you want to fight, or do you want to smoke?" he asked.

I looked at him. In the dark of the cabin, he was a blurry shadow. "Wait for me outside. I have to get dressed."

"I can turn around," he said, smiling that big smile again.

"You can also go fuck yourself," I said.

"You better not be messing with me," he said. "If you're not out in five, I'm leaving. I'm not going to wait out there all night like some asshole."

"Who said you were an asshole?" I laughed.

He turned from me, tip-toed over to the other side of the cabin, and jumped out the window. At least I had gotten the last word for once.

I put on my uniform and pulled my hair back in a rubber band. My bi-daily shower was definitely not doing the trick. It was stringy, felt as greasy as fries fresh from the fryer. I put on my boots. I looked over at Troyer, expecting a note to shoot out from under her sleeping bag, but she was still pretending she was asleep.

Fine, whatever, Troyer.

I met Ben on the porch. He was waiting with his flashlight on, aimed at the ground.

"So, give me one," I said, holding out my hand.

"Can't you wait until we're not inches away from the cabin?" he asked. He walked in front of me down toward the lake. I clicked on my own flashlight and followed him.

"No boats," I said. "There is no way I am getting in a boat with you."

"Don't worry, Cassie," he said.

Like I could ever listen to a guy when he told me that, but I continued behind him anyway.

"Okay, we're away from the cabin." I stopped on the trail and pointed my flashlight at the back of his head.

He turned, reached into his pocket, and handed me a cigarette.

"I want more than one." My hand was still out and waiting.

"One now, and more when we get there," he said.

"Where's there?" I asked.

"I told you, it's a secret," he said.

"I'm not doing anything with you if that's what you're after," I said, the cigarette unlit and hanging out of my mouth.

"I'm not after anything," he said.

"That would be a first," I said. Since when did a guy take you somewhere in the dark if he didn't want something?

I guess that was what sixteen days without MTV got you— insane paranoia.

I waited with the cigarette in my mouth, the night sounds all around us, that cold wet air that only comes out in the dark. Finally, he flicked the lighter. The area in front of his face lit up with the flame, his skin glowed orange. I leaned in and let him light the cigarette, let him touch my hand to steady it,

Lisa Burstein

let myself believe that was the only reason I was letting him touch my hand.

I took a long drag; the smoke made me lightheaded. I liked it. "Thanks." I exhaled, feeling the stress of this place blow out of me with that smoke. A small portion of it, anyway.

He put the lighter away.

"You're not having one?" I asked.

"I hate smoking and walking," he said.

He was right. Smoking and walking sucked, but I was too eager to smoke to have remembered that. I took another long drag, even though my head was already buzzing.

We kept walking on the lake trail, the bullfrogs croaking. There was also a humming in my ears from the nicotine.

It could only be from the nicotine. It had nothing to do with being outside, at night, alone with Ben. It had nothing to do with Ben coming to the cabin and taking me instead of Nez and it definitely had nothing to do with the stars above us shining like they were the sky's tiara.

I stopped on the trail and looked up, taking them in, when all of a sudden bright colored lights exploded in the sky—fireworks, one after another, on top of each other, huge kaleidoscopes of light, sparkling rainbow spiders.

"How did you know?" I asked, my voice going softer, like if I talked too loudly they would stop. It was so beautiful after weeks of so much ugly.

Ben turned to look at me, the colored lights in the sky turning his skin pink, blue, green. "I'm magic." He shrugged.

I geared up to tell him to fuck off, because that was some corny-ass shit, but then I realized that he really kind of was.

In that moment he was able to actually make me forget being me.

"Why didn't you bring Nez?" I had to ask. Fireworks? On a lake? What was more panty-dropping than that?

"I told you," he said. "I didn't want to bring Nez."

At least he hadn't said, *I wanted to bring you.* Even if we both knew that was what he meant.

"But why?" I said, still not convinced. I felt sick that I was asking. Felt sick that Aaron made me doubt everything, even something this simple, this perfect.

"Stop asking so many questions," Ben said, walking toward the lake again.

We reached the beach, the sky a tie-dyed shirt of colors, reflecting off the water.

"Did you bring me down here to remind me that you saved me or something?" I asked.

"I'm pretty sure I haven't totally saved you yet," he said, sitting in an Adirondack chair.

I felt my breath catch in my throat. Speechless yet *again*, I sat next to him, wondering why he'd chosen me to save and keep saving. My chair smelled like suntan lotion and wet bathing suits. I put my cigarette out in the sand.

"A beach and fireworks usually bring up happy memories. There isn't much here that does that," he said.

"I guess," I said.

"So?" he asked.

"Now you want to know my memories. What's next, my Twitter password?"

He didn't speak, just watched me.

I looked out at the lake. "It makes me think about my

Lisa Burstein

brother, Tim. When I was a kid, we'd light off sparklers on the Fourth of July. The only stuff we were allowed to use in New York. I was so stupid back then, I thought if we attached them to my butt I could fly up in the sky. We tried it one year—I think I was eight and he was fifteen. I didn't end up in the sky; I ended up in the emergency room. I still have a scar."

"That's not really a happy memory. Funny"—he smiled—"but not happy."

"Compared to my others," I said, "it is."

"I knew there was a reason I liked you," he said. "You're honest."

"I hate lying," I said. "Hate that it's something we have to do," I added, realizing I had done far too much of it to be allowed to just say that I hated it.

"You going to show me your scar?" He laughed.

"Only if you want to kiss my ass," I said.

"Amazing, huh, Cassie?" He whistled, looking up.

It was. It really was. It was *magic*: the fireworks reflecting off the lake, the sand under the chairs, the water lapping the shore.

I could let myself feel that.

But there was also the stuff I *couldn't* let myself feel. The heat that filled my skin when Ben got close, the shiver in my chest when he spoke to me, the way his touch made everything else vanish.

The way he could get me to talk about my brother, about *me*. The me I was before this place, before there was someone else inside me.

My hand went to my stomach. Why was I thinking about that now? Here?

"You should listen to me more often," he said, handing me two more cigarettes.

"No offense, Ben, but I don't listen to boys anymore," I replied, amazed that I'd said it to him.

"All boys, or just ones who make you nervous?" he asked.

"All boys," I said, staring at the sky.

"But I *do* make you nervous," he said.

He knew the answer, so I didn't bother responding. "I had some things happen to me before I came here that have nothing to do with how I feel about you," I said, even though that was a lie. What had happened with Aaron had everything to do with how I felt about Ben. Why I couldn't feel anything about him.

"How do you feel about me?" he asked.

"I'm not sure yet," I said. I was surprised that I hadn't said I hated him. That I didn't feel like I had to say it.

"I would try to kiss you," he said, "but I'm afraid you'd kick me in the balls."

"I probably would." I laughed, the sky filling with noisy color like paint launching from a giant popcorn popper. "But like I said, it wouldn't be about you."

"I guess I'll have to figure out how to make it about me," he said, taking off his boots and socks and standing. "Come on."

"There is no way I am getting near that water again," I said.

"I'll make sure nothing happens to you," he said, holding his hand out to help me up.

I looked at his palm, open, waiting, just wanting to hold mine. For once, I didn't think about anything except that there was a cute, sweet, smart-ass boy standing in front of me with his hand out.

Lisa Burstein

I pulled off my boots and socks and took it.

We stood at the lakeshore, our hands still clasped, the water licking our feet, fireworks decorating the sky.

I turned to him. He was looking up, his mouth open in wonder like he was trying to swallow the moment.

It was definitely one worth keeping.

Fucking Halfway Through

The good news is today was a shower day, complete with new bars of white, white Ivory soap and fresh, clean towels. I should have known that could only be followed by bad news, and it came in the form of a three-mile run around the campgrounds.

Leave it to Rawe to finally let us get clean and then make us sweat like pigs.

I guess it made sense, though, since that was kind of what she was doing with our Assessment Diaries. All day we were allowed to have our minds clear and clean, focusing completely on whatever task was right in front of us, and then at night she forced us to shovel out all the crap we had hidden in there and run around in it.

anything. Lila got a pass because of her face. I wasn't sure what she would get without it. No, actually, I *was* sure: she would get nothing.

Just like I got.

Lila turned away from me and added more shadow to the purple, shiny powder that was already there. She relined her lids below with black. Even for her, it was a lot of makeup. It was possible she had been sitting at the mirror putting makeup on for hours. Possibly even overnight, considering how bloodshot her eyes were.

"Lila, enough," I said, trying to bring her back to earth. "You're not even going out." I should have told her she looked like she had two black eyes, because she did. Well, two purple eyes.

"People are coming here and they expect something when they see me," Lila said, looking deep into the mirror. It was possible she was on something. Something more than alcohol, but I was kind of afraid to ask.

I lit a cigarette. Lila and I never got along great, even before Amy, but we had a history, we shared a secret. It was easier to blame it on Amy's arrival, but that was the truth. We tolerated each other. Maybe because we were both the kind of people that people tolerated. I guess Amy put up with us because she was the type of person who didn't know what else to do but tolerate.

"You know I hate it when you smoke in here," Lila said.

"You know I could give a shit," I said, blowing out smoke.

"Whatever," she said. "Give me one."

I launched the cigarette over to her. She turned to catch it and lit it, watching her reflection. At least she'd finally stopped putting on makeup. I was afraid her face was going to fall off from the weight.

"You going to step away from that mirror for a second, or is it your date for tonight?" I asked, trying to get back into our routine of giving each other crap. Anything was better than the weirdness that was flying around in Lila's mind right now like a bird with one broken wing.

"I wish," she said. "At least with it, I know what I'm getting." Lila lifted the cigarette she was smoking to her cheek. Turned it cherry-side in. "Sometimes I wonder what this would feel like," she said.

"It would fucking hurt," I said. Trying to give her crap wasn't working. I guess she wasn't coming back yet. I guess she was still out to sea on the insanity ocean.

"No," she said. "I mean after, to have something like that on your face." She held the cigarette an inch from her pink, pink cheek. It was possible all the makeup she was wearing would cause her whole face to go up in flames.

"No way in hell you could handle it," I said, trying to sound like I couldn't care less, even though my heart had gone as cold as the fall air coming through her open window.

"I've never had to handle it," she said. "Maybe that's my problem." She moved the cigarette a little closer. I was sure she could feel the heat radiating on her cheek, but she held it there like it was the black eyeliner pencil she had used earlier and she was about to add a fake beauty mark.

"Enough, Lila," I said. If she was about to mess up her face, there was no way I was going to sit there and watch.

"What do you care?" she asked, putting the cigarette back in her mouth and taking another drag. "What does anyone care?"

Lisa Burstein

"That doesn't mean you should mangle your fucking face."

"It doesn't mean I shouldn't, either."

This was definitely a different Lila. Maybe it was because Amy wasn't there, or maybe she was far drunker than I'd thought. It was also possible she really was on something else. Lila always talked about how Brian could get stuff, stuff that would make your mind and the walls melt.

"You're not scaring me if that's what you're trying to do," I said.

"I'm scaring *me*." She laughed, lifting the cigarette again. The tip was angry orange. She moved it closer to her cheek and squinted from the smoke. "Before you got here I was holding a razor blade like this, getting up the guts to cut my face on the diagonal. Like a peanut butter and jelly sandwich."

Was she fucking serious?

"I'm going to be too drunk to drive you to the emergency room," I said, taking another sip from my glass like I wanted to prove it.

She moved the cigarette closer. I saw her cheek contract from the heat.

"Lila, fucking stop!" I said. I could get up and tackle her if I had to, but did I want to? Did I want to see if she had the guts to go through with it?

"I wonder how many guys would try to get in my pants with an oozing blister on my face," she said.

"Seriously, enough." My voice was strained, like I'd been screaming all night and there was nothing left.

She didn't pull the cigarette away. Only stared at herself in the mirror, waiting. Maybe she was trying to decide if she could do it, if she was drunk enough, crazy enough, or really ready to leave the *burden of her beauty* behind.

Especially because I knew exactly what she meant when she said it.

"Doing that isn't going to prove shit," I said. I could feel my hands and arms start to tingle. Lila was scaring me. She was actually really fucking scaring me. I might not have been able to admit it to her, but that was the truth.

"What will not doing it prove?" she asked.

The door to her room flew open and Lila dropped the still burning cigarette on the vanity.

"Oh my God, give me a drink," Amy said. She was wearing a skirt, tights, and a puffy white sweater that she pulled off and threw next to me on the bed.

She stood in the middle of the floor in her bra and skirt.

"Amy," Lila said, picking up her cigarette from the vanity and showing it to her. "New rule: knock next time. I dropped my cigarette and almost burned the house down."

"Sorry," Amy said, pulling off her tights, throwing on a T-shirt she grabbed out of her backpack, and sitting on the floor.

I laughed, mostly because I was so glad Amy was there, so Lila would stop scaring the shit out of me.

"What have you guys been doing?" Amy asked.

"Missing the fuck out of you," I joked, pouring myself another glass of vodka.

"Ha," Amy said, looking at Lila. Maybe she noticed that she looked frazzled, or maybe she was just so relieved to be away from her parents that she didn't care.

Eventually Lila's house was filled with kids from our school, playing super-loud rap music and drinking out of a

Lisa Burstein

keg. As the night went on, Lila turned back into Lila—vain, pretty Lila—but even with our secret, I decided I would avoid ever being alone with her again.

Out on the road now, wherever the hell Lila is, my guess is she doesn't look like Lila anymore—that the freedom she got by running away had maybe finally let her leave the burden of her beauty behind.

For her sake, I hope so.

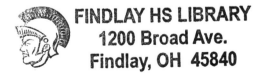

14 Fucking Days Left

I woke up with Troyer standing above me, her hand covering my mouth. It tasted like worms and fish guts. Leave it to her to pick the night after we had our training in fishing to surprise me above my bed.

I pushed her hand away and spit on the floor next to my bed. "Sick, Troyer."

She put one finger to her lip, spit, and wiped her hand front and back on her uniform.

"See," I said.

She looked at me.

"What do you want?" I asked. It was becoming standard at this camp that at least one person was standing above another's bed once a night, scaring the shit out of them.

She grabbed my shoulder, probably because she couldn't just tell me to get up.

I sat and looked across the dark cabin at Nez. She was still sleeping. Nez had actually been really good at fishing, talking about the correlation between catching fish and catching guys. She kept making kissy faces at the water, saying, *Here fishy, fishy*, and it was like they actually heard her and jumped onto her pole. If Rawe hadn't been there watching, I might have thrown Nez off the dock to see if any of her beloved fish tried to save her.

Like Ben had saved me.

Troyer steadied her gaze. I got it: Nez was not invited. Super. But since when did Troyer call the shots?

I guess since tonight.

I was kind of surprised that Nez wasn't gone already, into the arms of whatever boy would take her that night. Maybe she had her period. Of course, she kind of always acted like she had her period.

I guess I did, too, but that was more ironic than I wanted to admit.

That afternoon when we got back to the cabin we were supposed to write about what we feared most at Turning Pines. I hated that the only thing I could come up with was Ben.

I was terrified of the part of me that Ben was able to get to, which more and more was feeling like the soft part of a clam; before Aaron, I was all closed up and no one could get in there. Ben could easily. Maybe other boys would also be able to. Maybe I would never be able to shield myself again.

Troyer grabbed her pad back and wrote, *Get dressed. Let's go.*

"We better not be going over to the boys' cabin," I said. "I'll never hear the end of that," I continued, though I'm not sure why.

She grabbed the pad she had given me and scribbled, *I'm not stupid.*

"Hey," I said, but she was right. It had been stupid when Nez went, when I went. There was no way in hell I was ever going again. If I could avoid it, I was probably never speaking to Ben again.

But my guess was I couldn't avoid it.

I got dressed quickly and quietly, laced up my boots, and followed Troyer out of the cabin. She waited for me to step off the porch then closed the cabin door so lightly it looked like she was afraid it would burn her.

"Any chance we're breaking into the shower house?" I asked.

She wrote on her pad and showed it to me. *Even better.*

Nothing at that point would have been better than a shower—well, not to me, anyway. And from the smell coming off Troyer, she could have used one, too.

We walked in the opposite direction from the soccer field, our flashlights yellow planets on the dark trail. I didn't feel the need to talk this time, even though it was so quiet you could hear the bullfrogs croaking all the way down at the lake, like they had been the other night with Ben. But Troyer was in charge—silent, sneaky Troyer who couldn't talk was telling me what to do.

Well, okay, not literally.

I could see the lake coming up on the horizon, black in the night. The moonlight sparkled, sprinkled on top of it like

Lisa Burstein

Parmesan cheese. I couldn't help thinking about the day I found out I was pregnant. How I could no longer deny that something inside of me was spinning and sparkling like the water. The area just below my belly button filled with so much light and life.

"We're not going fucking fishing again, are we?" I asked.

Troyer shook her head but kept walking. Fishing once that day had been enough.

We hit the beach, walked past the canoes and past the boat house. The door to it was smacking open and closed in the wind. Everything in this place was locked but the damn boat house. I guess they figured if you wanted to go to the trouble to life jacket up and push a canoe into the water to try and escape, they were going to let you do it. I think that, and the fact that the land on the other side was far enough away that the windows in the houses looked like snake eyes in the dark, might have been discouragement enough.

I didn't know where Troyer and I were going. It was the first time I had been this far down the beach and for a weird moment I wondered if Troyer had brought me all the way out here to kill me—to drown me and leave me for dead. I let the calm of that realization fill me, because truthfully, I kind of deserved it.

Put me out of my misery, Troyer. Put me out of my misery once and for all. Make it so I don't have to think whether Aaron was my or Amy's sloppy seconds. Make it so I don't have to wonder why she was smarter than I was.

I looked down at the sand: little grain-specks twinkled in the moonlight, our footprints foot-shaped craters. We finally stopped at a cabin twenty feet down the beach. The lock had been broken off the door and a sign that said ARTS AND CRAFTS made out of uncooked macaroni hung from it.

Troyer pushed the door open. I could smell paint, clay, glue.

"Arts and crafts?" I asked.

She nodded, picked up a piece of sketch paper, and handed it to me. It was a cartoon drawing of Nez with her ass on fire. A thought bubble floated above her head that said, *Even fire is attracted to my ass*.

"Ha!" I laughed. "You drew that?"

She nodded again, her head dipping up and down like a bobblehead doll while she showed me a macramé necklace, a watercolor painting, a small clay bowl.

"Wow, you've been busy," I said.

She smiled.

"How did you get in here?" It looked like the art room at school but better; there were huge wooden art tables, easels, clay wheels, shelves and shelves of rainbow-colored art supplies. It was obvious why this door had been locked.

She turned to me but didn't say anything.

"Well, obviously," I said. "But *how* did you break in?" I was thinking about the other doors with locks: the dining hall, the shower house, the camp office.

She picked up an oar that was lying on the ground and broken in two.

"I hope we don't have to go canoeing again," I said.

Troyer laughed. It was nice to hear her voice, even if it was involuntary.

"When? When did you come here?" I asked, seeing there were a lot more art projects lining the table besides the ones

Lisa Burstein

she had shown me. "How?" I asked, thinking about all those times I was sleeping and Troyer was out, alone.

Without me, without Nez.

She shrugged and indicated a seat at one of the tables. She gave me a canvas, a brush, and a few jars of paint: red, purple, yellow. Why was she sharing it with me?

"I'm not very good at this," I said.

Troyer took her own brush and wrote *Paint* in purple on the art-supply-splattered table. She sat next to me and painted bright purple lines on her own canvas.

I looked at the paint. The only color that mattered was the red. I dipped my brush in it and started painting, one line, another, another, but it wasn't enough. It wasn't right. I picked up the paint jar and splashed it, over and over again on the canvas. All the kisses Aaron gave me that ended in lies, the blood I prayed I would see spotting my underpants day after day after day while I denied it, the skin on my stomach after I hit myself—raw, angry gruesome.

I tipped the whole thing over, red paint running like a waterfall.

I felt Troyer looking at me, her eyes wide. I had scared her. I was crazy. Aaron had made me crazy and she could see it. The red paint dripped off the table and onto the floor, forming a puddle like spilled nail polish.

"Sorry," I said. I grabbed a rag and bent over to start cleaning it up, but Troyer stopped me.

She spilled purple paint onto her canvas, a long sloppy drip, a melted grape Popsicle. She gave me the thumbs up, paint dotting her thumb tip.

I almost hugged her—almost.

I took the yellow paint and poured it, too, mustard covering the red, turning it orange, then blue paint, turning it brown. The thing was it took so much paint to change the red, to take away its power.

What will it take to change the red inside of me? How much more time will it take?

Will it ever be long enough?

Lisa Burstein

13 Fucking Days
to Go

When I woke up this morning there was still red paint under my fingernails. We'd tried our best to clean up with turpentine at the art cabin, but red paint, even when you use turpentine, has a way of staying behind.

Just like my red. I'd always sort of known it, but when I'd thought the night before about how long it would take for me to feel normal again, I couldn't even see a time where I would.

There is nothing I can do to make it go away.

It started the night I let Aaron in.

After he gathered up the balls to come and see me that first time at Pudgie's, our break time "dates" became routine. So routine that we did the same thing each time he picked me up: I got in his car, we lit two cigarettes, we drove to the park, we stopped the car, and we made out and humped on each other until our lips and hips were raw.

Usually he didn't ask for more and I never did. I'd had sex a few times before him but not with anyone I'd actually been with enough times to be able to pick out in a kissing lineup.

Aaron was the first guy who came back for seconds and thirds, and though he never said it, I sort of assumed he was my boyfriend.

He was the closest I had ever come to one.

It's not like we talked a bunch or had any deep profound conversations or anything, but there was something about when we were together. Something about the way I felt safe in his black convertible. How when I got in, the life I was living outside of it went away. Of course, looking back, that could have been because the life I was living outside of it was shit.

My prom night arrest had made sure of that.

If I was asked why I finally slept with him, I would lie and say that was the reason, but really I knew it was because I liked him. Really I knew it was because he liked me.

Boys didn't usually like me. They liked my face and body fine, but my personality was something else. Somehow Aaron found a way to hatchet through my bullshit.

Too bad I hadn't figured out a way to detect his.

"I wish I could have seen you in your prom dress," he said, stopping our make-out session to look at me. His hair was sweaty, like he had come from the skate park. We had been seeing each other for a month and it was the first time he'd mentioned the prom since the night we met. I should have known he wanted something.

"What?" I asked, even though I'd heard him. For some

Lisa Burstein

reason his saying that made me sappy, and I wanted to hear it again.

"I think you would have looked hot," he said.

"You mean you don't like my garlic-scented uniform?" I said, pulling at my Pudgie's T-shirt. It had a fat dude spinning some dough on the front and was stained with sauce, grease, and vinegar.

"That's the thing," he said, "you look hot in your garlic-scented uniform. Imagine how you would look all dressed up. Imagine the bra you'd be wearing."

I put my lips to his ear. "PS . . . I wasn't wearing a bra."

He clawed at me, went back in for more. I pushed him into his seat lightly.

"Well, because you're an asshole, I guess all you can do is imagine," I said.

"You might be saying that," he said, leaning in closer to me, "but I know you're lying." He kissed me again.

"You think you know it all," I said.

"No," he said, stopping to look at me, "I know you."

Normally, a boy saying that would have heard me reply, *You don't know shit*, but there was something about the way Aaron was looking at me. Something about the way his blue eyes floated over my face that made me believe. They were big like he'd shoved magnifying glasses on top of them. Seeing as I had so little to believe in back then, maybe I just needed to believe in something. Maybe it wouldn't have mattered what it was.

I guess it was just my luck that it turned out to be a sneaky-ass boy who was also doing my best friend.

He put both his hands on my waist. "You want to?"

I knew exactly what he meant, but I was stalling. "Do you?" I asked.

"I wouldn't be asking if I didn't," he said, leaning in to kiss me again. He pulled back and looked at me. "Wait, are you a virgin?"

"No." I laughed. I wasn't, but if I really thought about it, I sort of was. I'd never been with a guy I had actually let myself like.

"Okay," he said, and I could tell he was checking that off in his head, *not a virgin.* He looked at the digital clock, "I mean, we don't have to."

"No," I said. "No, I want to."

"You sure?" he asked.

"Yeah," I said, "as long as you have something."

He smiled, that crooked tooth poking out over his bottom lip. "I'm like an STD-free Boy Scout," he said, reaching over me and opening the glove box. A pile of condom wrappers shined back at me like coins stacked up by a banker. I tried not to think about the other girls he had worn them with. I didn't really have a right to think about them, considering I wasn't a virgin, either.

After that night our routine changed: I got in his car, we lit two cigarettes, we drove to the park, we stopped, and we got into the backseat, where we would pretzel into each other and shake the car, trying desperately to forget.

That was what I was doing, anyway, but it was hard with the seat belt always digging into my back and the clock on the dash ticking by to call me back to my old life. I had no way of knowing that this attempt to escape would take me into an even worse place than my post-arrest life.

Lisa Burstein

That post-Aaron life was worse.

There was a short time I considered telling Aaron about the baby, but I knew he would abandon me. As much as I wanted to convince myself that he had real feelings for me, I knew even before Amy's letter that being confronted with something *that real* would make his feelings seem like anything but. Besides, what could I have gained by telling him?

Looking back at that time, considering what I now know about Amy, I realize Aaron would have pulled out that old cliché where he asked me if I was sure it was his. Better to reject him first, to not have to even play that game.

Better to be the girl I should have been in the first place, the Cassie with thorns.

12 Fucking Days
to Go

Today was archery practice. I hope I'm not the only one who thought it was insane that they were giving any of us access to actual weapons, especially considering they made such a big deal about keeping us away from regular items that could be turned into them—dangerous things like cinnamon gum and hoop earrings. Yet somehow they made an exception for bows and arrows.

Rawe said we had to be prepared to hunt for our own food. Just in case. This too was part of our training—our never-ending, still-not-sure-what-for training.

We waited in a clump with the boys while Rawe and Nerone showed us how to pull back the bow and fix in the arrow, but it was hard to take that seriously when the arrows we had to use had bright, fake feathers on them and the bull's-eyes were bright gobstoppers of primary colors.

I watched as Nez whispered in Ben's ear. I saw him nod and look at me.

Oh, mother fucker.

Did Nez know about the other night with Ben, or was it sweet nothings she was whispering? I couldn't help wondering who Ben would pick if Nez and I were standing in front of him like the dream I'd had.

I hated that I wondered that.

There were only two targets, so while Nez and Eagan prepared their weapons on the range, the rest of us sat on up-ended boulders. Rawe stood behind Nez and Nerone stood behind Eagan, like human shields in case either one of them decided to turn around and go all *Hunger Games* on us.

Nez didn't seem like she needed Rawe's help. She knew her way around a bow and arrow, but Eagan was struggling. At least it kept him from telling us how many fatalities had resulted from kids playing Cowboys and Indians.

"Cassie," Ben whispered, "come and see me tonight." He had somehow found two sticks and was beating them against the rock he was sitting on, drum style, of course.

Troyer looked at me with her eyebrows raised.

Luckily, Leisner and Stravalaci didn't hear Ben. They were talking about Nez's ass.

I looked at Nez out on the range. If I was worried about what she was capable of before, watching her wielding a bow and arrow let me know immediately. She'd hit within inches of the red bull's-eye on every shot she'd made.

"Why don't you ask your girlfriend?"

"Who are we talking about?" he asked. "There's only one girl here who I want to be my girlfriend."

Troyer's face turned red; she got up and sat on a boulder far away from us. I understood. I was embarrassed enough to walk away, too. But I couldn't.

"Right," I said, bouncing my left leg up and down like a jackhammer, wishing I could break through the dirt and leaves below me and dive down and down and down and hide forever.

"Why are you angry?" he asked.

"I'm not," I said, my knee still bucking. *Anything* not to think about him, me, his hand holding mine tight enough to keep me from falling off a cliff.

"Cassie," he said, putting his hand on my knee and holding it to make me stop.

"Ben," I said, pulling away from him, standing and picking up one of the bows.

He stood too and grabbed the bow from the other side. He kept it away from me with one arm, one hand. "I really don't understand why you're mad," he said. The bow was taut between us, both of us pulling on it and getting nowhere.

"Can you let go?" I asked, looking past him at Nez and Eagan. "I'm trying to learn how to slice you in two with a bow and arrow."

Nez started hooting. She had gotten a bull's-eye, not inches away but right in the middle of the red. Eagan's target was still empty. He was as big as the bow and was definitely having a hard time maneuvering it. At least he was keeping Nerone busy.

"I kind of thought you might be nicer after the other night and everything," Ben said, holding tight to the bow and

Lisa Burstein

moving his face close enough to mine that I could feel the breath coming out his nostrils and onto my forehead.

"Nothing happened, Ben," I said. My words shot out one at a time like bullets.

"Maybe not that you're willing to admit," he said.

My arm was starting to shake. I wasn't sure how much longer I could fight to keep the bow away from him, but there was no way I was giving up. "Why me?"

"I like you," he said, his eyes tight on mine, like he was daring me to look away.

There was no fucking way that was going to happen. I locked onto those brown eyes like they were made of superglue. "Why?" I asked, my voice sighing out.

He stepped even closer to me, maneuvering to the side of the bow but still holding it, like he was dancing with it. "What would you do if I tried to kiss you?" His voice was breathy, hot in my face. He didn't move.

"Step back, Ben," I said. My heart felt like it was going to fly up and out of my rib cage like a helicopter.

"I might surprise you," he said. I looked at his lips, the edges of them turning up slightly.

"I doubt it," I said.

He let go of the bow and the force I had been pulling it with sent me flying right on my ass. My tailbone throbbed, my chest ached from shock.

"See?" He laughed. "Surprise."

My face burned like I had been out in the sun all day without sunscreen.

I heard Troyer spit-laugh. It was the most noise I'd ever heard her make when it wasn't just the two of us.

He held out his hand to help me up. "Come on, I was joking," he said, apparently his attempt at a truce.

"I'm not taking your hand," I said, like I was reminding myself not to as much as I was saying it to him.

"I'm patient," he said, starting to hum.

"You are a zombie that won't die," I said, looking up at him.

He held his arms out in front of him and shuffled his feet. "Brains," he moaned. "Mmmm, Cassie brains."

I started to laugh. I couldn't help it.

"Mmmm, Cassie laughs," he moaned, still acting like a zombie.

"You're seriously crazy," I said, finally standing up.

"But that's why you love me," he said, pretending to tap dance.

I started to laugh again and it made him dance harder, faster, his tongue lolling out of his mouth.

"I'll keep this up all day if I have to," he said. He was clearly out of breath, but he didn't stop.

Laughing at him, I felt warm, safe. Like I had at the lakeshore, in that moment when I had let myself hold his hand. When I had forgotten I needed to stay away.

"You can't keep dancing forever," I said.

He stopped, watching me. "Just like you can't keep pushing me away forever," he said, "eventually one of us is going to have to give up."

Lisa Burstein

11 Fucking Days
to Go

Toady we climbed what had to be every fucking tree in the forest with the explanation that we might have to escape "something" that was chasing us that we couldn't outrun.

My shoulders felt like they had been separated from my body in the process, but there was no way in hell "something" was going to catch me. I couldn't help thinking about Ben as I climbed. That was how I felt whenever he was near, like I was being chased, like I couldn't escape.

Like maybe I didn't want to.

Tonight, after everyone fell asleep, I grabbed a cigarette and set out to smoke and stare and try not to think about Ben.

It would be hard to do, considering the cigarette I hid in my palm had come from him.

Once I was off the cabin porch, I turned on my flashlight. The sky was filled with clouds. No stars tonight, only the moon—a big white egg pulling itself over the top of the clouds like it was trying to scale a brick wall. The only problem with my plan was that I didn't have a lighter.

I would need to find one. If I wanted to attempt to erase whatever traces of Ben were slamming around in my mind at that moment, I was going to need a lighter ASAP.

I looked at the soccer field and the dining hall about a half mile beyond it, hulking and dark, but probably my only chance. If worse came to worst, at least I would be able to light the cigarette on one of the stove burners. I guess I was finally breaking in to the dining hall.

Where was Troyer when I really needed her?

I made my way toward it, the wetness of the grass coming through my uniform and over the tops of my boots. I would walk over there and break in (somehow) and then smoke and forget.

Or at least, that's what I would try to do.

I jumped back, startled by the *thwack, thwack, thawck* of someone smacking a basketball against pavement. It echoed through the night, as constant and insistent as the thoughts in my head.

I turned toward the sound, expecting to see Leisner, desperate to expel whatever 'roids were left in his system by slamming a ball over and over again with the grace of a caveman. Instead, I found Ben shooting hoops, alone, lit only by the moon.

Lisa Burstein

I guess I wouldn't be forgetting that night.

I could have walked the other way and ignored him, but I did need a lighter. And while breaking into the dining hall might have been easier than talking to him, he was closer.

It was nothing but a rational decision, as you can see.

I put the unlit cigarette in my mouth and walked over. I stood at the edge of the court watching him. He probably saw me, considering the way he was dribbling, bouncing the ball back and forth through his legs before taking a shot, but he ignored me. Probably because he knew he had something I wanted.

"Where'd you get that ball?" I finally asked, my cigarette moving up and down like a heart monitor with every word.

"Is that what you really want to ask me?" Ben asked, sinking another shot.

I looked over at the equipment shed, the lock broken in half, hanging off the door like the Arts and Crafts cabin's had been. If it was so easy to break into all these places, what the hell was I doing wasting my time talking to him?

Maybe it was the way the moon lit up little hairs around his head, or the way he was sinking shot after shot without even trying.

Or, maybe it really was that no matter what I tried, I couldn't stay away.

"Aren't you scared of getting caught? You're being really fucking loud," I said, the cigarette still in my mouth. In the moonlight it looked as white as a fang.

"I'm not scared of anything," he said.

"Me neither," I retorted, touching my stomach.

"Liar," he said, catching his own rebound and bouncing the ball at me. I put my hands up and caught it with faster reflexes than I might have bothered with if I weren't desperate to smoke. The last thing I needed was for the ball to hit me in the face and break the cigarette in my mouth in half.

I dribbled, once, twice, the cigarette still dangling the whole time. "You got a light?"

He smiled. "You beat me in one on one," he said, "I'll give you a light."

"Come on." I bounced the ball back to him. "I'm not in the mood to play games." I knew I was talking about more than just the basketball court.

"You want a light, you play me and win," he said, dribbling the ball in front of me. "Or are you chicken?"

"I could probably find a lighter in that shed," I said, stalling. I knew how to play basketball okay. I'd played with my brother and he was pretty good, but I'd never played against anyone else. Especially someone who so obviously wanted to kiss me and liked getting close enough to my face to remind me of it constantly.

"I think a game of ball would be faster, don't you?" he asked.

"Against you?" I laughed, putting the cigarette behind my ear. "Definitely."

"Let's see what you can do, Wick," he said, pretending to throw the ball in my face and then catching it, that annoying thing that boys do that reminds you they are stronger and faster than you are.

"I want more than a light if I win," I said. "That's not enough."

"But that's what you want right now, so . . ." He spun the ball on his finger.

Lisa Burstein

"I want four more cigarettes," I said, holding my stance.

"Two," he said.

"Three," I responded.

"One." He smirked.

"Two," I said.

"Deal," he said.

I took my position in front of him—my hips wide, my legs shoulder-width apart. I rocked back and forth, ready to do whatever I had to with that ball to get my cigarette lit and get me two more.

"Well, look at you, Cassie Wick," Ben said, sort of sighing, sort of whistling, definitely surprised that I even knew enough to stand that way.

"I'm going to kick your ass." I smirked.

"I doubt it," he said, dribbling the ball between us. Each hit on the pavement felt like he was moving closer to me, felt like my heart was bouncing up into my throat.

"My brother's team at the Y went to the state championship," I said, my face contracting.

"But did he win?" Ben asked, pushing past me with a spin move. He faked me out and took a shot. It sank with a swish.

"Hey, cheater," I yelled to the back of his head. "We didn't even start yet."

"I say when we start," he said, his teeth white in the moonlight.

"Fine," I said. "One-zero. What are we playing to anyway?"

"Three," he said.

"That must mean you're scared," I said, dribbling the ball. "You might as well surrender."

"You haven't even done anything yet for me to surrender

to," he said, his voice thick with the words. I could see his eyes. They went right to my lips.

I needed to move. I faked him out with a bounce pass to myself, left him flailing for the ball behind me. My shot hit the rim but went in.

"We're tied now, asshole," I said.

"Impressive," he said, catching the rebound. "That won't work again." He moved closer to me so I could guard him. His face so near mine as he dribbled that there was no air between us. I could see sweat reflecting the moonlight on his forehead.

"Are we playing, or are you staring?" I said, the breath from his nose hot and sweet on my face.

He bounced the ball through my legs, caught it on the other side, and launched it in before I could even turn around. "Two-one," he said. "One more and you're screwed."

"How proud you'll be when you've beaten a girl," I said, going under the basket to grab the rebound. I dribbled slowly, like that part in the movie where the hero is going to make the winning shot.

"How proud I'll be when I beat *you*," he said, matching me step for step. He tried to slap the ball out of my hands.

I switched the ball into my other hand, spun around, and sank another shot. "Now that's all talent," I said. I felt myself smile, relax, that buzzing feeling you get when you do any-thing correctly with a ball—hit it, sink it in a hole, launch it in a basket.

"Look at you," Ben said, dribbling, and he was. Up and down, his eyes moving from the tops of my boots to the tip of my head. It was like he could see inside me. I could feel him

Lisa Burstein

melting through the skin on my chest, through my muscle, my rib cage, until he could see my heart jumping like it was on a trampoline.

"Maybe we should call it a tie," I said, suddenly desperate to get my cigarette lit and get the hell out of there.

"Scared?" he asked, one eyebrow up.

I faked him out and grabbed the ball. Fine, he didn't want a tie, but I wanted to end this game, needed to end this game. I ran past him and sank a lay-up.

"I win," I said, but I honestly didn't care about that. I just wanted the time I had to spend face-to-face with him to be over.

"You tricked me," he said.

"Never let your guard down," I said, as much to him as a reminder to me. I stuck my cigarette in my mouth, waiting for him to light it, but he didn't at first. He watched me, my lips and then my eyes.

"Ben, we're going to be sent home soon," I joked, anything to make him stop looking at me.

"Fine," he said, "I'm not a scammer." He flicked the lighter and brought it to my mouth. My hands were tight behind my back. No way was I risking possibly touching his skin again.

He walked over to the grass next to the court, lay down, and lit his own. "You going to stand there like a weirdo or smoke with me like a civilized person?" he asked, his cigarette protruding out of his mouth like the turret of a castle.

"I'm fine over here," I said.

"You want those two cigarettes," he said, "you'll come and join me."

I walked over and sat next to him. I did want those two cigarettes.

"I love the way grass feels at night," Ben said. He was still lying down. He pulled up his pant legs and pushed up his shirtsleeves.

"So can I get those now?" I asked, inhaling and exhaling quickly, my legs wrapped up like a pretzel.

"Patience," he said. "What's the rush?"

"I want to make sure you don't fuck me over," I said.

"Then you don't know me at all," he said, reaching into his pack and giving them to me.

"Thanks," I said, swallowing something else I was going to say.

"You should try it," he said, patting the ground next to him.

"What?" I asked quickly. Was he saying I fucked people over? Then he didn't know *me* at all.

"The sky looks pretty awesome from down here," he said.

"Listen, if you're trying to get me to lie down next to you, you can forget it." I took another long drag, blew the smoke out. It was the same color at the clouds above us.

"Cassie," he said, his cigarette a perfect straight line. "It's not always about you."

"Whatever," I said, pretending I didn't feel him saying that in my stomach. I had been so stuck in my head lately that it really had been all about me: what I was going through, what I felt. Maybe he was right. Maybe it didn't have to be.

I lay down on the grass, making sure to leave an arm's length between us. I rolled my sleeves up, the grass tickling my elbows. I rolled up my pants, the moonlight turning my legs ghostly white.

I could feel every blade of grass on my cold skin—thousands

Lisa Burstein

of them, millions, like each bright green piece was having sex and making tons and tons of baby grass.

I punched my stomach. How could I turn even a thought about grass into sex? Into babies?

Would I ever think about anything else?

"How did you even get cigarettes in here?" I asked, desperate to say something. To close up the silence that was actually starting to feel comfortable between us.

"I've got more skills than you give me credit for," he said.

"What does that mean?" I asked.

"It means I've been threatened with being sent to a place like this before," he said. "It means I know how to get away with things because of it."

"Why the hell would you do something again if you knew you were getting sent to a place like this?" I asked. I really wondered.

I'm still not sure what Turning Pines is doing for me, but I do know I will do whatever it takes not to come back.

"I guess I'm fucked up." He laughed. "Considering the way you keep shutting me down and I keep coming back for more," he said, "I obviously don't learn my lesson."

I felt the skin on my face prickle with heat. I looked at his profile, his cigarette sticking out of his mouth like one of the trees in the woods that surrounded us. Maybe he was fucked up. Maybe he was even more fucked up than me. I wondered what he could have done.

I wondered if he would do it again.

"Why?" I asked. "Why do you keep coming back for more?"

"I think I can make you happy," he said, his eyes on the sky. "I also think you're funny as hell."

"Thanks," I said, "but I'm pretty sure I've never been happy."

"Exactly," he said, putting one arm behind his head.

We lay there and smoked another cigarette, not talking, listening to the nighttime sounds and watching the clouds move over the moon like facial hair.

"Is tonight the night you're going to let me kiss you?" he asked, turning to look at me, moving his whole body closer.

"Who said I would ever let you kiss me?" I asked.

"Ever is a very long time," he said.

"You can hold my hand again if you want," I said, feeling so stupid as I did. There was no way I was pure enough to pull it off.

Since when was holding hands enough for me—or too much for me? The pregnancy had taken me too far. The only safe place to go was back to zero.

"I should probably hold out for a hug," he said, "but I'll take what I can get." His hand was warm, fit in mine like the last piece of a puzzle.

"Sorry," I said. I wished I could give him a hug, and at the same time I wanted to kick him in the nuts, because I knew if I gave him a hug I was done for.

I was kind of already done for.

"Wow, almost a full minute and you're still holding on," he said.

"Don't push it," I said. The sound of crickets all around us was like a room of cats purring at once.

He turned to me. "I'm not going to be the one to give up, Cassie."

Lisa Burstein

It was too much. All of this was too much. I had to get out of there.

"I should head back," I said, letting go of his hand.

"So, no hug," he said, not moving.

I stood. I guess I thought he might say something else so I waited a moment, then another. Maybe I wanted to say something else, or maybe I did want to be near him. Be close to someone who might possibly understand me just because he was as messed up and broken as I was.

I started back toward my cabin.

"Hey, Cassie," he called.

I turned to look at him, his skin white on the grass.

"You want a rematch, you know where to find me," he said.

I put my hands on my stomach. I knew our next rematch wouldn't be at basketball. I knew if we had a rematch, I might not be strong enough to win.

10 Fucking Days
to Go

woke up this morning trying to scratch my own skin off. I was either allergic to Ben or I had lain in something that had turned my skin to hot needles of itch. Considering the way I was itching, it was possible I'd been cloned with it. I thought back to the night before, Ben and me on the grass, holding hands, staring at the clouds in the sky and smoking.

I guess there was more underneath us than just grass. Fuck me for not listening to Eagan when he was geeking out about poisonous plants on our last hike. Not that I could have seen whatever it was in the dark anyway, but craaaap.

Troyer sat up in her bed and looked at me. Her big, empty face asked, *what?* I itched too badly to answer. My arms and legs were on fire. It felt like oven-baked itch ants were crawling everywhere I had rolled up my uniform.

Stupid Ben.

Stupid me.

This was not worth two more cigarettes. Not worth being close to him.

I was still in my bed scratching, Troyer staring at me, when Rawe came out of her room. She was morning-ready in her uniform, her face rigid, her braid tight.

"Ten minutes until breakfast," she said, walking into the middle of the cabin. She bent down to tighten her boots. Her braid fell over her shoulder, a black rope.

Nez stretched in her bed and glanced over at me, her eyes moving from my legs to my arms with each attempt of mine to keep ahead of the itch. I'm sure I must have been hopping around like I was having an epileptic fit, like a piece of bacon in a frying pan.

Nez's eyes continued to dance in their sockets as she followed the wild thrash on my cot. She mouthed, *Fleas. Sucks to be you*, and stuck out her tongue.

I wanted to get up and punch her in the face, but I couldn't stop scratching. I couldn't do anything but S-C-R-A-T-C-H.

Rawe pulled herself back up, taut like a rubber band. She was on me instantly.

"What's the deal, Wick?" Her expression was pinched.

"Nothing," I said, stopping my itch-fest for as long as I dared to try to prove my point. Little pin pricks of heat pushed up through my skin. All I wanted to do was douse them in water, flames, cold Greek yogurt, *anything* to make it stop.

"Doesn't look like nothing," she said, chewing on the inside of her cheek.

"Looks like fleas," Nez said, laughing.

Troyer jumped out of her bed and ran to Nez's side of the cabin. I couldn't blame her. Fleas would have made me do that. If I could have peeled my skin off and left it on my bed, I would have run over to the other side of the cabin, too.

"I don't even want to say what you look like, Nez," I said, tightening my mouth and trying not to scratch, but it was clear I was losing that battle.

"Fleas wouldn't make you itch that much," Rawe said, shaking her head. "You *are* itchy, aren't you, Wick?" She stepped closer to my cot.

"No," I said, *still* not scratching, even though I thought I might pass out from the lack of it.

"Let's see," Rawe said, holding out her hand.

"I told you I'm fine," I said, attempting to sit on my arms. "When's breakfast?" I guess I was even more stubborn than Ben gave me credit for.

"You going to show me?" Rawe asked, "or are we going to sit here all day watching you try not to turn your skin to confetti?"

I finally held out my arm. There was nothing else I could do. I had lost before our standoff even started.

Rawe held it lightly by the wrist, spun it one way, the other, and dropped it back on my cot.

"Anywhere else?" she asked.

I pulled my legs out of the sleeping bag and showed her. They didn't look as bad as my arms. Just my luck, the body

Lisa Burstein

parts I could scratch simultaneously were in better shape than the ones I had to count on one itchy arm for.

"Poison ivy," she said.

Fuck me.

Now that my secret was out, that she knew, that everyone knew, I started scratching again, my nails going at my skin with the force of a cheese grater.

"How'd you get it?" Rawe asked, looking at me through the slits of her eyes then looking across the cabin at Troyer and Nez.

"We don't have it," Nez said, her voice louder than it needed to be. "Well, at least I don't." She eyed Troyer and moved away from her.

Troyer shook her head hard—hard enough that she probably should have been wearing a helmet.

"I don't know," I said. My go-to answer for anything I didn't feel like answering. Well, that and *fuck you.*

"You must have come in contact with a plant," Rawe said, using her world-renowned sleuthing skills. "The question is where, or more accurately, when?" She continued to look at me, waiting for me to tell her more.

Waiting for me to confess to the suspicions she'd been having.

"Maybe I got it while I was up in that tree yesterday," I said, scratching again. I couldn't stop scratching even with her watching. Even with Nez beaming from her cot.

"Get dressed," Rawe said. "We're going to the infirmary."

"There's an infirmary? Like with a nurse?" I asked.

"No," Rawe said, sounding tired, "like with calamine lotion."

That was all I needed to hear. I got up. It was totally obvious to anyone with eyes that my arms and a portion of my legs were the only part of me covered with the rash.

"Interesting pattern," Rawe said.

I got dressed quickly, even though the fabric made everything itch even worse. I didn't want Rawe to keep staring at my rash waiting for me to admit something. That had to be what she was waiting for, because she had no proof.

"Okay, you two," Rawe said, turning to Nez and Troyer. "Clean the cabin while I'm gone."

"I want to go to the infirmary. I want medicine," Nez whined, pleaded.

"Nez," Rawe said, her warning shot.

"Why do we have to stay here and clean up this ship hole of a cabin while Cassie gets to lounge around in calamine lotion?" Nez asked. "It's obvious she got this last night, without us."

I looked at Nez, trying to squeeze her mouth shut with my stare. "I'll give you a reason to go to the infirmary," I mumbled.

Troyer stood with her arms wrapped around herself like she was afraid my skin would fly off and come in contact with her skin.

"I'll deal with Wick," Rawe said, looking at me. She held the cabin door open, waiting for me to walk out of it. "Today, Wick," she added when she felt she'd waited long enough.

I scratched as I followed her out onto the porch. I kept scratching as I followed her to the infirmary—honestly, I couldn't stop. I wished I could rip her braid off and use it to scratch my skin like a Brillo Pad.

"So," Rawe said, "do you want to tell me how this happened?"

Lisa Burstein

I guess this was how she was dealing with me. At least she wasn't yelling, but I knew her voice was soft because she wanted me to talk to her. Really talk to her. I kind of wished she were yelling.

"I don't know," I said again.

"You're lying," she said, but she didn't look at me. "I get that you don't want to open up to me, but you need to understand that each time you choose not to, you make it harder for me to help you." She kept walking, marching really, like she wanted me to have to struggle to keep up with her. Which I was.

I looked down and scratched at the parts I could as we walked.

We moved up toward the soccer field. I was hoping that Ben had relocked the equipment shed, or I might have had to not answer some questions about that, too. Not like an open equipment shed automatically equaled poison ivy, but it did equal something.

"You don't want to tell me what happened, fine," Rawe said. "Just do not do whatever you did again."

It seemed like I had gotten out of this a little too easily, but maybe Rawe figured that the result of what I had done was punishment enough.

For as much as I itched, it might have even been too much.

We didn't talk the rest of the walk. It was hard to speak anyway because I was SO ITCHY. The kind of itch where it is all you can feel. Like I felt when I found out I was pregnant—not itchy, exactly, but where it was all I could feel. So consuming that there was nothing else, only that, like a cannonball balanced on my chest.

We reached the infirmary, a building the color of a nurse's hat with a blood-red cross painted on it. Rawe pulled the key out from around her neck to unlock it, but it was already unlocked. She looked at me like I might have the answer, but my mouth stayed shut.

Rawe pushed open the door. We heard voices inside.

"Not your best day, Claire," Nerone grumbled.

"Yes, sir," Ben said.

"Well," Rawe said, turning to look at me, her eyebrows going up so high they hit her hairline. "Wonder why they're here?"

She wasn't asking like she really wondered, she was asking like she knew the answer. Like she knew that Ben was here for the same reason I was.

That we were both here because we had been together.

Nerone turned to us as we entered the room. "Oh, another one, huh?" he asked, seeming far less surprised than Rawe had been.

"Yeah," Rawe said, stretching out the word. "Some kind of epidemic." Her words hung in the air like the smoke from a just fired gun.

Ben had the rash on his arms, legs, and back. He was in his boxers—blue plaid—and even though I could tell he was in pain, he also looked pretty pleased with the fact that I had to see him this way. He didn't seem embarrassed, though I could feel my cheeks light up like fireflies.

Ben had managed to get poison ivy everywhere, which meant he had taken off his whole uniform after I left him last night. Maybe he really was totally fucked up.

Nerone was wearing latex gloves and slathering him with

Lisa Burstein

Pepto-colored lotion. If I didn't want to basically take a potato peeler to my own skin, I might have made a joke about Ben being covered in girlie-pink, but damn I wanted that cream. I wanted to swallow it and have it come out my pores.

"Is there a reason why both of you have poison ivy?" Nerone asked. Even if he wasn't surprised it didn't mean he didn't care.

"I already asked Wick," Rawe said, like I wasn't standing in the room with them. Still, she had no proof that we had been together last night, but our seared-red skin was a pretty decent clue.

"The first one of you to speak up is immune from punishment," Nerone said tightly. It was hard to take him seriously in his gloves covered with pink.

Ben looked at me. I could bust him, but he could also bust me. Both our mouths seemed ready to say something, but neither of us did. I would never do what Amy had done to me. I wouldn't even be here if it wasn't for what Amy had done to me.

"Uh-huh," Nerone said, his jaw pulsing.

"What are you going to do with him?" Rawe asked, pointing her chin in Ben's direction.

"Lock him in one of the exam rooms till he's no longer contagious. All we need is a real epidemic," Nerone said.

Rawe went to the medicine cabinet and found another bottle of calamine lotion. There were ten of them, stacked side by side like a grocery store shelf.

"Ben's already showered," Nerone said. "Make sure she cleans up first. It's important to get the resin off or, well . . . *Leprosy*," he whispered.

I looked at him. My mouth was open wide enough to catch flies.

Nerone laughed long, loud. He might have hit his leg, too, if his hand wasn't covered in pink lotion.

Asshole.

Rawe pointed to the bathroom. "Don't even think about locking it," she said, her face turning as red as the welts on my body.

I walked in and closed the door. Not only was there a shower, but there was a pretty white porcelain toilet. If I'd known poison ivy would have been enough to get me the use of a real bathroom, I'd have gotten it the very first day.

Considering they had enough calamine lotion to paint a little girl's room, it must have meant they knew poison ivy was an issue. Maybe they should have tried removing it from the camp before we got here. Of course, if you were stupid enough to lie on the ground with no clothes on, I guess you deserved it.

Ben had made me that stupid.

The water hit me, warm, heavenly. My body relaxed. It was too bad my skin felt like it was on fire, or I would have stayed in there for hours.

I got out of the shower, dried off, and put on my bra, underwear, and the robe that was hanging on the hook. The water helped the itching a little bit, but it was still there, wrapped on top of my skin like a web. When I opened the bathroom door, Nerone was *still* slathering Ben with calamine lotion. Either Nerone was really enjoying himself, or Ben was in bad shape.

"Okay, Wick, undress," Rawe said.

Ben looked at me. I could tell he was trying to stifle a laugh.

Lisa Burstein

"Um, here?" I asked, holding tight to the robe, even though it was probably dirtier than the floor we were standing on.

"Oh, right," Rawe said, like she had forgotten there was a difference between boys and girls. "Come on." She took me into one of the exam rooms and closed the door.

She looked at me and waited.

"I can do it myself," I said.

"I've let a lot slide this morning," she said. "Let's finish this."

I took off the robe and closed my eyes as her latex glove–covered hands slathered me in lotion. It was cold, soothing, amazing.

When she was finished, she took the gloves off, flicked them in the trash can, and handed me the bottle.

"Now," she said. "Try not to touch it. The more you touch it, the worse it gets, and it spreads."

"Okay," I said, holding the bottle close to me. I was still in my underwear and bra. I must have looked like someone at the beach who was only afraid of certain parts of her getting sunburned.

"Your Assessment Diary is on the counter," she said.

Couldn't forget this now, could she?

"Here." She handed me a small white pill and a cup of water. "Take one of these. It's a steroid so it will help with the swelling. I'll come to check on you later." She washed her hands in the sink.

"You're leaving me? Alone?" I asked.

"I'll lock you in," she said, pushing the little pieces that had come out of her braid off her face. "It's a precaution for forty-eight hours."

"Forty-eight hours," I repeated, like I couldn't believe it. I felt anxiety build, traveling up from my toes to the middle of my chest where it sat on my heart, knocking around with the force of something falling down the stairs.

"You'll be safe here," Rawe said, like she could see what I was fighting so hard to keep in.

I opened my mouth to talk, but I couldn't. My throat was dry. My windpipe felt like someone was squeezing it shut. Tears started to form in the corners of my eyes. I wasn't even sad. Why was I crying?

Because Rawe was leaving me?

No, because Rawe was leaving me *here*.

It didn't make sense and then all at once I knew.

The thing I had tried so hard to keep in—to never, ever talk about, write about, think about. I was sitting in it, the place where the thing that happened because of the thing that happened with Aaron happened.

I was in the exact surroundings of the *after*.

The place where I'd been broken.

This room reminded me of the clinic. Smelled like it, looked like it. Had the cream-colored walls that were supposed to calm you, the waxy black floor, the white, white sheeted bed, the cabinets filled with instruments to take care of whatever "problem" you were there to solve. Surely it wasn't as sterile, but that was it, and I really didn't want to be locked inside here.

Not for half an hour and certainly not for forty-eight.

"Can't I stay in the cabin?" I pleaded quickly. "I won't touch anything." I felt my body start to shake, each of my

Lisa Burstein

joints rocking on its axis. I tried to slow my breathing, but it came out in gasps.

"What's wrong?" Rawe asked.

I looked down. The floor was blurry from the tears. They felt as hot as my itchy skin.

"Wick?" she asked. "Talk to me."

I looked up and tried to focus on her. I was not going to do this. Not in front of her.

"Nothing," I said, too upset to even realize I was answering her previous question. I dried my eyes and willed my body still. Doing anything to show her I was fine with her leaving me, because I was afraid I would crumple up into a ball on the floor if I didn't.

She watched me. "It's okay," she said, reaching out for me.

"Don't," I said, pulling away from her touch. If I let her I would lose it. I didn't *do* losing it, as much as my current actions made total bullshit of that statement.

"I want to help you, but I can't if you don't want to be helped." She looked at me and waited. I almost spoke and then I saw her eyes, wet like mine with pity, but people didn't feel sorry for me. I felt sorry for people.

"What?" I spit angrily. "You're locking me in, so lock me in already."

She breathed through her nose and shook her head in that way people do to let you know you've disappointed them. "You've already locked yourself in," she said. She walked out the door and closed it behind her. I heard the bolt turn, the sound as heavy as a boulder falling.

The day my brother drove me to the clinic was hazy, from the drugs they gave me, from the sick shame I felt about what I had to do.

I don't remember much of it. I remember the pain, an empty ache, like the howl of a cavern in my guts. I remember my brother sitting in a chair next to the bed I slept on at the motel we drove to after. The bed with the too-thin comforter and sheets that were so rough they felt like sandpaper.

Each time I woke up moaning, my brother was next to me with a wet washcloth for my forehead. In the night, his silhouette was like the trace of a pebble thrown in a pond. But he was there, like always. My brother, the only man I could count on.

I didn't even want to tell him, but I needed someone over eighteen to drive me to and from the clinic and there was no way I was telling my parents. I wasn't sure how much more they could punish me beyond what they already had, but I knew they would figure something out. My mom would figure something out.

I also knew they would have made me keep it, which would have meant that my mother would have to help raise it and there was no way I was putting someone else through that.

When I told him he started to cry, which made me start to cry. It was late, almost midnight, my mother already passed out in her bedroom. Tim and I were in the dark living room with the crappy half–grandfather clock we had that ticked and ticked filling the silence that only held our tears. At that moment it made me think of the heartbeat in my belly that I was asking my brother to help me snuff out like a spent cigarette.

Lisa Burstein

He asked and asked and asked who the father was so he could go and castrate him, but I never told. The thing in my belly and fuck-face Aaron and I were the only ones who knew I had been stupid enough to sleep with him.

Now, only Aaron and I knew.

I think the weirdest part of all of it was how routine it appeared to be to everyone but my brother and me. The nurse at the clinic acted no differently than the guy who gave us our room key at the motel. I guess both of them were only doing their jobs, regardless of what doing that job meant.

I guess that's what Rawe is doing when it's the three of us and she has to "stay on script." To be honest, it's easier to deal with. I would much rather have someone holding me at arm's length than trying against all odds to hold me.

I blinked, once, twice. I had to get it together. I had to calm down. Even if this room did look and smell and *feel* like the clinic.

I heaved myself up on the bed and sat in the corner of it. Pulled my knees up to my chest, bent my head down so my mouth rested between them. Nothing could touch me if I sat this way. The only trick was not to move.

There was a knock on the wall.

"Anybody home?" Ben asked. Even when he was covered with an itchy, pus-filled rash, he was still fucking adorable.

"Go away, Ben," I said.

"I can't; I'm locked in," he joked.

I looked up at the ceiling. It had the same fluorescent lights as the clinic. The ones that sounded like a mosquito trap and made your eyes water if you stared at them.

Yes, it was the lights that made my eyes water.

"Aren't you itchy?" I said, scratching at my own arms. I was surprised Ben wanted to use any part of his energy talking to me, when he could have used it annihilating the little pinches of itch all over his skin.

"Sure, but I'm also bored," he said. "I can compartmentalize my feelings."

"How?" I talked into my knees. They were rough, prickly hairs covering them like porcupine needles.

"What else do I have to do?" he asked.

I couldn't answer. My arms felt numb, my chest ached. I was pretty sure I was having a panic attack and I had forty-eight hours to go.

"Cassie?"

"I can't breathe," I said. I felt nuts. No wonder there were so many crazy people in insane asylums—it was because they were all forced behind closed, locked doors. All forced into rooms that left them with nothing to do but think.

"Just try to stay calm," the wall said. "Everything is going to be okay."

"It's not," I said. His words should have made things better, but they were making things worse. Probably because I knew nothing would ever be *okay*. Whatever I had tried desperately to leave behind that day at the clinic was here now. And maybe it always would be.

"I'm here, Cassie," he said.

I covered my ears. "You, you want to hurt me," I said, the tears coming again and I wasn't even looking up at the lights.

"What are you talking about?" he asked.

What *was* I talking about? What hole had this room pushed me into?

Lisa Burstein

This room, this stupid fucking room.

"I just don't like being alone," I said. I could taste soap on my knees. It was my attempt at some kind of explanation, because I couldn't explain.

"You're not," he said. I could hear him scratching at the wall, making circles on it like someone might in water.

I pictured him being able to break through, to come in here and comfort me with the words I kept telling him I didn't want to hear. But he was locked in, too.

I lay back and stared up at the ceiling, the same way I had in the clinic, from one corner to the other and back again. Anything to not have to see the doctor with his surgical mask covering his mouth and nose, like a monster hiding the scariest parts of his face.

"Cassie? You still there?" Ben asked.

"Where the hell else would I be?" I asked.

"You're just so quiet," he said.

"I don't want to talk, Ben. Talking last night is what got me here." It was true; I was finally starting to let him in. Was this the universe telling me not to? Was God punishing me again?

Would I ever stop being punished?

"Does this have to do with the stuff that has nothing to do with me?" he asked.

I closed my eyes, tears rolling and hitting the tops of my ears. I was shaking so hard my teeth were chattering. Why was I afraid of a room?

But I knew it wasn't the room. It was how it was making me feel. How it was taking the anger I had built up to fight my sadness and shattering it.

"How about I try to guess what happened?" he asked.

I wiped my eyes and nose. "Knock yourself out," I said, letting myself focus on his voice.

"You were abducted by aliens," he said.

"No," I said, tears still flowing.

"You're really a demon," he said.

"No." I felt myself laugh, one of those cry-laugh combos that makes you start to cry harder.

"You were forced to perform in a circus by your demented uncle," he said.

"Are you fucking kidding me?" I choked the words out through growing sobs. I knew Ben was just trying to make me feel better, make me laugh, but it was obvious he didn't take what had happened to me all that seriously.

Not that he could have known how serious it was. Not that until I was locked in here had I allowed myself to feel how serious it was.

"Why are you crying?" he asked.

"I'm fucking sad," I said, in full-on snot-faced cry. "I'm really, really fucking sad."

"You sound sad," he said.

Luckily Ben couldn't see me, but he could hear me. He knew I was crying. I could tell in his voice that he was afraid I couldn't stop.

I was afraid I couldn't stop.

"Wow, Ben, you're a fucking genius. When we get out of here remind me to call the Nobel Prize people."

"Cassie," he said, "I—"

"No, you're seriously amazing. You can tell when someone is having a fucking mental breakdown, what they act like

Lisa Burstein

when their heart has been stabbed with twenty thousand acid-covered metal toothpicks."

"I was just trying to help," he said. "I'm sorry."

"You shouldn't be," I said. "This has absolutely nothing to do with *you*."

"Okay then," he said. "I'll let you be." I could hear Ben scramble up onto his squeaky bed and away from crazy, crazy me.

He had been the one to give up.

9 Fucking Days to Go

I woke up and found a tray with food and a bottle of water in the corner of the room.

It was some kind of meat sandwich that I would not eat. I'd never been a vegetarian before the clinic, but after that day, I felt sick to my stomach when I thought of eating anything that bled, when I thought of eating anything that had once had a heartbeat.

When I thought about anything, really.

There was another white pill on the tray. I took it without even thinking, anything to make my skin turn back to normal. The door was still closed and locked. I guess that was Rawe coming to check on me. Since she feels like she can do a half-ass job caring for me, I have decided to do the same with this entry. The only reason I'm writing is because there's something I want to remember.

There's something I've realized I can never forget.

I've tried everything I could think of to bury it, like the baby or whatever it was that had been inside me and never was.

But burying it is not enough.

What I want to remember, what I need to remember, is that no matter what I do, I will never be the same.

8 Fucking Days
to Go

When I woke up it was dark and I'd forgotten where I was. For a moment, I did think I was back in the clinic, my brother about to open the curtains around my bed, look at me with his sad smile and ask me if I was ready to go home—the fleabag motel room we rented—where I bled and sweated all over the sheets.

I sat up in bed. I could see that my locked door was open and the light in the hallway was on. I could see through the windows outside that it was dark. The tray from the day before was gone. Maybe Rawe had actually come to check on me instead of leaving food and slinking away like a scared servant. Maybe she was out there waiting for me now.

I hoped she had some water. I was thirsty, very, and I realized it was the first thing besides itchy that I'd felt in hours. I hoped it meant that maybe the itching was getting better.

I put on the clean uniform she'd left for me and stepped out of the room. I checked both sides of the hallway: no Rawe, no Nerone, no nobody—empty. I grabbed a bottle of water that had been left on the table and gulped it down so fast it hurt.

The door to Ben's room was open, too, but he wasn't there, and his bed was made. How long had I been sleeping? Had I really just slept through an entire night and day? How tired must this place have made me that I could stay asleep in daylight with my skin on fire, my head full of confused, terrible feelings? I guess Rawe had succeeded in her attempt to break me. My body, at least, was done.

Ben must have already gone back to his cabin. I wondered if he had come in and watched me sleep before he left. If so, he would have probably seen my fists clenched, my face tight. That was how I woke up every morning, like I wanted to tear up the air around me like paper.

Or maybe he had left without even checking on me. Maybe I had finally succeeded in pushing him away. I felt that familiar emptiness in my stomach, craved it, knowing it was the only thing that would keep me safe.

Before I left the infirmary I took another shower, cleaning off the calamine lotion that had dried on my skin like old pink cake frosting. In the shower, my skin felt less itchy than it had yesterday and was healing, from what I could see. I got out, dried myself off, reapplied more calamine lotion, and got dressed.

I left the infirmary door wide open and walked in the dark back to my cabin, a bottle of lotion under my arm. I was more than halfway back when I realized I hadn't even bothered to check the medicine cabinets in there for real drugs. Was I really too far gone to even want to get fucked up? Or was some part of this weird place working?

The air was full of that sweet pine tree smell, like the needles had been tossed with sugar and cooked in an oven. I walked quietly back into the cabin, but the door still creaked as I closed it. Nez didn't stir in her cot. She was out like she'd been hit in the head. Whatever training they had done that day and the day before had put her into a coma.

Even though it felt like I'd been through hell, at least I'd missed that.

I slipped onto my cot and could see Troyer was still awake, lying in bed, her eyes wide like bowls of milk with two blue-berries in the middle. I did a small wave and pulled my sleeping bag up and around me, realizing that it was weird to feel comfortable here. That when I thought of leaving the infirmary, even though I could have gone anywhere, could have left the grounds if I had the guts to disappear into the night and turn into a different person on the other side, I came back here.

To this.

Troyer wrote something on her pad and showed it to me. *Where have you been?*

"Infirmary," I whispered. Better to say that than, *The place of my nightmares.* The place I wished I could pretend had never existed. The place that took me back to the place in my mind that I wish had never existed.

Lisa Burstein

You okay? she wrote, like she could tell.

"Compared to what?" I whispered.

She shrugged.

"Exactly," I said, turning away from her and trying to go back into the nothingness of sleep. She was trying to be nice, I guess, trying to make me feel better. Unfortunately, even coming from her, I was way beyond that.

7 Fucking Days to Go

woke up still in my uniform, sweating in my sleeping bag. I gasped and looked around. I was so hot that I wondered if the rash had gotten worse. So hot that I wondered if the fever I had after my time in the clinic had come back.

I must have looked insane, because Troyer got out of her bed and put her hand on my shoulder and squeezed. I guess her way of saying, *You're okay, you're awake, you're here.*

Not like it mattered.

So what if I was *here*? Was here really better than the clinic when it was obvious I would never escape it?

Nez rose up out of her sleeping bag and stretched—her brown arms and neck reaching toward the ceiling like tree branches.

"Oh goody," she said, furrowing her brow, "Cassie's back."

"Fuck you, too, Nez," I said.

Troyer let go of my shoulder and sat on her bed.

"Already starting things out the way we left them," Nez said.

"Well, I haven't changed and my guess is you haven't either," I said, trying to match her expression. Even though I *had* changed. Being locked up in the infirmary had unlocked something in me. Something I wasn't sure I would be able to contain anymore.

"How was the infirmary? Get a lot of rest?" Nez asked, her last word hissed on the *s*, extending it, her way of letting me know that she and Troyer had not.

I could feel Troyer's head moving back and forth between us, like she was a cat watching a bird fly from one end of the cabin to the other.

"It was hard to sleep with your boyfriend trying to break into my room the whole time," I said, hating myself for it.

Nez's mouth opened, her chin almost touching her chest.

"So, no, not too much rest," I said, embellishing the *s* with my own hiss.

Nez's eyes went smaller, the black balls in them turning to thin dashes. "You're a liar."

"That would be easier, wouldn't it? For all three of us," I said, not dropping my gaze. "But no, I'm not."

It was bad enough I didn't know how to deal with Ben, that after what happened in the infirmary, it appeared he didn't know how to deal with me. But now I was using him like this.

"You were probably delirious from your flesh-eating virus," Nez said, brushing her hair so hard I thought it would scream.

"Save it," I said. "Oh, and Ben doesn't say 'Hi.'" I pulled myself out of the oven of my sleeping bag and gave my left arm a quick scratch, then scratched the right one. Whatever Rawe had given me was working—my skin only looked like it had been sautéed in oil for ten minutes instead of for an hour.

Troyer was smiling at me like she was waiting for me to give her a piece of candy. "What'd you guys do yesterday?" I said. I could have asked about the day before too, but this was Troyer and I knew she would need to write it down. I wasn't in the mood to wait for her to pen a novel.

Troyer scribbled on her pad and handed it to me: *Packed.* A look of fear settled on her face, the same look she got when she had to go into the canoe alone with Stravalaci.

"Packed what?" I asked, scratching at my arms again. My legs didn't feel itchy. It was progress.

"Oh—" Nez laughed. "You'll see. I almost couldn't sleep thinking about your reaction."

Rawe came out of her room, a backpack secured to her back. She didn't look at me, didn't even mention that I had returned. Maybe she was mad at me. Or whatever you could be toward someone who was doing everything she could to keep you out of her head.

"Take a good look around the cabin," Rawe said, staring at the front door, "because it's the last time you'll see it."

"That's what packing means," Nez said, smirking at me.

"Where are we going?" I asked, looking at Rawe, but Nez was not about to let her answer.

"Out there," Nez teased, pointing at the door.

"Like, for good?" I asked, suddenly experiencing everything I'd felt the day I arrived here in the van come rushing

Lisa Burstein

back. Somehow I had gotten used to being here. Sure, we had to be outside a lot, but we did get to be in the somewhat-safety of our cabin at night.

Well, at least we *had* been allowed to.

"You didn't think this was going to be a spa vacation forever, did you?" Rawe asked, finally noticing I was alive.

I didn't bother answering. I guess I had. Not that any of this was pleasant, or even close to what Rawe was referring to as a "spa vacation."

"What do you think you've been training for? To hide in here with your tail between your legs?" I could feel her saying that directly to me. For each time she'd tried to talk to me and I'd shut her down.

My stomach and lips sank. It felt like my skin was rolling down from my forehead to my chin. We were going out there? For good?

"That's the face!" Nez yelled. "That's the face I was waiting for." She clapped her hands together like a trained seal. "It almost makes having to actually do this myself worth it."

I looked at Troyer. She seemed like she wanted to apologize; I wasn't sure why. None of this was her fault.

Nez laughed again. "Surprise, Cassie. We're spending the rest of our stay out in the woods," she howled. "Aren't you excited?"

"Fuck you, Nez," I said, trying to slow down my heartbeat. I could hear it in my ears, feel it banging on the inside of my skull like a cymbal.

"No fighting," Rawe said. "This is important. You need to be a team. Out in the woods *we* need to be a team."

I didn't want to go out into the woods and I definitely didn't want to be a team. Fuck. Fuck. Fuck. Whatever breakdown I had experienced in the infirmary was about to be eclipsed if I found anything in my tent with more than two legs.

Would we even be allowed to use a tent?

"Wick, let's move," Rawe said.

I sat there. Moving meant leaving. Meant being *out there*. I wasn't moving.

"It's time to use your training," Rawe said.

"I don't want to use my training," I said.

"Okay." Rawe's hands were tight on the straps of her backpack. "Let me put it another way. We're going. You have no choice."

"We already did this yesterday. It didn't help." Nez shrugged.

"Well, I wasn't *here* yesterday," I said, grasping at anything.

"We know," Nez said, rolling her eyes.

"We leave in ten," Rawe said, marching out the front door. It was obvious the conversation was over.

"You better keep your *disease* to yourself," Nez said, blowing me a kiss.

I was about to be in the middle of nowhere with bugs, bears, and *Nez*. If we had to share a tent I might be sent back here for attempted murder.

I hiked between Nez and Troyer, Rawe in front of us, leading us into the gut of the woods. I had a pack on my back. It was heavy, slogging, as much weight as carrying another one of myself.

Lisa Burstein

The tall pine trees above us rustled in the wind, doing a really shitty job at keeping the sun off our faces. Up the trail ahead of Rawe, the boys' camp walked in a line behind Nerone. They moved like they were each dragging a sled behind them, their backs bent and chins jutting out in front of them.

When we met up with the boys that morning, Ben kept looking at his boots, staring at them like they were going to tell him the secrets of the universe, which let me know he didn't want to look at me.

I guess my freak-out in the infirmary *had* scared him off. It was hard to want a girl who turned into a pile of snot and estrogen at a moment's notice. At least I wouldn't have to worry about him anymore.

But without him, would anyone worry about *me* anymore?

As I hiked, I could feel the three cigarettes I had left, stored horizontally in my bra strap like bullets. Sweat was starting to pool on my lower back, dampening my shirt, making it stick to me. We had been walking for hours when I finally had to stop. I sat down on a log and took a drink from my canteen. Troyer ran over and tried to pick me up and pull me along, her lips almost pointing toward Nez and Rawe up the trail. It looked like it was hurting her face—seemed to me it would have been easier to talk.

"What?" I asked. "I need a break." She shook her head, hard, fast. I wished she would tell me what she was thinking for once.

"Wick!" Rawe yelled from fifty feet ahead. She didn't look tired at all. Nez stood next to her, grinning. Troyer ran from me to where they were standing, a blur of white-blond hair.

"Wick," Rawe said again.

"Yes," I huffed, "here."

"Here." Rawe chuckled. "No," she said, halting her laugh to let me know no part of this was funny. "Here!" She pointed to the ground in front of her, like I was a dog.

And, like a dog, I had no choice but to obey. I got up, hung my canteen back at my waist, and walked, head down, to where they were standing.

"You didn't get the rules yesterday, so I'll give them to you now," Rawe said.

I looked at Nez. If she were smiling any harder, her teeth would fall out.

"No breaks till I say there's a break," Rawe said, ticking off a finger. "No talking till I tell you to talk. And no fighting. I will not put up with that crap out here. We have enough things against us to be against each other."

"You should talk to Nez about fighting," I said.

"I'm not doing anything, Cassie," Nez replied.

"Did you hear what I said?" Rawe asked.

"Yes," I said, not moving.

"You don't look like it," Rawe said. "What's rule number one?"

"No breaks," I said.

She looked at me, stared, really, her eyes fixed on my very tired ass. I started walking before she could say anything else. We kept moving in silence, the breaking branches below us and the birds in the trees above. Every so often something would buzz past me—a fly, a bee, a mosquito, and because we weren't supposed to talk I couldn't say, *Fuck! Get this fucking thing away from me.* All I could do was smack at it or run from

Lisa Burstein

it, the pack on my back working to push me down into the ground like a nail being hammered.

After a ten-minute lunch and pee stop, Rawe started leading us in this weird march call. The silence had been better.

"How far will we go?" she yelled.

As far as we need to, we were supposed to answer. We did, but certainly not with the gusto she had.

"How far will we go?" she yelled again.

"As far as we need to," we answered again, with about as little energy as I'd ever heard from people who were supposed to be shouting. Of course, Troyer wasn't saying anything, so I guess even my and Nez's sad attempts were better.

I knew Rawe was making us say this for more than the distance we were walking. I didn't need a psychology degree to understand that going deep into the woods was supposed to help us go deep into ourselves.

Lucky me.

I'd had enough going deep into myself via my Assessment Diary and at the infirmary. I still felt like an empty husk from what had happened there. Writing and thinking about the things inside my head had turned me into a girl I didn't recognize: quiet, scared, ready to cry or scream at a moment's notice. I couldn't find the anger that I'd used to hold it all together anymore.

"Wick, tell us something you've never told anyone," Rawe yelled from the front of the line.

"Why?" I complained.

"What's rule number three?" Rawe said, not even stopping to yell.

"I'm not fighting, I'm asking," I said.

"Stop stalling," Rawe said.

I *was* stalling. There was really only one thing I hadn't told anyone, and there was no way in hell I was about to reveal it here.

"Wick, answer or we keep walking," Rawe said.

My guess was we were going to keep walking anyway. It didn't look like the boys were stopping anytime soon. It made sense to keep us moving, make us tired — less chance we would sneak out of our tents at night. Not that I had the balls now that we were out here to even unzip my tent.

"I've never kept anything from anyone," I said, but I'd kept everything from everyone.

Even my brother didn't know the whole story. Even Aaron didn't. I knew that even *I* really didn't. I had kept myself from the pain, the real pain. I had to. That was what I had felt at the infirmary.

That was what had scared Ben away.

"Uh-huh," Rawe said, turning her head to make sure I knew she was yelling at me. "I'm waiting."

"It's not my fault I got poison ivy," I said. I knew she was still angry about that. Angry because she didn't have proof to punish me, but she wanted to. I guess this was how she was going to.

"Jeez," Nez huffed. "I'll tell you two things if it means we don't have to hike anymore and Cassie stops whining."

"Wick!" Rawe stopped to yell. "Don't you dare test me. This forest is five hundred miles across and we will hike every step of it until you speak." She turned and started walking again.

She wasn't letting up. I had to say something, but it couldn't

Lisa Burstein

be *the* thing. It could never be *the* thing. Besides, I was afraid if I said *the* thing I would melt into a pile of mush again.

I turned to Troyer. Her forehead looked like it was going to pop out of her skull. Her way, I guess, of saying, *Fucking say it Cassie, I'm tired.*

"Fine." I sighed. I looked down at my feet, one boot moving in front of the other.

"Still waiting," Rawe said.

"I never told anyone I got stood up on prom night," I mumbled.

"Again," Rawe said, "I don't think your chin could hear you."

Rawe wasn't going to make this easy. But why should she?

"I said—" I tried to speak more loudly, even though my throat was so dry the words felt like sand. "I got stood up on prom night."

"That's dumb," Nez said.

"Well, it's true," I retorted quickly. That was all I was sharing. Rawe could make us walk until my feet fell off. I was keeping my mouth shut.

"You're going to accept that?" Nez asked Rawe. She was probably hoping I would say something that she could use against me later—something even more embarrassing than what I shared. What must Nez have been through to think it wasn't?

"And why didn't you tell anyone?" Rawe asked, still leading us down the trail and thankfully ignoring Nez. Maybe she was happy that for once I'd finally answered her.

"Because it was humiliating," I said, thinking quickly. "People who get stood up are losers." I looked at the trail. At least the boys were too far ahead to hear me.

"Well, that's true." Nez laughed.

"Shut up," I said. "No one cares what you think."

"No fighting," Rawe said.

"Hey, I'm agreeing," Nez said. I could see her hold her hands up like someone was aiming a gun at her.

"Wick, is that what you are choosing? You can pick anything you've never told anyone," Rawe said.

"That's what I pick," I said. It was the safest. And if I wanted to get deep about it, which I didn't, that was how it all started, wasn't it?

"Okay," Rawe said. "Yell it."

"What?" I asked.

Nez laughed.

"Yell *I was stood up on prom night*. It's the only way you can free yourself from it."

"I don't need to free myself from it," I said.

"Well, I say you do," Rawe retorted.

"C'mon Cassie," Nez said. "Loud enough so Ben can hear."

I lifted my hands up to push her but stopped myself. I turned around and glanced at Troyer instead. Her face was sad, but of course she didn't say anything.

"I was stood up on prom night," I said.

"Louder," Rawe said.

"Yeah, louder," Nez hissed.

I looked at Nez's back and repeated it, again and again, until my throat ached. I wanted the sentences to be like bullets going through her pack and her uniform into her perfect brown skin.

I could yell and scream those words easily. What I couldn't do was even say the word for the thing I had really kept from everyone.

Lisa Burstein

One word that I couldn't even whisper, that I couldn't even write down, like Troyer.

If Rawe was right and saying something out loud freed you from it, how would I ever be free from something I couldn't even admit to myself?

We sat around the campfire, all nine of us: a man, a woman, and seven fuckups against the wilderness.

Probably not the best odds.

The whites of our eyes looked pink in the firelight. Each of us had our lips around a metal mug, our only utensil for the next six days. We slugged at it like it held one hundred sleeping pills. Apparently there would be a lot of drinking, and not the kind I liked, in our future.

We sipped on lip-scalding broth in silence while Nez stared at Ben and he tried not to stare at me.

The fire was pretty sad, like what a homeless guy might have been able to build with the scraps he found in an alley, but we had to keep it small so we didn't alert anything that we were out here. Anything that included a rescue plane and, more importantly, the grizzly bears Rawe warned us would break us in half like a candy bar.

When we first arrived at the camp that afternoon, Rawe and Nerone had us dig the holes that would be our toilets for the night while they went and "checked the perimeter." As I worked, I couldn't help wondering what the clinic had done with whatever was inside me. I'm sure no one dug a grave for it. I don't think anyone at the clinic said a prayer or did anything special. I think whatever was inside me went into a plastic biohazard bin. Which I guess was supposed to make you feel like it wasn't just a garbage can, but really it was, just with a fancy sign on it.

I kept looking at Ben. I needed his fucking lighter. I figured we could get a quick smoke in before Rawe and Nerone got back, but Ben was acting like he was Superman and my face was kryptonite.

Perfect fucking timing.

Troyer was working next to me. At least with her I didn't seem like a total zero, even though that was what I felt like. I felt the way I did in middle school before I realized I could scare people, when I used to be afraid of them instead. Ever since I had come here, ever since that day at the clinic weeks ago, the same vulnerability was just below the surface of my skin. Like someone could reach in and rip my heart out by looking at me. Or not looking at me.

Stupid fucking Ben and stupid fucking boys.

Troyer wrote on a piece of paper and passed it to me. *You really got stood up for prom?* That was what she chose to ask me about. Not why Ben was pretending I didn't exist, not why I was fuming, trying to pretend I wasn't fuming.

I guess being stood up for prom really was that bad—not like Troyer knew what I was comparing it to.

"Yes," I hissed. "Did you even go to your prom?" I sounded angry, even though I wasn't at all mad at Troyer. It was easier to be cold than to let people be cold to you. That was something I'd learned from my mother.

The only thing I'd learned from my mother.

Of course, she wrote.

Lisa Burstein

Of course she'd gone to her prom. Eagan had probably even gone to his prom; Eagan who had already fallen in the hole he was digging. That's what normal kids did, even what abnormal kids did. Total fuckups like me got stood up for their proms, got arrested, and then got in "trouble" and had to do something about it.

Total fuckups liked me scared away total fuckups who were actually being nice to them.

I dropped my shovel and punched deep into my stomach, once, twice, till the pain made me nauseous.

Why do you do that? Troyer wrote. She had noticed. I didn't think anyone had because no one ever asked me about it. Maybe everyone had noticed but it was too weird to ask me about.

It was definitely too weird to explain.

"Why don't you talk?" I asked. It was mean, but I didn't know what else to say. I couldn't answer her, so I attacked instead.

Troyer ripped a blank piece of paper off the pad and dropped it on the ground next to me. I guess that was her way of saying she wasn't talking to me anymore.

Fine, now I was totally alone. Even Troyer had deserted me. Not like I could blame her.

I guess I crave loneliness. I certainly try to create it. I do anything I can to cover up the loneliness that comes from knowing I had something that would have been connected to me for my whole life and I destroyed it.

I can never be alone enough to snuff that out.

6 Fucking Days to Go

woke up alone in my tent, which was good considering that was how I'd fallen asleep. I don't know what I was expecting. That Ben would come and see me during the night? That he would actually not have given up on me, so I could push him away again? At least his attention had been something I could count on, until I'd fucked that up, too.

I should have known I'd push him too far. I push everyone too far.

I looked at the red top of my tent and couldn't help wondering if this was what the thing inside of me saw before it was no longer inside me—safety and red and soft all around. If it was floating in that light, until I forced it out into the world.

Kind of like me, except I was waiting for Rawe to come wake me up and tell me how far I was going to have to hike before I was allowed to get in here again. The thing that had been inside me had no choice to come back.

I had made the choice for it.

Choice.

Calling what I had to do a *choice* was a joke. Anyone who described what I had to do as *freedom of choice* has never had to do what I had to do. There is no choice in it. Who would actually choose what I put that thing inside me through? What I put myself through? What I'm still going through?

I listened to the birds. Felt the sun filtering through the red of the tent. It was going to be another long day of Rawe trying to break open our shells. Well, really just mine. She didn't seem to be pushing Nez and Troyer the way she was pushing me.

I pictured Rawe like someone at a seafood buffet, a plate of crab legs and lobster tails in front of her. She was wearing a bib, drooling, waiting for my shell to open so she could get her claws into the soft parts I hid from her. The soft parts that probably even she herself hid.

The soft, scary parts Ben had seen at the infirmary. The ones that were too much for him.

"Breakfast in ten," I heard Rawe call. I knew she'd put her hands around her mouth like a megaphone. Knew her braid was tight, tight, tight.

I unzipped my tent and stepped out, feeling even more bleary-eyed than I had when I was sleeping in the cabin. Newsflash, sleeping on the ground makes you feel like dog shit.

Everyone was milling around the dead fire from last night, waiting for instructions from Rawe and Nerone. I guess it was sort of the way it had been in school, where you would be sitting in the auditorium with your classmates waiting for someone to go up on stage and tell you something you were going to ignore, or in my case, that you would skip out on entirely. Except here Rawe and Nerone had our undivided attention and they were far too boring to deserve that.

"Troyer, Eagan, you're on breakfast duty," Nerone muttered.

Rawe stood next to him like they were bookends, one with a square head and one with a pointy head. I guess they weren't picking our duties without thought. Considering Stravalaci's past, it was probably a good idea to keep him away from anything he could poison.

"Yes, sir," Eagan lisped.

Troyer stood there.

"Leisner, Stravalaci, Claire, you're on tents," Nerone said.

The three of them grumbled and walked with scuffing feet to the first tent. I thought about my tent. Was there anything inside it I wouldn't want Ben to see? Why the hell did I care?

That left Nez and me, and I knew before Rawe even said it that she was planning to fuck me royally.

"Nez, Wick, you two go gather some wood," she said, looking right at me to let me know she knew she was fucking me royally.

"Can I trade with someone?" Nez asked. I saw her look over at Ben, who was taking down Eagan's tent. At least I didn't have to see Eagan fumbling and struggling with it again.

I knew she was saying it because of me and not because of the wood, which was fine—I felt the same way. I didn't have the energy to ask to switch partners, mostly because I knew it wouldn't make a difference anyway.

Lisa Burstein

"No," Rawe said, clenching her teeth. Nerone stood next to her and clenched his teeth, too, a united front of different-headed bookends.

Nez and I didn't move.

"That means today," Nerone said. "We're all waiting for breakfast."

Nez huffed and started walking quickly toward the woods at the north of the camp.

"And get enough for a decent size fire," Rawe called after her, like she wasn't satisfied with Nerone having the last word.

Nez was walking so fast I had to run to catch up to her. And I wanted to catch up to her. If I had to go look for wood while other things looked for us, there was no way I wanted to be alone.

It felt immediately cooler when I entered the woods, the shade from the trees coloring everything gray.

Nez stopped and turned to me. "What, are you chasing me now?"

"I wouldn't have to if you weren't walking so fast," I said, surprised that I was actually out of breath.

"I want to get this over with," she said. "The less time I have to spend alone with you, the better."

"Fuck off, Nez," I said.

"Do you ever say anything else?" Nez asked, her lips puckered like my words were something she didn't like the taste of.

"I never want to say anything else," I said, then added, "to you."

"Because you're jealous," Nez said.

"Of what?" I laughed.

"Me," she said. "Ben and me."

A breeze blew through, whipping her black, black hair in front of her face like shadows. The look of it made me shiver.

"You're delusional," I said.

She shrugged. "Ben says you're jealous and he's right."

"You don't know shit and Ben knows even less," I said, feeling hot needles start to poke at my hands, trying to force them into fists.

"I see the way you look at him," Nez said, almost sang.

"I don't." I paused. "Look at him."

She snorted. "We always want what we can't have."

A crow cawed and bounded from one tree to the next.

"You suck, Nez," I said, starting to walk past her. I should have kept walking. I should have ignored her. I never did what I should do.

"I suck?" She laughed. "At least I use your first name, *Cassie*. Do you use mine? Do you even *know* mine?"

"I never asked you to use my first name," I said, spinning to look at her, not wanting to admit I actually didn't know hers.

"You call Ben by his first name. Ever think about that?" she asked.

"How do you know what I call him?" I asked, immediately feeling silly for it. It didn't matter. Nez could see right through me. Regardless of how much I said I hated Ben, how much I acted like I wanted him to leave me alone, she was right—I did use his first name.

"You don't even call Troyer Laura," Nez said, her voice rising to meet the top of the trees.

"Neither do you," I retorted.

"But I'm not her friend, am I?" Nez asked. Her face was calm, as still as the sky far, far above us.

Lisa Burstein

"I wouldn't know," I said, searching for something to say next. "I don't know what you are, Nez," I hissed. If it bothered her so much I was using her last name, I was going to use it so much it made her ears bleed.

"You think you're so tough," she said, "but I see you. You're scared, scared of everyone, scared of yourself."

"You're the one who should be scared," I said, even though her words hit me right in my lower stomach, punched me there, like I usually did.

"Oh really?" she asked. "I know things, Cassie. Things about you."

"Don't," I said, though I'm not sure why. I didn't have any idea what she was going to say, but for some reason I knew that once she said it, that would be it.

The last straw.

"I saw your file." She smiled evilly. "Troyer's, too. You know it has medical info in it, right?"

"You're a fucking liar," I said, like I was responding to any annoying thing that came out of her mouth, but really I felt the woods around me start to spin like I was in the center of a merry-go-round. The trees were the horses, the leaf- and dried-pine-needle-covered ground the beach-ball-colored base. Could Nez be telling the truth? Could what I'd done that day at the clinic be in some "file" that had been forwarded to Rawe? Did that mean other people knew? Ben? Or worse, my parents?

Was that why Ben was ignoring me?

My stomach felt like the hull of a ship riding wave after wave.

"Listen," Nez said matter-of-factly, "I'm not the one you should be angry with. You should be angry with yourself."

I couldn't talk. The hot needles were back in my hands, my neck, my chest. Angry little pricks, buzzing like bees.

Nez looked at me, waiting.

When I didn't move, she spoke again, the words seeping out. "You should be disgusted with yourself."

I felt myself zoom over to her like a magnet. I couldn't help it. I was right in her face, my teeth bared. I said nothing, but I felt a growl in the pit of my stomach that wanted to well up.

"Forget it," Nez said, turning away from me. "You're not worth it."

For some reason, that sentence went right to the center of my chest. The same place I still felt the sting from Aaron's actions. Felt the pain of being sent here and having my father seem not to care either way. Felt it in the lack of words from my mother for years and years.

Nez bent down in front of a tree to gather some sticks and, without even thinking, I lunged for her. I meant only to shove her, to let her know I wasn't going to let her fuck with me, that I wasn't going to let *anyone* ever again. That was what I'd meant, but instead I pushed her off her feet and she fell. Hard. Hard enough that her face smacked the tree and I heard her nose crunch.

She screeched, loud. So loud her voice broke through the shadows around us like harsh, angry sunlight.

"Nez," I said, reaching out for her. I hadn't meant to hurt her, just scare her. Maybe I had sort of meant to hurt her, but really this wasn't even about her. I tried to pick her up, but she squirmed away from me. Her hands covered her nose like it was going to fall off.

"I didn't mean to," I said.

Lisa Burstein

"You did mean to, and now you're in deep," she said, standing up, still covering her nose as she ran toward camp.

Fuck.

I followed behind her, could hear her pushing through the woods, calling for Rawe. She moved like she was running through the jungle with a machete—fast, thunderous. If she was really that hurt, she didn't seem like it.

From up ahead, I saw Nez enter the clearing where our camp was. I wasn't ready to face Rawe. To face whatever being "in deep" would really mean. I hid behind a tree and watched as Nez fell to her knees and started to wail.

Rawe ran over to her. Troyer ran, too, and stood behind Rawe, who turned and grimaced at her unexpected shadow.

"What the hell happened?" Rawe asked.

"Wick pushed me," Nez cried through her hands. "She hit me. Look at my nose."

I could tell she was making herself cry, that though she might have been in pain, it wasn't as much as she was claiming. But I *had* pushed her. Her nose was swollen and bleeding, so it didn't matter what had really happened. I knew that about this. I know that about everything.

"Wick, get over here," Rawe yelled.

I was still hiding behind the tree. I didn't move.

"Now," Rawe growled; she must have sensed I was there. It's not like I was known for my tracking or camouflage skills.

I walked over to the three of them with my head down. Nez's hands were covering her nose and mouth like the mask the doctor wore at the clinic, but her black eyes hit mine. Her way of saying, *I told you so.*

"What happened?" Rawe asked, looking at me.

"Nothing," I said, unsure why I was bothering to lie. Something had definitely happened.

"What's rule number three?" Rawe asked, putting her arm around Nez and helping her up.

"No fighting," I mumbled.

"What's that?" Rawe said, cupping her hand around her ear like a smart-ass.

"No fighting," I said. "But I didn't hit her." I wanted Rawe to know that.

I looked over at Troyer. She was shaking like she was either afraid of me or afraid *for* me.

Probably both.

"She did," Nez said, her voice thick with tears. "She pushed me."

"Did you?" Rawe asked. Her lips were a thin pink line while she waited for my answer. "This will go a lot better for you if you tell the truth."

"I did," I fumbled, "but—"

"But what? I don't see a scratch on you," Rawe interrupted. "Did she hit you first?"

How could I tell her Nez had started it with words? With words that hurt me more than her nose hurt her? I couldn't.

"You know what happens now," Rawe said gravely.

I didn't. I looked at Troyer, her eyes filled with tears. I guess she knew what happened now. It must have been something else I missed while I was at the infirmary.

"I get sent home, or jail, or whatever," I said, a question in my voice even though it was a statement, even though it was *so not* whatever. But I had a new low to compare my life to now, one that began and ended at the clinic. There was no way I was

Lisa Burstein

breaking down with Nez standing there. With the boys staring at us and straining to overhear what was happening even though Nerone kept yelling at them to get back to work. If Ben couldn't look at me before, he was more than making up for it now.

"No," Rawe said, shaking her head, "we are way past that. There's less than a week left."

"I apologize?" I asked, realizing I hadn't even done that yet.

"You're going into solitary," Rawe said.

I heard Nez start to laugh, then cover it up with a wail.

"What, like, alone in a tent all day?" I asked, wondering how I could be locked up in so much open space.

"No," Rawe said, crossing her arms so tight it was like she was afraid her ribs would fall out. "Like you, alone, in the woods for the night."

"No fucking way," I said. But I could feel my voice waver.

"Now it's two nights," Rawe said, her chin jutting out.

I opened my mouth, but nothing came.

"Talk again," Rawe said, waiting.

My mouth was still open—I couldn't close it, but I didn't dare say a word. Two nights? Alone in the woods? What? The? Fuck?

"Let's go; grab your pack," Rawe said, her words as tight as her braid, letting me know there was no room for debate.

"Please," I said, so quietly I could barely hear myself.

"No!" Troyer yelled. As soon as the word was out, she covered her mouth and nose like she and Nez were twins.

As scared as I was to go into the woods, Troyer actually making a sound blurred that fear for a moment.

"Holy shit, you can actually talk?" I said, touching Troyer's shoulder.

"We'll deal with that later," Rawe said, pointing to my tent.

"She hasn't said a word in weeks and you want to deal with it later?" I said. It was possible I was stalling. It was possible it wasn't all about Troyer.

"Unless she wants to talk again, and then she can join you," Rawe said.

"You're punishing her for talking when she never talks? That's so backward," I said.

"You want three nights?" Rawe asked, holding up as many fingers.

I looked at Troyer, her hands still on her mouth. She was crying, maybe for me, but probably because she had finally let words escape. She had finally let words escape and it was because of me, who was such a sucky friend I didn't even use her first name.

I looked over at Ben. His face was angry, undoubtedly because I had messed up his girlfriend's perfect face. I was surprised he hadn't run over and hugged her, but maybe he was afraid if he did he would also end up alone for two nights in the woods.

Two nights alone in the woods? That hadn't really sunk in yet.

"Wick, today," Rawe said.

"This is really happening?" I asked. I felt dizzy, like my head wasn't attached to the rest of my body.

"You have no choice," Rawe said.

Well at least for once someone realized that.

Lisa Burstein

5 Fucking Days
to Go

am in the middle of nowhere, the sun so far from going
down. Luckily I have my trusty Assessment Diary so I can
write it's the next day, even though it isn't.

I want it to be the next day *so badly*. Bad enough to trick
my mind into pretending it is by writing it at the top of this
page. That date would mean my first night alone in the woods
was over. It would mean that I was only one day away from
Rawe coming back for me.

Honestly, I don't know how I am going to survive it. I can't
even really think about it without feeling like I'm going to
puke, scream, and explode all at the same time. Sure, I had
wanted to push Nez. I *had* pushed Nez, but does that mean I
deserve this?

Maybe I will die alone in the woods. Sure, eye-for-an-eye seems fitting, but it doesn't mean I'm not scared shitless to face it.

After everyone left me here and moved on to the next camp, I put up my tent with shaky hands. There was no way I was letting it get dark without having a place to crawl into and hide.

Rawe had told me being alone out here would help me, change me, allow me to find strength inside. But so far that was a pile of bullshit.

I looked up at the tree above me as I put the tarp down. It was massive, its trunk as wide as a kiddie pool. If I wanted to get all nature-y, I could have told myself it looked maternal. I could have told myself it was going to watch over me, but I knew I didn't deserve any of that. I deserved for Mother Nature to fuck me sideways.

I deserved for the tree to be struck by lightning and fall on me. It seemed like one of the least horrible scenarios that could kill me in the night.

Rawe had left me with a knife so I could hunt if I needed to, but there was no way I was killing anything. I had already made a dead thing. I had paid to make a dead thing.

A thing so small, it was amazing how huge it felt.

Once the tent was up, I got inside. No fire for me. No dinner for me. Safely zipped up in my tent was about all I could handle, even though I knew if a bear came along—hell, if a raccoon came along—it could claw my tent into angry red ribbons.

It was hot in there, the sun baking it like it was a Hot Pocket and I was the filling. I took off my uniform and lay on

Lisa Burstein

my sleeping bag in my bra and underwear, red, fire-engine red all around. The red tinged my skin so all of it was the color of the poison ivy sores that were starting to heal. All my skin turned to blood.

Red was what I saw when I closed my eyes at the clinic. When I first closed them and the florescent lights hit my lids, I saw red—bright, angry. My mind had swirled with drugs, making the murmured voices around me echo, making the cold hands that touched me turn my skin warm and gooey. As they put a breathing mask on me, the antiseptic smell hit my nose and the red I saw went to pinpricks—the middle of a bull's-eye surrounded by black that drowned it.

It was all here now, again.

So much red. All the blood I shed, all the beats of the heart I prevented.

Over the last few days, my feelings had lodged loose from where I kept them in a little wooden box in my brain. I had pushed the lid down for weeks. Sat on it, punched it closed when it tried to open, but now I guess the memory was going to come out whenever it felt like it—uncontrollable, drowning me, making it hard for me to breathe.

Maybe death by raccoon mauling was better.

I closed my eyes, trying to make the red go away. That day at the clinic there had been so much red and so much white and so much black, colors that felt more like suffocating blankets, like knives.

The warm sleeping bag on my skin was the only thing that was keeping me in the now. Barely. It was a sick irony that I was stuck in a tent, but it made sense. The day my brother had driven me to the clinic, we'd lied to our parents and said we were going camping. We'd even brought a tent with us, the old stinky tent that sat in our garage unused for years, used only as evidence for a disgusting lie. We put the tent in the trunk of his car, along with a cooler, a flashlight, and our sleeping bags, hoping that would be enough to make them believe.

When we got back to the house the next morning and my brother pulled the tent out of the trunk, it felt so crappy—a sick, sick lie that began and ended with an un-popped tent.

My brother tried so hard to make it true, even took the time to put the tent up in our backyard to air it out like we really had used it. I remember seeing it through the window at dinner that night—tan like skin, empty like I was. Shaking in the wind like it was laughing at me.

My brother kicked me lightly under the table, his way of telling me to *stop staring at it, stop thinking the things you're thinking*, like he knew.

He always tried to do the best he could for me, was the only one who ever did, and in this terrible moment back in a tent, I realized that he never had anyone like that. I should have been that person for my brother, but I never could be because I was selfish.

In yet another sick irony, I'm not even that person for myself.

The ache in my lower stomach had started when I woke up at the clinic. Once it went away, once my body had healed, I recreated it by punching myself over and over, so I would never forget. That was what I couldn't tell Troyer when she asked. I hit myself because I needed to remember. I deserved to have to remember.

Lisa Burstein

I closed my eyes and punched myself in the stomach, once, twice, harder, harder, knocking the wind out of me, hoping to make myself pass out from the pain. Again, again, my knuckles getting sore. Again, my body curling in on itself on the floor of the tent like a flower wilting.

Again, letting out a breath as the red all around me went black.

I woke up in the middle of the night to branches cracking outside the tent. Something was coming. It sounded heavy, lumbering, and moved with that kind of force like it knew what it was looking for. I sat up. This was it. I was going to be eaten by a bear.

Not that I was happy about it, but this was supposed to happen. I kept trying to punish myself with punching, with anger, with the bile that I spewed from my mouth. It wasn't enough. Mauling was what I deserved. Mauling and being eaten alive by a big, hairy, rabid bear.

I sat motionless, silent in the tent. Sucked in a breath and held it. It was so dark. I considered clicking on my flashlight to scare the bear away, but I knew it would make the tent look like an enormous cherry lollipop in the night. Exactly the type of thing a hungry bear who was about to eat someone who deserved it would not be able to resist.

I heard the sound coming closer: *branch crack, leaf shuffle, branch crack, leaf shuffle, branch crack.* A light flashed on the red canvas of my tent.

I exhaled. Not a bear. Rawe? Probably feeling like shit

for making me stay out here all alone and too guilty to sleep. So guilty, she had to come all the way back here to see if I was okay.

Fuck her, I wasn't okay.

"Rawe, you scared the shit out of me," I yelled from inside the tent. "Way to warn me it was you."

"It's not Rawe," a male voice said.

Ben's voice.

Ben?

Ben had come in the middle of the night into the ass-crack of nowhere to see me. He must have been seeking revenge for Nez. Only anger would push someone who had been ignoring you to walk in the dark-wooded night to find you. Only blind, over-the-top anger. I knew that anger.

"Are you going to come out of your tent or what?" he asked, his flashlight still illuminating it from outside.

"Wasn't planning on it," I said. I was crouched in the middle of it, like a pearl in an oyster. If he lunged for the tent, he probably wouldn't be able to reach me.

"Are you going to let me in?" Ben asked, his flashlight running circles on the red canvas like he was trying to see where I was sitting.

"I *definitely* wasn't planning on that," I said, my lips on my bare knees. I could hear him standing so close and breathing, could see his shadow. "What do you want?" I waited. It was possible he wasn't angry. If I was angry I would have ripped the tent in half trying to get in. I would have blown it down with hot, stinking air like a fairy-tale wolf.

"I wanted to make sure you were okay," he said.

Lisa Burstein

"I'm fucking great," I said, my defenses going up without me even being able to stop them.

Was stupid Nez right? *We always want what we can't have.* Now that Ben was back, wanting me, I was pushing him away again.

"Cassie, do you want to have a cigarette or not?" he asked impatiently.

I did, desperately, and maybe I kind of wanted to see him, too.

"Fine, come in," I said. It was about as much niceness as I could expel.

Ben unzipped the tent, so loud in the woods it was like someone ripping someone else in half. I felt like *I'd* been ripped in two; half of me was melting from Ben being so close and half of me was freezing from it.

His flashlight entered the tent before he did. It went from my face, which made me squint, to my chest.

"So I guess you were waiting for me." He laughed, ducking his head as he stepped inside.

I looked down. I was still in my bra and underwear. "Oh, fuck you, Ben," I said, hiding myself under my sleeping bag. "I was hot, okay?"

"You are hot," he said, his eyebrows going up and a smile quivering playfully on his face.

"I thought you weren't talking to me," I said, my cheeks going as red as the tent as I desperately tried to change the subject.

"I was worried about you." He looked at his hands.

"I don't need you to worry about me," I said, even though

his words fell on me like raindrops after a blistering hot day, the kind of rain you open your mouth and try to catch.

"You're lying in the middle of the woods half naked. I'd say you do." He held his flashlight at his waist. I saw he had his backpack with him.

"You running away?" I asked. "If so, I'd keep going. This place sucks."

"I figured if I got caught I could say I was gathering wood, since you guys kind of messed that up today."

"Thanks for the reminder," I said.

"I think you're sitting in the reminder." He laughed.

I looked down. Until that moment, I had forgotten that I was still essentially naked aside from my sleeping bag and I hadn't kicked him out of the tent yet.

I guess he realized it, too. "I'll go outside and wait while you get dressed so we can smoke," he mumbled, zipping up the tent behind him.

I pulled my uniform on in the dark. My brother would have come out here in the middle of the night to make sure I was okay.

And Ben had, too.

He sat against the tree next to my tent. His cigarette was already lit. In the night it was orange, glowing like the way the sun looks in outer space.

I sat down next to him, clicked on my flashlight, and put my bra-strap-crumpled cigarette in my mouth. He pulled out his lighter and lit it. I sucked in smoke. It seemed like it filled every empty part of me, like air inflating a ball. I looked up. The stars were tiny crystals above the trees, so bright it seemed like they were whistling with heat.

Lisa Burstein

"Is Nez okay?" I asked, exhaling heavily, the smoke gray in the flashlight beam. I could have asked him so many things: *Why did you come all the way out here? Why did you risk everything to do it? Why do you give a shit about me at all?* But I knew I couldn't. Sitting next to him felt like all I could handle right then.

"Do you care?" he asked.

"Not really. I mean, I guess a little," I said.

We sat there for a moment in silence, except for the quiet shush of cigarette paper burning as we inhaled.

"You weren't really with Nez, were you?" I asked.

"With her?" he asked, like he really didn't know what I was talking about.

"Don't make me ask again," I said, looking at my cigarette, staring into the cherry of it like it could hypnotize me into saying the hard things I was starting to be able to say, feel the things I was starting to let myself feel.

"No," he said, the pebbles underneath him crunching as he shifted. "Why? Did she tell you I was?"

"Yeah," I said, feeling so stupid that I'd ever believed her.

"Nez is fucking crazy," he said, shaking his head, smoke dancing around him.

"You think I am too, don't you?" I asked.

"No," he said.

"Then why were you ignoring me? I know it's because of what happened at the infirmary."

"I—" He paused, took a long drag. "I just don't want to let you down again."

"Again?" I asked. "You're, like, further up my ass than Rawe."

He laughed.

"At least you were," I said, unable to look at him when I did.

"I understand it's not about me," Ben said, his face illuminated in the flashlight beam, his eyes big, like they were the brown paint from two watercolor sets, "but I figure it's got to be another guy." He exhaled smoke.

"You finally guessed right," I said, taking a long drag. "I wasn't abducted by aliens."

"Anyway," he said, ignoring me in the way people do when they need to say something no matter what you've said first, "I get why you keep pushing me away and if that's what you want, that's what you want."

"I don't know what I want," I said.

"I'm just trying not to hurt you," he said. "It seems like you've had enough hurt in your life."

I felt a warmth in my belly that glowed like my cigarette when I inhaled. Ben's words were like oxygen stoking a fire, and my body a spark. I reached for his hand in the darkness. He rubbed his thumb on the underside of my palm so gently, so deliberately, the kind of touch that, if you let it, has the power to make you go blind.

"You really came all the way out here to have a cigarette with me?" I asked.

"I guess." He laughed, picking up our hands. "Well, and this."

For the first time, I wasn't afraid to hold on.

I woke up; the sky was gray. Ben was snoring next to me, a spider web like a lace canopy above us. We had fallen asleep

Lisa Burstein

outside the tent with our hands still clasped, sitting in the silence of the woods.

The early morning was gauzy with dew. I looked at Ben's face, his soft skin, so calm. It was obvious that he didn't have nightmares when he slept like I did. Whatever reason he was here for, whatever he kept doing, it wasn't something that caused him to scream in the night. Unlike me, it was something that allowed him to sleep. Sleep soundly, even.

I guess it took my brain a few seconds to really wake up and realize Ben shouldn't be here at all. That sleeping next to me meant he wasn't in his tent, where Nerone would be looking for him in a matter of minutes.

"Ben, crap, you slept here!" I said, shoving him.

He snorted and turned over. Yes, this boy slept just fine with his guilt.

"Ben," I said, smacking the back of his head.

"What the hell, Cassie?" He rubbed where I'd hit him. I guess it had been harder than I thought. He didn't look surprised to find himself here, waking up next to me. I tried not to think about that.

"You need to get up," I said, grabbing his shoulder.

"What?" he asked, wiping his doe-brown eyes like this was any other morning he was waking up to. Except it wasn't; he was waking up to getting his ass kicked by Nerone if he didn't get a move on and get the hell back to camp before the sun came up.

"You need to leave. You're going to get in trouble," I said, talking to him like he was drunk. I mean, he was sort of acting like it. I considered asking him what he had in his canteen.

"I'm going to get in trouble," he said, yawning. He closed his eyes again. The sun was about to come up, like a diver hesitantly standing on a diving board.

"Ben, seriously, go," I said, pushing him.

"All right, all right," he said. He stood up and stretched; his brown hair had leaves in it, pine needles. I didn't bother to tell him, but I combed at my own hair.

"Don't worry, you look great," he joked, his smile as wide as the open sky above us.

"I'm certainly not worried about that," I said, glancing past his shoulder. What would happen to him if he got caught out here with me? What would happen to me?

"You going to be able to make it through another day and night?" he asked, looking down. It seemed like he wanted to add *without me*, but he didn't.

"I'll be fine," I said, not really wanting to think about it. I could have said, *No, no don't leave me*, and held onto his leg like I was about to fall into quicksand, but I think we both knew I wasn't going to do that. I think no matter what he'd said, I would have told him I'd be fine.

He turned to go, then stopped like he remembered something. "I'll try to come back tonight," he said. His face was hopeful, as hopeful as the sun that was about to rise.

"You sure are willing to go through a lot for cigarette smoking and hand holding," I said.

"You need to try and remember that." He watched me. Maybe for the way the sun was starting to color my face, or maybe for the way my eyes were on his, unable to look away.

Finally he ducked into the woods. I could hear him start to run, the sticks on the ground beneath him breaking with each

Lisa Burstein

step. I listened, his footsteps getting quieter as he went back to a day of using his training.

I went back into the tent. Ben had left his backpack there, and I wondered how he would explain not having it. He would probably get busted, get sent into his own solitary. Would probably be unable to come back tonight by no fault of his own. It was easier for me to consider that than how I was afraid he would decide not to. Would decide that it wasn't worth it for cigarette smoking and hand holding.

I opened his pack, hoping there was some water inside. I knew I could go and try to find some to fill my own canteen, but the woods weren't any less scary to me during the day. I understood that there were predators that arrived when the sun came out that I didn't want to see. Snakes, for instance, or deer that could bore me like a charging bull with their horns. I would much rather boil in my tent than deal with whatever I might find outside of it.

Luckily, Ben's canteen was full and, as excited as I was to see that, I was even more excited when I found his Assessment Diary.

Well, maybe the word wasn't excited, it was *interested*. If I read it I would be able to know exactly what he thought of me. His words were nice and I was starting to believe them, but reading his real, uncensored thoughts . . . that was something else. I took a long gulp from his canteen and picked the diary up. It felt hot in my hand—or maybe my hand felt hot holding it.

I stared at it. From the outside it looked like my Assessment Diary, but it wasn't mine. It was Ben's and it held every secret thought he'd had since he'd been here. Like mine did. I knew I shouldn't open it—if anyone read mine I would seriously skin them alive—but there were a lot of hours between now and when Ben might come back. A lot I could learn about him if I took a peek.

When I cracked the notebook open, I swear my crazy-solitary mind heard it squeak, like it was an attic door or something. He wrote so neatly—print, not cursive, his words little match sticks. The first pages were a lot like mine: *What am I doing here? I shouldn't be here. This place sucks. It is not my fault.*

Blah, blah, blah. Whine, whine, whine.

I looked for my name, but it wasn't in the beginning entries. I guess Ben was smarter than me and understood that he needed to keep some secrets hidden. Maybe everyone was smarter than me. I considered that I was the only bozo stupid enough to actually use this thing for my real thoughts. I kept looking, but my name wasn't there. Whatever he felt about me was hidden deep in his brain.

I guess what he'd said was true: it wasn't always about me.

The name *Andrew* was mentioned a lot. I thought about the guys in the boys' camp. None of them was named Andrew and as I continued to skim I realized Andrew's name was on every page. *I did what I had to do for Andrew. Andrew would have done it for me. Of course, I don't think I would have put Andrew in that position. Especially not twice. But I'm under eighteen and have done this for him before and that matters more than the truth.*

What was the truth?

I knew a lot about hiding and denying the truth, more than I would probably want to accept. More than I would be able to defend if someone went behind my back and read

Lisa Burstein

my Assessment Diary. I knew I should stop reading, but I couldn't. Maybe I wanted to see if anyone was as fucked up as I was. Maybe I wanted to see if the reason why it seemed that Ben sort of liked me was because he was that fucked up.

Maybe I wanted to try to understand one person, since I found it so hard to understand myself.

I read on, flipping through, looking for the name *Andrew* to try to get some answers, when I found my name.

HEY CASSIE, I KNEW YOU LIKED ME AND I LET YOU WIN AT BASKETBALL. —BEN

Mother fucker.

I heard branches crack outside the tent. Finally, Rawe was coming to check on me.

Perfect fucking timing.

I stuffed the Assessment Diary back in Ben's pack and hid it under my sleeping bag. I felt my heart start to pound, my forehead start to sweat. Maybe Rawe wasn't only coming to check on me. Had Ben been busted and now it was my turn? I crouched on my sleeping bag and waited.

Rawe banged on the tent, like it was a front door and she was locked out. I unzipped it, bracing myself, and found Troyer standing there.

I was relieved not to see Rawe, but it also meant *she* had still not come to check on me. Yet another person from camp had snuck over to see me, but the person who was supposed to be "caring" for me had left me to swing in the wind. I wasn't sure what that meant.

Before I could say anything, Troyer walked over and sat down against the tree in the same spot Ben had, like this was a TV show or a movie and I was the one everyone went to for advice. The tree was my bathroom stall, or backseat, or whatever. It was a good thing it wasn't really a TV show because there was no way I should have been giving anyone advice.

Troyer's blond hair was almost as light as a cobweb in the sunlight.

"Troyer," I said. "Laura," I corrected, "what are you doing here?" I didn't sit down right away. Mostly because I wasn't sure she wanted me to. I still wasn't sure what had happened to her the day before, and I'm sure she wasn't, either.

I expected her to shrug, to pull out a pad, but instead she spoke, her voice so quiet it was almost like it wasn't there. So quiet it was like a woodland fairy flying out of her mouth.

"I don't know," she said. It was so strange to hear her talk, but yet, it felt familiar. She was no different, just louder.

I could have asked her why she was talking, but the big deal I'd made about it yesterday didn't seem like it had gone over very well. Yesterday? Fuck, it seemed like weeks ago.

"Aren't you going to get in trouble?" I asked, still not sitting. Maybe it was really because I didn't want her to get comfortable. Fucking up Nez's face and Ben having probably gotten busted for staying last night were about all my overflowing conscience could handle.

"I'm gathering wood with Eagan," she said, looking up at me. That was what she was supposed to be doing, but instead she'd come here.

"Don't punch him in the nose," I joked, even adding a laugh, but it was stupid. It made me wish I couldn't talk, like Troyer hadn't been able to until yesterday. I kind of understood. If you kept your fat trap shut, you didn't say stupid shit

Lisa Burstein

you would regret. You could keep other people from saying regrettable stupid shit in order to keep up with the regrettable shit you kept saying, which meant you wouldn't have to hear their stupid shit replaying in your mind like a song on repeat.

I didn't know what else to do, so I sat down next to her on the cool ground.

"So are you talking again?" I finally asked. I'd decided it was weirder not to mention it. If any part of this could have gotten weirder.

"Not really. I guess only to you."

"I'm sorry," I said. I could have taken the time to explain, but I hoped she understood. I was sorry for opening the dam that had held her words safe. It had been my fault and now she was struggling to put them back in, like bunnies jumping from a cardboard box.

"It's okay," she said. Maybe she knew. Or maybe she didn't want an apology from me.

I got that, too.

An apology from me probably felt like a fly buzzing in her ear. It would have been like getting an apology from Nez. One from Nez would be one I felt like swatting away. One I felt like smashing under a magazine. I had much bigger apologies to deal with.

She looked at me and waited. The skin on her arms was so pale, it reminded me of a peeled pear.

I felt the words behind her lips. The words she wrote in her Assessment Diary, that she thought were like her own song on repeat. Just like me.

"You don't have to tell me," I said, still staring at her arms, wanting to look anywhere but at her face.

"You either," she said. Her voice was hoarse. You would have expected it to be clear and bright from being rested for so long, but it was the opposite. Her voice was a rusty bike that squeaked when you rode it for the first time after the winter.

"I can't anyway," I said, pulling my knees up to my chin. I guess she could see the words behind my lips, too. I guess everyone could. I probably didn't hide them as well as I thought.

She nodded. She knew all about not being able to say things. In that moment I saw her as epically strong. The restraint it had taken her to stay silent for so long, it really was incredible. Swearing and yelling and saying words to cover up the words I couldn't say, that was weak.

"It's not the same without you at camp," she said, pulling her knees to her chin like mine.

"That's because Nez is a bitch," I said.

Troyer turned to me and did something I didn't expect: she laughed, long and hard. Her laugh was deep, beautiful. It made me hate whoever it was who made her feel like she had to hide it. It made me hate me for not having laughed like that since I'd been here—since the clinic. It made me hate myself for wondering if I could ever laugh like that again.

"Ben told me he came to see you last night," she said, wiggling her eyebrows.

I guess he hadn't been busted. There was that at least.

"You like him, don't you?" Troyer said.

"No," I said quickly, instead of being a smart-ass and saying *Who?* like I usually would. It made me wonder if the answer wasn't really no, wasn't as easy as no. It was complicated, that was for sure.

Lisa Burstein

"So, you okay?" Troyer asked.

"Yeah." I looked around. "Rawe said I'd get into the solitude." I pushed my hands straight out, like a surfer guy trying to balance after catching a wave.

"Rawe's kind of an idiot," Troyer said. "Not in a mean way, in a regular way."

"Most people are idiots," I said. "I'm kind of an idiot." I was honestly surprised I was admitting it. But my time at Turning Pines had made me realize that. Only idiots let themselves get in fucked-up situations with horrible boys that made it hurt to breathe when they thought about it.

Only idiots let that situation keep ruling their lives.

"Ha," Troyer said, "that's true."

If anyone else had agreed I would have throttled them, but Troyer agreeing with me felt right. She deserved to agree.

"What else did Ben say?" I asked. I thought about his diary. I shouldn't have read it. I shouldn't have even looked at it. That was another thing that made me an idiot.

She shrugged.

Of course, *now* she was silent.

"I came here because I want you to understand," Troyer said.

"You don't have to tell me." I understood that better than anyone.

"I have to tell someone," she said. Her face was so small, like a softball with a wig on.

"Okay," I said, breathing in. I don't know what I was expecting. Her deepest, darkest secret? The reason she was here?

Was it worse than the reason I was here?

The real reason?

It didn't matter. I would listen. I could at least give her that.

"I don't talk because people take your words and do what they want with them," she said, looking at her feet. "When I got in trouble before I came here I had a lot of people try to tell me what I meant when I said things. What I was really saying. I had people try and take my words and throw them back at me. So I stopped talking. No words, no confusion."

It made sense. It made more sense than anything I had done that hadn't worked yet. Maybe I needed to try keeping my mouth shut for once.

"I guess it seems stupid now," she said.

"Not to me," I said.

She leaned into me. Her breath smelled like peanut butter. It made me remember I hadn't eaten in hours, yet I wasn't hungry at all. "When I stopped talking they said it was because I couldn't steal anymore. They said it was like I was stealing my own words. Isn't that crazy?" she asked.

It honestly made sense, not like I had the guts to tell her. "Who are 'they'?"

"My parents. They're psychologists," she said, flattening the word.

"And they sent you here?" It seemed like there were way better places they could send her. *Way* better places.

"When your kid won't talk and you make your living talking, I guess it freaks you out enough to get drastic."

"Here is drastic," I said.

"No—*here*," she said, patting the ground below us, "is drastic."

"It's not so bad," I said.

"You don't have to lie to me," she said.

Lisa Burstein

I knew she wouldn't believe me. I was learning that Troyer was wise in ways I hadn't yet realized. "I know," I said, "I guess I'm kind of lying to myself."

"When you're ready to tell me, you will," she said. I could tell she was talking about more than me being out here alone. She was talking about everything.

If it was anyone else I would have scrunched up into an angry ball and told them I would never fucking be ready to tell them anything, but for some reason I couldn't say that to Troyer—having her offer to listen, I felt a wash of relief.

She stood up and grabbed something out of her pocket, putting it in my palm. "Here," she said.

It was a pack of matches: so small, so flammable, so my pilfered cigarettes' BFFs.

"Where did you get these?"

"It's better if you don't know," Troyer said, standing. Then she sort of bowed and walked into the woods. I watched the back of her white-blond head moving back toward camp, a ghost floating in the trees.

I looked at the matches. I could smoke whenever I wanted. I could start a fire if I dared to. I could do *anything*. One thing I'd learned in my time here was that in the wilderness, fire was power.

But beyond that, Troyer would listen when I was ready. Even without the matches, she had given me power.

4 Fucking Days Left

woke up to the sound of rustling leaves and cracking branches outside my tent.

Ben.

I didn't know what time it was, but the absence of light and the sound of only crickets and owls aside from Ben's boots let me know that as far as time was concerned, we had progressed past midnight and into the next day. I would take that. It meant I was hours away from not having to be by myself anymore.

I unzipped the tent and stepped into the night before Ben could say anything. I wondered why. It wasn't like me, and I felt like a total asshole, but it's tough to play hard to get when you've been in solitary confinement for the last ten hours.

"You came back," I said, my mouth, along with my body,

doing stupid, girlie things that made me feel like an asshole. Rawe was right: being in solitude was changing me. It was turning me into a total drooling dork.

"I told you I would," he said, his flashlight buzzing past me and over the inside of the tent like an angry bee. "Where's my pack?"

"It's inside," I said, pointing behind me.

His flashlight finally landed on his pack and he reached around me to pick it up.

"Do you need to get back or something?" I asked. He seemed anxious, which was my only guess as to why, unless Nez had poisoned him with the terrible truth about me.

He reached inside his pack, like he was trying to make sure everything was there.

"I didn't steal anything, if that's what you're worried about," I said. I thought about the note in his Assessment Diary, *I knew you liked me*. It made me step back from him.

Maybe when he got here he was expecting me to jump into his arms and say, *I do like you, I do*. Maybe that's what he was all worked up about, but I didn't think any amount of solitude would bring me there, even if I was sort of thinking it.

Ben pulled out his notebook and shook it at me. "Did you read this?"

"No," I said, probably too quickly.

"I would have read yours," he said, balancing the notebook in his hand, his lips turning up at the corners.

There was his smile.

"Well, I'm not you," I said, not giving in that easily.

"You *did*," he said, moving his face closer to mine. "I can tell."

"How?" I laughed. Having him that close made my neck feel hot. Made my hands feel cold. "Did you memorize the way the pages were folded over?"

"No," he said, "it's the way you're looking at me. The way you acted when I first got here. You're being nice to me." He tilted his head back like he'd figured something out, like he'd figured me out.

I felt my whole body tense. I had been nice to him. I had wanted to see him. "Oh, so that's why you were acting like a dick," I said, hoping he didn't notice that I paused before I said it.

"I was acting like you usually do," he said. "So yeah." He smiled. "I guess that makes me a dick."

"Seriously, Ben, fuck you," I said, keeping my arms tight at my sides, afraid if I moved them I might touch him. "I'm not being nice to you."

"You were. For you, that was nice," he said.

He was right, but there was no way in hell I was about to admit it. "By the way, you didn't let me win anything. I beat you. I know it's hard for your macho brain to accept."

He smirked; the realization that I had seen his note made him stand inches taller.

"Like it's hard for your macho brain to accept that you like me," he said, stepping closer, so close that I could feel the heat off his skin. "That I like you."

Words caught in my throat. I looked out into the woods behind him. The trees were like black skeletons in the dark.

He was still so close to me. "I think you owe me a secret."

I looked at him. If Nez had gotten to him he already knew my secret—the only secret that mattered. There was nothing

Lisa Burstein

I could tell him that would surprise him, except maybe that I did like him. But considering he was within millimeters of me and still had both his balls, that might not be a secret at all.

"I don't owe you shit," I said, my lips tight.

"If you don't want to tell me, you can show me your notebook," he said. He pointed at the tent. "I know it's in there."

"Forget it," I said, strengthening my stance, letting him know the only way he was getting into my tent was in a body bag. There was no chance I would show him my notebook. I had been stupid and had put everything into it. Had vomited my words all over it, the things I wanted to keep from everyone and the one thing I was still denying to him. That I did like him. Even if he had all the evidence he needed that it was true.

"I can stay up all night," he said, walking over and sitting against the tree we'd slept under the night before.

The tree. The place where I entertained visitors out here in the middle of nowhere.

"So can I," I said, grabbing my notebook out of the tent and sitting down next to him.

"Then I guess we're in for a long wait," he said, leaning back, getting comfortable.

I held my notebook tight to my chest. I considered that if I really could tell him everything, it would have been better than him reading it, but he was asking for more. He was asking me to let him in, really let him in. I didn't know if I could.

We sat there in silence, not even smoking. We waited, like our notebooks were pistols that we'd kept in our holsters. We were cowboys in a duel trying desperately not to fall asleep. Eventually I couldn't take the silence anymore. Silence when you're alone is one thing, but silence with someone sitting next to you is enough to make you sick—especially when that someone sitting next to you is someone that you kind of like, and who most definitely drives you crazy.

"You said you would have read mine." I sighed. Not that he had asked me to defend myself, but I guess I wanted to let him know that I was no more interested in him than he was in me, or whatever. Because that's what this was about.

"Okay, let's have it," he said, holding out his hand.

"No way," I protested. "I didn't really find out anything other than that you are obsessed with some guy named Andrew and that you maintain your masculinity by telling yourself that you let girls win."

"Andrew is my brother," he said, ignoring my other comment. "My older brother." He put his notebook down and lit a cigarette, like he was getting ready to talk.

"It's okay," I said. "You don't have to tell me." It made me think about my brother, how he would have liked Ben.

"If you think that's you being nice, think again." He blew smoke out angrily. "I didn't leave my pack here by mistake. I want to tell you, I want you to tell me, but as usual you have to make everything difficult."

I turned to him, but I couldn't talk. He was so direct. So available. So never giving up. Maybe I was scared to hear what he wanted to tell me. He had almost been to a place like this once and still did something to be sent to Turning Pines. Whatever he did had to be pretty fucked up.

"Fine," he said, "if you don't want to know, it's your turn." He put his hand out palm open, like my words were going to sit on it.

I took out a bra-smashed cigarette and lit it with one of

Lisa Burstein

Troyer's matches. I went cross-eyed to look at the flame, wanting to focus on that instead of Ben staring at me, looking for any way in—a prowler trying to get into a locked house.

"You're really not going to tell me," he said. "After everything."

I inhaled smoke, still not saying anything. I knew my answer, but it felt nice to let him think I was the kind of person who might have told him. Who would have felt safe enough to. I wondered if I would ever be that kind of person. At least if he was still asking, I knew Nez hadn't told him yet.

"I'm sorry," I said. The ache in the pit of my stomach came fresh and new, without a self-inflicted punch. It wasn't even about saying the word. It was about him looking at me differently once he'd heard it. Right now he thought I was strong, fierce, and angry. That was the Cassie I wanted to be. The Cassie *he* wanted.

When I'd cried, it had freaked him out. I couldn't let him see that Cassie again. I didn't want to be that Cassie again.

"If you don't tell me, I'm going to kiss you," he said.

"You know what will happen if you try," I said, even though him not asking for once was kind of hot.

"I mean it," he said, turning to me.

"You are signing your death certificate," I said, not moving.

"Get ready," he said, starting to lean in.

I pushed him. "Try it and I bite your tongue off." The cigarette bobbed in my lips as I spoke.

"I hadn't even thought of using tongue," he said, leaning toward me again, "but thanks for the suggestion."

I watched his face, his eyes, and his lips, my heart flickering like a flame.

"Last chance," he said, grabbing the cigarette out of my mouth.

"Are you fucking serious right now?" I asked, my eyes on the cigarette. It was in his hand and not in my mouth and he was still breathing. Maybe I did want him to kiss me. Maybe I needed him to make me so I didn't have to admit wanting to.

Ben didn't answer, just stubbed out our cigarettes and threw them up above and far past my tent.

"What the fuck, Ben?" I said. Even though him doing that made the ache in my stomach turn to butterflies—hot, sticky butterflies.

He sat in front of me, put his hands on my thighs, and leaned closer, so close that our noses were touching. So close that I could feel his heartbeat through his forehead, as fast as one of his drum solos.

"Don't do it," I said, but there was nothing behind the words.

"Then tell me," he said, his breath hot on my lips.

His mouth inhaled the words I couldn't say. I felt his lips hit mine like someone had pushed him into me.

And I pushed back . . . I pushed back.

We kissed for seconds, minutes, our lips hot in the cold night, our hands grabbing for anything in the darkness.

He stopped and looked at me. "I didn't think you'd kiss me back, Cassie."

"I guess I let you win," I said. It was hard for me to breathe. It was weird, but when I was kissing him, my mind wasn't wandering the way it sometimes would when I was with other boys. I didn't even think about the clinic. About how what might happen between us had the power to send me

Lisa Burstein

back there. All I thought about were his lips. How I wished he would kiss me so hard that not only would I stop thinking, but I would forget my name.

"I've been waiting to do that for a long time," he said.

"I'm still not going to tell you," I said playfully, or at least what was playfully for me.

He leaned in again, put my cheek in his palm. "You'll tell me," he said, "but not tonight. We have better things to do."

For once I agreed.

When I woke up against the tree, I smelled smoke. Not like a *campfire that has been put out* smoke, but *smoke that makes you cough* smoke. Smoke that made you crave oxygen like you couldn't get enough. My eyes were barely open and I could hear and feel the flames before I saw them: engulfing my tent, the ground underneath it, and the trees around it.

Another ten minutes and it would have been Ben and me who were on fire. Another ten minutes and Rawe would have felt like shit for the rest of her life. I covered my mouth and coughed like it was my job.

It was dawn. I could tell that even with the smoke in the air and the fire turning the sky red. Quickly my brain attached it to the cigarettes that Ben had thrown the night before.

"Fuck, Ben," I said, shaking him. My notebook lay next to me like a discarded stuffed animal. He was using his as a pillow.

"What?" he asked, coughing. He jumped up, which seemed like a good idea, and one I wasn't sure why I hadn't thought of.

I hopped up, too, and stood next to him, our backs flat against the tree.

"What the hell did you do?" he asked, speaking loud to be heard above the rumbling of the fire. He put his arm over his mouth and coughed again. I could see the red reflecting on his skin.

"Nothing. I woke up to this." I covered my mouth with my hands, but the smoke was still coming. The heat felt like it was burning the hair on my arms. "It was probably that cigarette you threw."

"That cigarette wasn't lit," he said, like his denying it meant anything considering the fire-breathing dragon staring us in the face.

"Well, Mr. Science, obviously it was," I said, wondering why we were still standing there, knowing it was only because we were both stupid and stubborn and didn't want it to be our fault.

"We have to put this out," he said.

"With what?" I asked. "You got a hose on you?" A huge smoldering branch fell and smashed my already burning tent into pieces like an apple smashed with a hammer.

I screamed, the kind of scream that embarrasses you when it happens.

"Fuck, Cassie," Ben said.

"Yes, Ben, fuck," I said. There was nothing we could do; the only water we had was in the canteen, which was in what used to be my tent.

"We need to get out of here. We need to tell Nerone and Rawe. We need to warn them," Ben said, his thoughts coming fast. He grabbed my hand and led us into the woods and away from the fire. He started running and I followed him, the heat

Lisa Burstein

dissipating as we moved farther and farther away. He kept turning to make sure I was keeping up, but other than that, I couldn't see anything but the back of his hair bouncing up and down as he ran.

A few paces before camp Ben stopped and looked at me. We were both bent over and out of breath.

"What?" I asked. I wasn't sure what I was expecting him to say, but it was certainly not what he did.

"I want to tell you about Andrew," he said.

"This is not the time, Ben," I said.

"When is the time?" he asked.

"Listen, if you want to tell me your fucking secret, then just tell me," I said. I was uncomfortable. I didn't want to think about why, but I knew. I could feel myself caring about what he was going to say next. It was a scary feeling.

"He didn't do anything to me," he said, exhaling. "I did something for him."

I waited.

"I lied for him," he said.

I waited some more, but he didn't say anything else.

"Big deal," I said. I'd lied for my brother a ton: when he was late for curfew, when he'd broken the back window with his baseball, when my mother's car had less gas than it had when she'd last driven it. Of course, I knew none of those lies made up for what I'd burdened my brother with. But I knew about lying for a sibling. I knew my brother knew about it, too.

"No," he said, "that's why I'm here."

"I don't understand," I said, even though I thought I sort of did, but that's what people say when someone is telling you something and you know they aren't done.

He exhaled, pushing his breath out like he'd just put something heavy down. "He stole a car, but it wasn't the first time. It wasn't the first time he'd done anything, and he's over eighteen so I stole the car," he said. "I stole the car," he repeated, "just like I slashed that guy's tires the last time."

"Wait," I said, my brain going clickety-clack as I put his sentences together. "So you're saying you're not even supposed to be here? There's nothing wrong with you?" The last words spilled out fast. Faster than I meant them to, but I was able to stop myself before I kept going, before I added *like there is with me.*

"I wouldn't say that." Ben laughed. He didn't get that it made him different from me, separate from me. Whatever was between us couldn't be because he was not a fuckup. He was a good guy who did something because he loved his brother, like my brother had.

"But you're not here because of anything you've done," I said, feeling myself pull away from him. His allegiance to his brother was definitely something I could relate to, but not being a total fuckup like me, well, that was something else.

"You're no worse than I am," he said, like he could see it.

But he was wrong. I was. I was here for something I'd done and for everything I'd done. He was a good person and I suddenly felt disgusting standing next to him.

I could feel him leaning in to kiss me. I pushed him away. "No," I said.

"I told you the truth. Why are you mad if I told you the truth?" he asked.

"You don't understand," I said, feeling my voice crack. I couldn't even control it. My notebook was stuffed in my back

Lisa Burstein

pocket and with his admission I knew it would stay there. I could never tell him. He was too far from the kind of person I was for him to to ever understand. "You're not like me," I said quietly, "and when you find out who I really am, you'll leave."

"If you don't trust me by now, you never will," he said.

It was true that he'd done plenty to make me trust him, and I did, but I liked him, too, and that made me not trust myself.

"Ben, seriously, it's bad," I said, looking at my shoes, their laces not even tied because I'd put them on so quickly. "Worse than you think."

"What, did you kill someone or something?" He laughed, making his jokes again.

The irony made my stomach ache. I looked at him. I could say *yes*, but then he would really know. Then he could throw *me* away.

He reached out to hug me and I didn't move. He hugged my motionless body, my arms at my sides. "What's wrong?" he asked when he noticed I wasn't hugging back. He was really clueless. I guess all boys were. I guess that was how they were able to stomp on your heart without even noticing.

"I don't know," I said. How could I admit, *You, you're what's wrong*? How could I have let another boy become my problem?

"You seem mad at me," he said, stretching his whole body, rolling his neck.

"I'm not anything at you, Ben." I sighed. It was a lie, but it was all I could think to say.

"Oh," he scoffed, "that's nice."

"You need to go," I said.

"Okay, Cassie," he said, "I'll go."

I watched as he slipped through the trees and away from me.

Was that really what I wanted?

I gave him five minutes and entered the camp. It was silent when I got there. If it wasn't for the smell of smoke growing in the distance, filling my nostrils like something burning in an oven, I might have let everyone sleep. I might have crawled into Troyer's tent and listened to her crackly voice talk until the crackly fire came and got us all.

Instead I let out a bloodcurdling scream. I couldn't decide what else to do. I had to admit it felt pretty good. Maybe Rawe thought I needed solitude to get through my issues, but honestly what I needed was destroyed vocal chords.

Nez was the first to unzip her tent and peek out, but when she saw it was me, she zipped back up before even asking what was wrong.

Fine. Given the choice I probably would have let her burn anyway.

Rawe bounded out of her tent in her uniform. It was probably why she had come out after Nez—either that or she slept in it. I didn't want to believe she had heard me screaming and decided to take the time to dress, so I went with slept in it.

"Wick, what?" She looked confused, by me standing there and by me screaming. She was probably asking as much about why I was screaming as what the hell I was doing there.

Rather than bother answering, I screamed, "Fire, fire!"

She looked at me strangely and I remembered that I was talking about something that was more than a mile away that she couldn't see.

"There was a huge fire at my camp," I said, trying to pretend

Lisa Burstein

I was out of breath. I held my hands wide like you might when describing the size of a fish you caught.

Her eyes went as big as if someone was pulling the lids of them on strings. "What do you mean, huge?" Her mouth sort of dropped.

"Very," I said. "Very huge, tent- and tree-destroying huge," I explained.

She didn't ask why. She didn't ask how. *Thank goodness*. Instead she started banging on tents and screaming, *Wake up, fire, Wake up, fire*, like there was someone in each tent named *fire*.

Everyone ran out looking flat-haired and bleary-eyed, including Ben, who had added the extra touch of taking off his uniform so he was wearing only his boxers. He either really wanted Rawe and Nerone to believe he'd spent the night in his tent or he was determined to show me what I would be missing if I really never let him kiss me again.

"What the hell?" Nerone asked. He was in his uniform and it was wrinkled, which meant he definitely slept in it, as opposed to what I wanted to believe about Rawe. That made sense. He seemed like the kind of guy who would never take it off, like someone wearing a flag pin or something.

"Wick said there's is a wildfire near where she is camped," Rawe said.

"That seems odd," Nerone said, sniffing the air like he almost didn't believe me. *Of course* he would do that rather than try to get us to safety. Because he was a robot.

Troyer ran over and asked me if I was okay. Her lips didn't move, like she had a ventriloquist's dummy on her lap. I guess she really hadn't yet shared with anyone else the fact that she was talking.

I nodded slightly, even though that was really only true in the physical sense. Yes, I had avoided being burned alive, so as opposed to everything else, I guess that was a positive.

I hadn't noticed before, but Nez's nose was covered with a bandage, which on her actually looked cute. She watched Troyer and me but didn't say anything, even though her look said, *Oh, so you're back. You didn't die a horrible death in the woods.*

I looked at Ben. He was playing with the waistband of his boxers, which meant I wasn't getting any help from him unless what I was trying to do was remove his boxer shorts, which *I was not.*

"If there's a fire coming, we need to get out of here," Eagan said. "Most wildfires move at a rate of five to ten miles per hour, and that's way faster than us."

"Faster than you, maybe," Leisner said, pushing him.

Stravalaci laughed.

None of them seemed nearly as scared as they should have been, but that could be because they hadn't seen my tent turned into a smashed-up sun like I had.

"Maybe she's lying," Nez said. "She's lied before." She looked at me but didn't say anything else. I could see the secret she knew just under her lips. I felt the needles start to form in my stomach, instead of their usual place in my fists, which meant I was scared. Nez was going to say something, and I didn't want Ben to hear. If she said it, it wouldn't matter that I knew Ben was nothing like me because he would know it, too.

He would more than know it.

It was easy for me to dismiss him because of what he'd

Lisa Burstein

done for Andrew, but I was pretty sure I couldn't take him dismissing me for what I had done.

Nez stared at me. She could say it right now. She could find me on Facebook years from now and torment me with this. As long as I lived I would have this secret and there would be people who would be able to use it against me because of the power I gave it. Because of the power it had over me.

"We don't have time for this," Rawe said. "Start packing up."

Nez walked toward her tent. She had spared me, but in some ways that was worse. She still held the secret over my head like a boiling pot of water she could pour onto me and anyone I was with at any time. Yet I knew she would probably never tell, because power was a hard thing to give up and an even harder thing to get back.

Rawe clapped her hands, trying to move us along. "Come on, we have to haul it back to Turning Pines. We can call the Forest Service from there and see what they want us to do."

Everyone started breaking down tents, packing up packs, tying up boots.

Nerone slapped on his pack. "I'll run ahead and make sure the van starts okay," he said, moving with the force of a stampede of horses through the woods.

I guess that means we are leaving. Where will they take us? Jail? Another camp? Or worse than that: home?

3 Fucking Days Left

T he Holiday Inn at the airport was where they took us. We're each going to fly home as soon as they can find an open flight for us. All I've wanted the whole time I've been stuck at this stupid place is to leave and now that it's coming early—even three days early—it feels too soon. Maybe it would feel too soon three days from now, anyway.

This is probably my final and absolute punishment while at Turning Pines: go home and face what I have to face even earlier. *Surprise!* Your life back home sucks more than here, in case you forgot.

The Forest Service was working on containing the fire and we were in one hotel room, the boys in the other, adjoined by a door that we were not allowed to walk through.

That was fine by me. I was still trying to figure out how I felt about what I now knew about Ben; still trying to figure out if I wanted to figure it out.

Even in our own rooms, we weren't supposed to do anything other than sit on our beds and wait for the phone to ring to let us know when it was time for one of us to leave. Nez sat on a bed, Troyer and me on the other. Looking at their faces it was clear I wasn't the only one scared shitless to go home.

Luckily, the airport we'd flown into was the same rinky-dink one we were waiting to fly out of and likely wouldn't have extra room on the few flights that came through it. Even a twenty-by-twenty-foot room with Nez was better than going home. Sharing the closet with the ironing board attached to it with Nez for the next six months would have been better than going home.

I'm not better yet. How can I leave?

After we all showered, Rawe went to the vending machine to get us some breakfast, which meant we weren't eating any better on the outside than we had on the inside. Nez had her own bed because everyone hated her, Troyer and I shared one, and Rawe had slept on the loveseat at the front of the room.

Nez's honor of being most hated would have normally been bestowed on me, and it made me wonder if my time at Turning Pines really had made me soft. I mean, Troyer actually liked me. I actually liked her. In my old life I probably would have made her cry on an hourly basis. I definitely wouldn't have been the special chosen person she decided to talk to. She definitely wouldn't have been the special person I had decided to talk to.

Troyer hadn't said a word in front of anyone but me since

the day before yesterday in the woods. I felt like I was in one of those movies where someone has an imaginary friend that only she can see.

We were supposed to wait for Rawe to come back, and not use the phone, and not turn on the TV, but honestly I don't think any of us wanted to anyway. We were shell-shocked. TV and a dial tone were a bit much to deal with when the lamp on the nightstand made us squint.

"What's the first thing you'll do when you get home, Cassie?" Nez asked, lying on the bed like she was lounging in an Arabian tent. I knew she was asking because she could tell I really didn't want to go home, just like she really didn't want to. I knew she was asking to remind me of this.

"Dunno, Nez, who's the first person you'll do when you get home?" It was easier to just deflect. I couldn't get past crawling into my bed and pulling the covers over my head and sleeping for the rest of my life.

Doing anything, going anywhere in Collinsville meant possibly running into Amy. Into her apologies about Aaron, which even the thought of made me nauseous. I wasn't angry at Amy anymore. I understood more than ever why she did what she did, but because of what I knew about her and Aaron, I didn't think I could ever be her friend again.

I had enough reminders of what had happened with Aaron without a living, breathing one in my face asking me for forgiveness.

"Funny," Nez said. "I think we know what Troyer's *not* going to do."

I didn't respond. I wasn't in the mood to fight with Nez. It made me nervous. I had bigger problems now.

Lisa Burstein

Troyer went into the bathroom and started the shower. It had to be the fifth shower she'd taken since we arrived last night. It seemed excessive, but I understood why. It was the only place in this room you could actually be alone.

I looked at Nez, her black hair so clean and shiny from her own recent shower, it looked like an oil slick on water.

"You're not really going to tell anyone about me, are you?" I whispered. It was what I had been thinking since the day before, *dreading* since the day before.

Nez turned to me, her head cocked and waiting. "You really are stupid." She laughed.

I was about to say, *Fuck you Nez, you're the one who's stupid*, like I normally would, but I knew if I did that it would just take us around in our circle of hate and insults again. I needed answers.

"What does that mean?" I asked, trying to keep my tone even. If anyone else had said what Nez had just said to me, she would be nothing but a stain on the bed she was lying on.

"Oh, Cassie, I never took you as naïve," she said.

I listened to the water in the shower, the noise like the static on a TV, like the roar in my ears as the medicine took effect at the clinic.

"I am *so not* naïve," I replied. If anything, I was jaded. If anything, I had been through a hell of a lot more than most seventeen-year-olds had. I certainly knew the world wasn't ice cream and unicorns and fake swear words.

I knew that even a boy's kiss wasn't enough to make everything okay for more than just a moment.

"You're gullible," Nez said, her head propped up on her hand. "It's the same thing."

She was right, even though I wasn't sure how she knew. I had believed that Aaron had liked me, that Ben *was* like me. I was stupid. I was gullible, but what the hell did that have to do with her?

"Just answer my question so I can stop talking to you," I snarked, pulling at a string on my jeans, freshly washed—they felt tight after wearing the uniform for so long. "Will you tell anyone about me?"

"I can't," Nez said. "I don't know anything." She shrugged.

"What?" I couldn't believe it. She didn't know anything. What the hell was all that about in the woods?

What the hell was all that about the morning of the wildfire?

"What?" Nez mimicked, like she didn't owe me an explanation, which I guess she really didn't.

I could feel my mouth open and close. She didn't know. No one did. Nez had fooled me. But worse than that, I was speechless. Gullible, weak, stupid, *speechless*—was this the new Cassie? Or had I always been this way and been able to hide it with mean words, fists, and raging anger?

"Oh please," Nez said, putting a fluffy white pillow between her legs, like a cloud against the branches of a tree. "Of anyone, you should know that what people say doesn't mean poop. Maybe you have a file," she said, "but I've never seen it. I just figured there had to be something majorly wrong with you or you wouldn't be here."

"You just figured," I said, my mouth finally able to make words.

"Yeah," she said, "I mean there's something majorly wrong with *me*," she said. She pointed at the bathroom door. "And there is definitely something majorly wrong with Troyer."

Lisa Burstein

"What's majorly wrong with you?" I asked. I needed to know. Maybe she didn't really know my secret, but I needed to know hers. As far as I was concerned, she seemed pretty together, aside from her need to pounce on everything with a penis.

"I lie. Can't stop lying," she said. "Apparently it's 'compulsive,'" she added, making air quotes.

"You're kidding," I said, thinking back to our twenty-seven days together, wondering if anything she'd said was true, and then remembering Ben's answer when I asked if he'd really been with her. *Nez is fucking crazy.* I guess she really was.

"I never had sex with Stravalaci or Ben. I've really never had sex with anyone." She shrugged. "I wrote all the letters I got myself, except for one. I sent them right before I left. I knew I wouldn't have mail, or enough to make people think I had that many guys who liked me."

"But why?" I asked.

"Do you need the definition of compulsive?" she asked, looking at me like I was an idiot.

"No, I mean, why do you do it?"

"Does it matter?" she asked, her coal-black eyes filling with what might have been tears, if she'd let them fall.

I watched her. Nez was just like me, majorly messed up and too afraid to admit why. Like Troyer, like everyone here, I guess, except Ben.

"No," I said.

"Whatever your deal is," Nez said, sitting up and putting the pillow on her lap, "your secret is safe with me, because I don't know what it is."

I should have been really pissed off at her — and I was — but

I also couldn't help thinking that Nez was no worse a person than I was. Sure, she had lied to me, she'd made a disease out of lying, but who *hadn't* I lied to?

"So what's your name anyway?" I asked.

"Cassie," she said, her face as empty as a starless sky.

"You've got to be fucking kidding me," I said.

She shrugged. "Wynona," she said.

"Are you still lying?" I asked.

"Not right now," she said, her eyes flicking to the closed bathroom door. The shower had stopped.

"Nice to finally meet you, Wynona," I said.

"Nice to finally meet you, Cassie," she said.

"Sorry about your nose," I said.

She touched it, like she had forgotten. "I guess I sort of deserved it."

"You did and you didn't," I said.

"Story of my life," she said.

I laughed. "Mine, too."

Troyer exited the bathroom, pink-cheeked. She sat on the bed next to me and started to comb through her hair, which looked like cooked spaghetti. She turned to me and Nez like she could tell something had happened, but like the friend she really was, she didn't ask what.

Rawe entered the room and threw granola bars at us. She was wearing her uniform, even though we were all back in our civilian clothes. I guess it was hard for her to let it go.

"So is this what we're doing today?" Nez asked, crunching on her granola bar.

It was something I would usually have asked, and I hated this middle-ground person I had become. It reminded me

Lisa Burstein

of Amy, someone who let other people talk for her because she was so afraid to talk for herself. But unlike Amy, I wasn't afraid. I was just filled up with other shit, my thoughts making it hard for me to be as quick with a comeback as I used to. That was what I decided to go with instead of the apparent truth that being able to write down my feelings, *feel* my feelings, actually made me lose the need to lash out as much.

"What did you have in mind?" Rawe asked.

Honestly, what was she going to do? Hike us around the parking lot in a circle? Have us canoe in the indoor pool? Make us chop up our headboard?

"I don't know," Nez said. "Anything other than stare at this cottage cheese ceiling."

"You are still under my supervision. You are not free yet," Rawe said.

What I thought but didn't say was, *I will never be free. Not until my secret isn't a secret anymore.* What I knew but couldn't believe was, *I really never was.*

"The calls will come soon," Rawe said.

I looked at the phone. Would the calls about our flights come before I could tell my secret? Did I want them to?

"We could talk," Rawe said, looking right at me when she did. I guess she was still trying, and that said something about her. She had more faith than the rest of the girls put together. She was like Ben. She didn't give up.

"Sounds like just what I want to do," Nez said. "I hate Cassie and Troyer doesn't speak . . ."

"I hate you, too," I said. Even with my new, easier silence I wasn't able to let that one go. Nez admitting she was as messed up as I was certainly didn't make us best friends, but I guess it did make us best enemies. We'd come to an understanding, but that didn't mean we liked each other.

Rawe chewed on her granola bar. There was no way she was going to fix Nez, or any of us, in the next forty-eight hours. Whatever had started at Turning Pines wouldn't be complete just because we weren't there anymore. We were messed-up cases, sent here because they didn't know what else to do with us. People who were normal didn't stop talking, or lie all the time, or hate themselves so much that it was easier to just hate everyone else.

"Fine, turn on the TV," Rawe said.

Troyer grabbed the remote and clicked it on. She moved through the channels quickly, letting each one get a word out, like she was trying to have the TV say a sentence for her.

Rawe looked at me and shook her head. I suppose she pictured each time she'd tried to talk to me, how I'd turned her down cold. Like she'd said, she can't help someone who doesn't want to be helped. But what about someone who *needs* to be?

Lisa Burstein

2 Fucking Days Left

N o one left today. The phones stayed silent. We fell asleep with the TV on, wrappers from the vending machines covering our beds like shed cocoons. I woke up and saw the light on in the bathroom with the door ajar. I found Troyer on the white tile floor with a watercolor set and papers with muted paintings all around.

"Close the door," she whispered.

"What are you doing?"

"What's it look like?" she asked, like I was stupid.

She had really turned into quite the smart-ass since she'd started talking again.

"Grab a brush," she said, pointing to where they were piled

next to her on the floor—black sticks, like the kindling we'd used to start our fires.

"You took all this from the art cabin?" I asked.

"I didn't know how long we would be in the woods for." She shrugged. She was painting a sky—a sunset, full of oranges, purples, and reds.

I sat against the tub. It felt cold, clammy on the back of my arms. "I'm not in the mood to paint," I said.

"When are you in the mood to do anything?" she asked, not looking up from her paper.

"You've really fucking gotten your voice back, haven't you?"

"Sorry," Troyer said, turning to me, her skin almost colorless in the overhead light. "It's just been a long time since I've been able to tell someone to do something." She smiled. "I kind of like it."

I picked up a brush and put a piece of blank paper in front of me on the floor. I was all ready to go for the red, but Troyer covered it with her hand. "Use a different color. It's time for you to use a different color."

I didn't fight her; she was right. If I'd learned anything in the woods, she was right.

I knew which color I needed to pick, but I also knew what picking it would mean. I stared at it and waited.

"Go on," Troyer said.

I dug into the blue, painting a wash over the paper at first, then I pointed the back end of the brush to stipple dots on top, all the tears from the day in the infirmary—small tears, big tears, falling down the page like rainwater, soaking through to the white tile.

Lisa Burstein

"What is that?" Troyer asked, pointing at my painting.

"Sadness," I said, without even thinking about it.

"That's a lot of sadness," she said.

I nodded. It was.

"Is it yours?" she asked.

Troyer was newly confident and I could do nothing but applaud and surrender. "Yeah," I said. It was and there was more. Coming from the red I never thought would end, now there was blue. But the red had ended. Maybe the blue would, too.

I looked at Troyer's painting. It had transformed from a sunset to a beach scene, complete with a cottage, chairs, a striped umbrella.

"Our summer house. My favorite place," she said.

I looked down at my painting. Why couldn't I paint my favorite place, or a flower, or a fucking sky full of birds that looked like spastic *Ws*? Why did I paint blood, tears, the colors that coated me like a constant cloud?

"You okay?" Troyer asked.

"No," I said, the tears starting to come in real life.

"Why are you so sad?" Troyer asked.

"I'm not. I mean, I don't know what I am," I said, wiping my face, but they still came. I couldn't stop them.

"You should flush it," Troyer said.

"What?" I asked.

Troyer waited—strong, solid. "Your sadness," she said, picking up my painting and dismissing it. "Flush it down the toilet."

"That's not going to make it go away," I said, even though I didn't have any better ideas.

"It's symbolic, Cassie," she said.

I looked at her, Troyer, back and talking, in her real-world jeans and paint-splattered light blue T-shirt—such a different Troyer than she was when I first saw her. Such a different me than I was when I got out of the van that first day.

"You really are the daughter of psychologists," I said.

"Unfortunately, yes," she replied.

I wiped my eyes and caught my breath. The room looked fuzzy. My body felt bare, like someone had picked it clean of my organs. I had thought I was empty at the clinic, at the motel after, and then in the infirmary. But now I knew being empty would mean finally being free.

"Do it," she said.

"You're serious?" I asked.

"Unless you want to keep feeling like this," she said, "I am."

I stood, slowly, getting my bearings, deciding if I was really ready to let it go, even as the symbol that Troyer suggested. I lifted the toilet lid and seat and lay the paper on the water. It floated there, rippled, the blue paint bleeding into the bowl.

"Flush it," she said.

I looked at it, moving in the water—waiting. My sadness, the symbol of it turned by Troyer into something I could just get rid of.

It seemed impossible, but I pushed the handle. The water rushed from the sides of the bowl and drowned the paper. It spun in a tornado of blue, sucked into a hurricane of white, before it was forced down the bowl.

"Do you feel better?" she asked.

"No," I said.

Lisa Burstein

"At least you're honest," she said, touching my back, "but you will."

"I was pregnant," I said, the words feeling like marbles in my mouth. I'd never really said them before, never really admitted them. Not even to my brother. I just told him I was in trouble and needed him to drive me to the clinic. That was all I had to say. He knew me enough to know I didn't want to elaborate and loved me enough not to make me.

"Wow," she said.

"Yeah, wow," I said.

"Was?" she asked.

"Yes, was," I said, making myself look at her. I felt the room spin, moved my fist to my belly, but I didn't hit. I let myself feel the hurt that was there, for once not trying to mask it with more pain, with physical pain, with anger.

"I'm sorry," she said. "I'm so sorry, Cassie."

"I did it," I said, like I'd had to do that day in the judge's chambers with my parents, when I admitted that the huge bag of pot we were found with was my fault, even though Lila was the one who snatched it, even though Amy was in the car, too.

I had. I'd made the phone call. I'd given the folded-up twenties to the receptionist. I'd signed the piece of paper that said: *I understand that if something terrible happens to me it isn't their fault.* It seemed ironic to have to sign that. Something terrible was going to happen whether their estimation of something terrible happened or not.

"You know you couldn't have had a baby, right? You're seventeen," Troyer said.

"I know," I said, starting to cry again. It didn't matter if I'd flushed the sadness—it was still there.

She reached out and hugged me, just held me, the fan in the bathroom going above us, humming and swirling like we were in a snow globe. I could smell her hair, clean with the scent of flowers from the hotel shampoo. "You need to live this life," she whispered. "You can live it with regret, or you can let it go."

And even though I had no idea how, with the two of us having helped each other get here, get to this place, I knew she was right.

Lisa Burstein

*Well, you can count
how many Fucking Days
are left.*

woke up in an empty bed. It made me wonder if the night before in the bathroom had been a dream. I lifted my head—no sound coming from the shower, no light coming from under the bathroom door, just the soft snore of Nez sleeping in her bed next to me. It was still dark. Maybe Troyer had snuck out to get a soda. I felt her side of the bed, but it was cold. If she'd snuck out it had been a while ago.

I looked over at the love seat where Rawe slept—it was empty. She must have noticed Troyer was gone, too. Crap. I pictured Rawe out in the hotel hallway calling Troyer's name. Would Troyer even answer? Or would she sit with her knees up to her chest next to the soda machine, hoping for just a few more seconds alone?

Even after last night, I still didn't think of her as Laura, but I guess that was because we now knew each other so well that names and their meaning made no difference.

The hotel room door opened. Light from the hallway pierced the bed, sheets glowing white for a moment as the door was propped open then closed. I lay back down quickly but watched as Rawe tiptoed to the love seat. I guess that meant she hadn't found Troyer. She was trying really hard to be quiet, but that wasn't easy to do in hiking boots, so she bent down to untie them. Why was she still even bothering to wear them?

"Where's Troyer?" I whispered into the dark hotel room. I knew it was no surprise to her that Troyer was gone if she was awake.

"Shhh," Rawe said, pointing at Nez. Not like I would have cared ordinarily, but I definitely didn't care at that moment that Nez was sleeping.

"Where is she?" I asked louder, like I could already kind of tell from the way Rawe was acting that maybe she wasn't just missing; I needed Rawe to tell me what I didn't want to hear.

"Nez is sleeping," Rawe said.

"Not anymore," Nez said in a raspy voice.

"So where is she?" I asked, looking at Rawe. It was pretty obvious, even in the dark, that she was trying not to look at me.

"Wick," Rawe said, "we can talk about this later."

"Just tell me," I said, even though I knew what Rawe was going to say next. Even though I didn't want to hear it, I was asking for it.

"She went home," Rawe said.

I felt the ache in my stomach and immediate nausea. Why

Lisa Burstein

didn't Troyer wake me up? The one person in the world who it seemed had kind of understood me felt like she could leave without even saying good-bye.

And, worse than that, the one person I had finally, really let in was gone.

"She left you a note," Rawe said, walking across the dark hotel room to hand it to me.

I took it from her and flicked on the light that was stuck by a brass arm to the wall above the nightstand. It was a piece of paper from Troyer's Assessment Diary—just plain notebook paper like all of us had. She'd folded it down so small that the edges were sharp.

"Oooh, love letters," Nez said, in bed with her back to me. "Feel free to highlight the interesting parts for me for later, because like I said, I'm sleeping."

"Screw you, Nez," I said. I stared at the note. I was glad she hadn't left me with nothing, but it seemed ironic that Troyer was going to have the last word.

I wasn't sure I wanted to know what it would be.

"Turn the light off," Nez said. She covered her head with her pillow.

"You're awake anyway," I said.

"Not by choice. Just because your girlfriend left you a note doesn't mean I need to be awake, even if your lady parts are."

"Fuck off, Nez," I said.

"Hey," Rawe said, finally jumping in. I always wondered why swearing was the last straw with adults. I guess it was because they were the sucker punch of words. "Nez, go take a shower."

"It's the middle of the night," Nez whined, her hair all around her head like a shadow.

"No, actually it's morning," Rawe said.

I turned to the clock. It read five a.m. in angry red numbers. Five a.m. meant it was my last day. It meant tomorrow I would be sent home. Unless I was unlucky enough to get an earlier flight like Troyer had.

Nez got out of bed and slammed the bathroom door behind her.

"I didn't read it," Rawe said, indicating the note that was still folded in my hand.

"Thanks," I said, because I couldn't think what else to say.

Rawe watched me while I opened it. Indicating that even if she hadn't read it, she was still interested in seeing what it said via my face. I tried my best to keep my mouth tight as I opened the note, fold by fold by fold, and read:

You need to forgive yourself

It wasn't addressed to me and it wasn't signed, which made me wonder if Troyer had written it as much as a reminder for herself as for me. That was it, one line in the middle of a sheet of paper.

I knew it was true. I knew that last night was the first step. Without her, I just wasn't sure what the *next* step was.

"You okay?" Rawe asked.

"Fine," I said, folding the note back up, as tight as Troyer had.

"Do you still want to use marijuana?" Rawe asked, like we had just been talking about that.

"What?" I asked, dropping the note on the bed. It fell like a rock.

Lisa Burstein

"I'm trying to see if our program worked," Rawe said, like that made more sense. "Do you still want to use marijuana?"

"If the program worked?" I laughed, but not because it was funny.

"I'm supposed to ask," she said.

"And you're choosing now?"

"We're alone," she said, looking at the closed bathroom door. "And it's not like you were open to any of my other invitations to talk."

Awesome. She hadn't sent Nez to the shower to punish her. She'd sent her to the shower to punish me.

I shook my head. "Marijuana, no." I couldn't help laughing again. Prom night seemed so far away now. I was a different girl then. That was the girl she should have been asking, not me.

"Great." Rawe smiled. Her smile wasn't soothing or pleasant. It kind of made it look like there was no skin left on her face.

"Yeah, great," I said. I picked up the note and unfolded it and refolded it.

"There's something else?" Rawe asked.

Maybe she had read the note.

"You keep asking me to talk," I said. "What about you?"

"We're not talking about me," she said, what all adults say when they are too afraid to answer your question.

"What are we talking about?" I asked.

"Okay, I'll tell you my name," Rawe said.

"Not good enough," I said.

"You haven't heard it yet." She crossed her hands over her knees.

I waited.

"Fanny," she said.

"Fanny Rawe," I replied.

"Yup," she nodded. "Bad, right?"

I laughed. I couldn't help it.

"School was—" She paused and flipped her braid from one shoulder to the other. "Not fun." She smiled her skin-ripping smile, looked down, and rubbed her hands against her thighs like she was gearing up for something. Like what she was about to tell me was something she needed generated energy to say. "People don't really like me much," she said, still looking down. "I guess I work with kids like you because your reasons for hating me have nothing to do with me personally."

It was weird, but hearing her say that reminded me of what I did with my words and fists and anger. I was afraid people wouldn't like me, so I made them hate me. I made them fear me.

"I get it," I said.

"I know there are things you don't want to tell me," she said. "I understand, Cassie, I do. I just hope you'll choose to tell someone, someday."

"Thanks," I said.

She smiled, like she was surprised that I hadn't shut her down again. I guess I was, too.

"Words aren't magic," Rawe said, "but talking, opening up can be."

"I know," I said and I did. Rawe might be the one saying it, but it was Troyer who made me understand. Rawe meant well, but she wasn't cut out for this like Troyer was. I guess Troyer had her parents' genes. Wherever she ended up, I hoped she decided to do something to help other people, because she was good at it.

Lisa Burstein

The bathroom door opened and we jumped.

Nez walked out and looked at Rawe, at me. It was obvious the words we had said were hanging in the room like smoke, making the room smell.

"You guys done making out or what?" Nez asked, twirling her towel into a turban on top of her head.

"Yes," Rawe said, getting up, stopping to squeeze my shoulder and then entering the steamy bathroom. "We're done."

I opened the note that Troyer gave me. Rawe might have thought I needed to talk to someone else to heal, but I knew I needed to start with myself. I needed to say and keep saying three words.

I forgive you.

When Nez and Rawe left the room to have their own *Are you cured?* talk, I picked up the phone on the nightstand and dialed my brother's cell. I had to have some idea of what was waiting for me when I landed.

"Tim, it's me," I said when he answered in his *This better not be a telemarketer or I'm going to kick someone's ass* voice.

"Cass, where are you?" *Cass.* My brother was the only one who ever called me Cass.

Ever.

"Some hotel," I said. I looked at the pad on the dresser. Actually it was the *Holiday Inn at the Arcata Airport.* I wondered how many other people had used this phone in the same way I was—to figure out what was waiting for them on the outside.

Maybe a guy who had been kicked out of his house for cheating on his wife. Like me, he was trying to figure out what shit was waiting for him if he was actually allowed to go home.

Except I was more than allowed to go home, I was being fucking forced to go home.

"Are you back?" he asked.

"No," I said. I was surprised by the question and wondered how he wouldn't know that. Maybe more had changed than I thought.

"Tomorrow," I said. That word had a different meaning now. I remember having said only that to him when I saw him at the breakfast table the day before he took me to the clinic. And now again, *Tomorrow*. When you said it like that, you didn't want it to be tomorrow.

"You need me to pick you up at the airport?" he asked. I guess that meant there weren't other plans to come and get me, not that I was surprised.

"If you want," I said, even though I did want him to, needed him to. I thought about the $40 in the wallet that would be returned to me tomorrow. Half of it would be gone if I used it to get to my parents' house via taxi and once I got there, what would happen if I showed up alone? *Hi, I'm home, or whatever.*

"You staying with Mom?" my brother asked, like he could feel my hesitation. Yes, he knew me that well. He knew my parents that well.

"Where else am I going to stay?" I asked. Sure, I had thought about it, but the answers all came up empty. I had no one else and as sad as that was, I was still trying to find *anywhere* else to go.

"You could stay with me," he said.

Lisa Burstein

"What? Like in your room?" I joked, even though I could tell something was different. He was different.

"No, Cass, like in my whole apartment." He laughed.

"Since when?" I asked, playing it cool, even though my insides felt like they were buzzing like a phone. Maybe going home wouldn't be bad at all. My brother and me in our very own apartment. It would be the perfect place to hide until I figured out what the hell I was going to do with my life.

"Yeah." He paused. "I moved in with Marcy."

I stayed quiet on the line, trying to connect the dots. Marcy had been my brother's girlfriend since he got back from Afghanistan six months ago. I'd met her a few times and she reminded me of a Cocker Spaniel. Had hair the same color and texture and the same expectant face, like she was always waiting for someone to say something she could get excited about. I didn't think they were serious enough about each other to move in together, but maybe they had gotten that serious in the thirty days that I'd been gone. Maybe my being gone made him realize he needed to get his own life, allowed him to get his own life.

"She would be totally cool with you crashing here," he quickly added, like he was trying to cover up the words he'd just said.

"Oh," I said, knowing I needed to say something. There was a difference between crashing and living. Crashing meant a month tops — a month to figure out what the hell I was going to do next. Awesome.

That's what this last month was supposed to have accomplished and I'd only gotten as far as realizing I needed to forgive myself. It took thirty days to get there. Who knew how long it would take to figure out *how*.

I picked up a pen and drew a circle on the *Holiday Inn at the Arcata Airport* pad, kept outlining it over and over until it bled through to the next page.

"I thought you liked her," my brother finally said.

"I do," I said, still drawing that circle. But liking someone and living with her are two different things.

"Awesome," he said, "this is perfect." I could hear the nod of his head, his hundred-watt smile through his words, but he had a real, steady girlfriend now, so of course he was happy. Like I had been with Aaron before, well, before.

Like I had almost been with Ben.

Hopefully Marcy wouldn't turn out to be a total slime wench who would chop my brother's heart into cat food. Hopefully my brother had really finally found someone who would treat him the way he treated me. He deserved it. I didn't want to ruin it and I knew if I moved in with them, I would probably ruin it.

No, I would definitely ruin it, but where else did I have to go?

"I'll talk to her about it tonight," he said.

"Sure," I said, agreeing on the surface, agreeing because I had no better options, but inside I was tired of being a burden to him. That was never clearer than when he finally had the chance at a life.

"We can work it all out tomorrow when you're home," he said before he hung up.

Home.

It's Mom and Dad's house or my brother and Marcy's apartment. Home doesn't exist.

Lisa Burstein

The End
Fuck

Rawe was finally in her civilian clothes: high-waisted jeans and a denim button-down that made her look like she was ready to head to a rodeo. My time here was over, not like I needed Rawe's mom-jean-assed reminder in my face while she packed up her duffel.

Fanny Rawe's fanny saying good-bye in the way only it could.

She didn't even take the shuttle with me to the airport. Instead she walked me to the entrance of the hotel, shook my hand, and wished me luck. I tried not to think that I kind of really needed a hug. Not necessarily from her, but from anyone.

But this was what I got: my earrings, my brother's dog tags, and my cinnamon gum, followed by a handshake, *Good luck*, and her mom-jean ass walking away from me.

I knew that was what people said to you when your life was so shitty they didn't know what else to say. It's not like they could really say, *Have fun*, or, *See you around*, so they said, *Good luck*, like your life was magically going to improve from the truckload of suck it had been just because they told you that.

Like Rawe had said, though, words weren't magic. If my life was going to improve, it was up to me now.

Words hadn't been magic when Nez and I said good-bye, either. There was no *Abracadabra, we've been through a ton of shit together and now I finally like you*. There was just *Later, Cassie* and *Later, Wynona*, though I had to admit it was progress we used each other's first names.

Ben and I hadn't said good-bye. Not that, considering the way I'd left things, he would have gone out of his way to find me. But he'd been so constant, relentless, even. It felt strange that he'd left a hole on the end. Of course, if I really thought about it, that had been my fault.

I didn't want to admit it, but I was a girl who'd given up when I got here and was still giving up. Even when faced with the possibility of something good, I gave up, because it was easier than knowing it wouldn't last.

I guess it was for the best. Ben was dangerous, the kind of boy who made me feel.

I waited for the squat little van that was going to start my journey home. Maybe I would take the airport shuttle and make my flight and maybe I wouldn't. Rawe was gone and she

Lisa Burstein

didn't care. I was not her problem anymore. I wasn't anyone's problem anymore.

The shuttle pulled up and stopped. The helpful guy took my duffel and threw it on the rack. My earrings were back in my ears, my brother's dog tags were back around my neck, and I was chewing the recently returned cinnamon gum—sticking it in my mouth like French fries. My saliva was thick and sweet and made me feel like I was going to puke. I wanted to feel like I was going to puke. I wanted to feel anything other than the chilly fear I felt when I thought about what I might find when I landed.

Sure, my brother, but would Marcy be with him? Would he have told her anything about me? Would he have told her *everything* about me? Would she give me the same sad look the squeaky-white-shoed nurse did when she walked me down to the exam room? If my brother told her, she would.

I knew it was the look I would get every time she saw me: when she was getting me a blanket, a towel, making me eggs, treating me so much better than I deserved to be treated because she felt sorry for me.

I felt my brother's dog tags, cool from the air conditioning. I wondered if I would have to give them to her now.

I was the only person in the van. I could have gotten rid of the driver and taken his Holiday Inn Airport Shuttle all the way to the ocean. I pictured it parked on the beach. I would have started a bonfire, a new life, alone on the sand. It wasn't the worst idea I'd ever had—well, aside from the grand theft auto part.

The van stopped at the airport's passenger drop off and I got out. The helpful guy handed me my duffel bag, and I gave him a dollar even though I only had the $40 I'd come here with. I probably should have kept it in case things with my brother and his girlfriend went south.

Considering things until that point, how could I expect my life to go any other way? It was south and deeper south. It was the South Pole and hell.

I checked my duffel bag at the curb, walked into the airport, and looked up at the screen, searching for my gate. Even after having been back in society for two days, it still felt odd. All these people going places, living their lives, probably not crumpling into a mess of skin and sobbing when they got behind closed doors. Or maybe I was wrong. Turning Pines had taught me that there are a lot of different kinds of fucked-up people. It could only mean there were a lot of them.

They were all just dealing with their shit like I was. Some of them were just better at hiding it.

I found my gate number and started toward it, even though with each step I took, my mind was asking me the same question over and over. Was I really doing this? Really going home?

I could keep asking, but the truth was it didn't matter. I had nowhere else to go.

There was more than an hour until my flight. The gate was empty, just black leather chairs lined up in rows. Even the little desk up at the front where everyone went to complain was deserted. The screen behind it didn't even have my flight listed yet. Maybe my gate would change and I wouldn't even notice. Maybe I would get lucky enough to miss my flight. Yes, that would have felt lucky today.

Lisa Burstein

An earthquake without fatalities but rendering the airport nonoperational would have felt lucky today.

I wasn't tired, but I lay down on one of the benches and closed my eyes, listening to the sounds of the airport around me. The nasally voice over the intercom asking people to pick up white courtesy phones, the wheels of suitcases whirring, the sound of babies screaming and people murmuring to each other that they hoped that baby wasn't on their flight. And of course worse than all that—the sound of planes taking off. Planes that would eventually become the sound of one plane.

My plane.

I felt someone flick my nose. This person would be killed. Annihilated. My eyes shot open. My hands went immediately to fists.

"Don't say it." Ben held up his hands. "Fuck off, Ben," he said, moving his arms like a conductor indicating we were going to recite it together.

"Yes, that," I said, sitting up and rubbing my nose. I was acting like I couldn't care less that Ben was standing in front of me, but I was relieved, the wall around my heart melting with warm, sweet heat. He had come to say good-bye.

"We meet again," he said, sort of fake bowing, still trying to be cute. The thing was he didn't have to try that hard. He did look cute all cleaned up and ready to go home.

We were both in our street clothes, jeans that were as dark as the night had been at camp and T-shirts, but we were the same people we had been in the woods—the same lost people who found something in each other and were still trying to figure out what it was.

"Yeah, well, this is the only airport," I said, not knowing what else to do except to make my lips shoot out stupid small talk. I now understood why sometimes people just talked about the weather or the long line they were standing in. It was because intimacy was hard. Saying real things was hard and sometimes saying nothing was hard.

Especially when there was so much to say.

"Right," he said, nodding, waiting.

"So," I said.

"Well," he said.

"Uh-huh," I said.

"Yes," he said.

"Exactly," I said.

I just needed to say good-bye to him, but I couldn't stop thinking about our kiss. I hoped it was only on my mind because he was standing in front of me. I hoped this wasn't a new addition to the thoughts I couldn't stop. If so, there were way too many boys stuck in my head.

"This is dumb," he finally said, putting his hands in his back pockets and rocking on his heels.

I was glad he had the guts to point that out, because I didn't. He was right. There were a lot of things we needed to say to each other and they weren't one-word niceties. Not that I would have been willing to admit any of those things before he did.

"The thing is, Cassie," he said, rubbing the back of his neck in that way guys do when they are exasperated, "I don't really know what else to say. You don't want to hear what I have to say."

Lisa Burstein

"I do," I said. I did, but I also knew it wasn't fair for me to keep asking him to *tell me, give me, reassure me,* when I wasn't able to respond with the same.

Ben stood, waiting, maybe for me to jump into his arms, maybe for me to punch him in the nads.

I understood that, with me, it was hard to know what to expect.

"What am I supposed to do? We're leaving." I felt my eyes start to burn. I closed them. I was not crying, no fucking way, not again.

"I know," he said.

"So, whatever this was—" I moved my hand back and forth between us. "It's not anymore. Can't be anymore." My stomach felt queasy. It was wrong and I knew it, but I also knew it was necessary.

"We were a *was*?" he asked, those brown eyes of his trying to say a million things.

"No, Ben," I said, "we *are* a was."

"Who says?" he asked. He leaned down and kissed me and I let him, his lips taking me away from the airport and back into that night in the woods when it was just him and me, our lives on a beautiful pause that started and ended when our lips touched. He stroked the side of my face, barely touching it, like he was afraid I would wake up.

But I stayed in the dream. My abdomen filled with a yearning, an ache that might have made me fall to my knees if I were standing. I kept kissing him until the thought of him being so close to me, and soon being so far away, made it hard to breathe.

"You said you didn't want to hurt me again, so don't," I said, pulling away from him and touching my mouth. But I could still feel his lips there. Still wanted to feel them.

"You could come with me," he said.

"You're joking, right?" I asked. We'd known each other for a month. It was crazy for me to go with him. It was crazy for him to want me to. There was no way he could mean that.

Even though it sounded so good.

"This is sad," he said. "This is not how I wanted this to end."

He'd said it: *end*. The word I knew would come eventually. At least it was coming now.

"How did you want it to end?" I asked because I wanted the fantasy. I knew I couldn't have the reality, so I needed that at least.

"I didn't," he said, looking down. "I wanted you next to me. That's pretty much it."

It was what I'd wanted, too. Why was I still too scared to take it?

"You make it sound so easy," I said, picturing it in my mind. We were in a garage, he on his drum set, me sitting in front of the bass drum, so close I could feel the thump of it. Just listening to him play and not thinking, not wanting anything else but him next to me.

I hated Aaron for taking that away from me. I hated myself for allowing him to. But there it was. He had. Even with a boy like Ben, who was nothing like Aaron, who had proven it by getting to miles less than first base for most of the time we knew each other, he had.

"It should have been," he said, shaking his head and turning. Was I really going to let him go? Considering we both

Lisa Burstein

had different planes waiting for us, different lives waiting for us, was it even my decision?

"Ben." I didn't know what I was going to say, but I didn't want him to go.

"Cassie," he said, his back still to me.

"I'm sorry," I said.

"For what?" he asked.

I wanted to go to him. To kiss him again, right there in the middle of the airport like two people in the movies. If only it could be a movie so it could have ended there—with us kissing, with us not having to answer all the unanswered questions.

"For being me," I said.

"And you are?"

"Scared," I said, the word coming out shaky.

His eyes flicked to mine. "That's not you," he said. Then he walked out of the gate and away from me.

I guess this really was the end.

I sat there and told myself I wouldn't do anything until someone else came to the gate. Made a weird game of staying put. It was a good excuse, but the truth was my body hurt too much to move. It was the ache I'd felt at the clinic, multiplied exponentially, and I knew it was because I'd lost something I wouldn't have the chance to care about—again.

After ten minutes, I finally got up and went into the bathroom to splash cold water on my face.

The bathroom was empty. Good news, considering I couldn't deny it was possible that I went in there to do more than splash cold water on my face. I felt like maybe I was going to cry.

I stared at myself in the mirror, trying to fight the sting. It had been a long time since I really looked at myself. Even at the hotel I scurried out of the bathroom after brushing my hair, probably because I was afraid to. Afraid of seeing the girl I had become. I'd turned pale, thin, certainly not someone who had been in the wilderness for a month. Honestly, I looked more like someone who had been underground for thirty days.

I turned on the cold water and cupped it with my hands. So cold it hurt. I splashed it on my face, once, twice. I gulped handfuls of it. It dripped all over the front of my T-shirt. My wet chest burned in the air conditioning. This was the end. I might have been able to deal with that if I wasn't facing the beginning ahead of me alone.

Without Ben.

I was jolted by a male voice behind me. "What are you doing in here?"

I turned and found a policeman standing in the middle of the bathroom, hand on his holster.

My first thought: *Oh shit, not again*. My second thought: *This is a women's restroom and he is a man*.

My third thought: *Maybe he will take me somewhere and I won't have to go home*.

"Washing my face," I said, indicating the running faucet, my wet skin and shirt.

"Didn't you hear the announcement over the loud-speakers?" he asked, glancing behind me at the still running water. I took that as a cue to turn it off.

"Announcement?" I asked.

Lisa Burstein

He grimaced, which meant he wanted an answer, not a question.

"No," I said, looking up. There were no speakers in the bathroom that I could see.

"You can't be in here. The whole airport is being evacuated," he said, staring at me with cop eyes—anger with a touch of superiority.

"What?" I asked, still not understanding.

"Get moving," he said, not explaining, and waved his hand in a pushy scoot.

"Why are we being evacuated?" I asked. This was too weird. Too much like what I'd wanted so badly to come true that I couldn't even believe it.

"Less questions, more moving," he said, then added, "Don't make me tell you again," for emphasis, just like Rawe would have. I walked out into the terminal while he stayed behind in the bathroom looking for feet under stall doors.

The large hallways that lined the gates were filled with people streaming toward the exits. They weren't running but were definitely walking with purpose. It was organized chaos, people flowing out of the building, asking the same question I had with no answers. Policemen on megaphones and the overhead announcements were telling everyone to leave in an orderly fashion and that all their questions would be answered once they were safely outside.

Safely outside?

What was unsafe about being inside? I guess it wasn't an earthquake.

I couldn't help thinking about those alien movies my

brother loved. This was what they did when the space monsters came: rounded everyone up and forced them into pens like cattle. The thing was, unlike the scared and confused people around me, I didn't really care what had happened. I was glad to be doing anything other than waiting for my flight.

Other than thinking about Ben.

Aliens?

Sounds good to me.

Lab tests?

Sure thing, let me just bend over.

I followed everyone else out into the sunlight. The policemen had us line up in the parking lot like we were at school and had just had a fire drill.

Cops stood around the perimeter of the building along with TSA agents, their uniforms looking very navy and the emergency lights on their cars flashing very red and blue. Two officers were stringing yellow crime scene tape over the entrances. Two more had German shepherds on leashes sniffing around the passenger drop off area. Whatever had happened, it was major.

Alien major.

I heard two businessmen talking in line behind me, bitching about how they better not miss their flight because of this, something about a very important meeting with a very important client that would fuck up their very important life if they missed it. I could almost hear them sweating through their suits.

"I'm going to ass rape whoever is responsible for this. I cannot miss this flight," one of them said.

Lisa Burstein

The other one just said, *Mmm hmmm.* About as sad an agreement to someone's statement as I'd ever heard.

I was probably the only person in this whole airport who wasn't thinking what the guy behind me was thinking. Who was instead thinking the exact opposite—well, minus the ass rape part.

It was possible Ben was thinking it, too, or he could have finally decided he was so done with me that he wanted to get as far away as possible. I deserved it. He'd done everything he could to make things work and all I did was push him away.

"We meet again," he said, walking up next to me.

I almost jumped, so freaked out that I had just been thinking about him and he appeared. Though I had really been thinking about him since he'd left me at the gate.

"I already said good-bye." I was trying very hard to be the old Cassie, but he'd seen the new me, the girl whose layers had been stripped away like onion skin, who kissed back, who smiled, who slept next to him under oceans of stars. Who couldn't really say good-bye.

"Not properly," he said, tapping his thumb ring against my hand. "I really didn't like the way that went down."

"So does that mean we're saying good-bye again?" I asked, not telling him to move his hand. Liking the way the metal of his ring still felt cold from the air conditioning while his skin felt hot.

"Well, maybe not," he said, still tapping his thumb ring but not taking my hand, like he was testing me. Maybe he was. There was something about the way he kept trying. There weren't many boys who could deal with my bullshit and still want more.

"So what are we doing?" I asked.

"Good question," he said. "I guess we'll find out." His eyes moved to the front of the airport, scanning the nodding cops and the TSA agents standing like columns on a building.

"What does that mean?" I asked.

He whispered in my ear, his breath like the heat of an oven, "This might be my doing."

"This?" I asked, looking around me: the cops, the crime scene tape, the cars with siren lights blaring, every person in the airport lined up like they were giving away free donuts.

He nodded, so imperceptibly that if it were a sports game, they would have needed a slo-mo replay to see it.

"What the fuck did you do?" I whispered. If Ben really did do this, the guy behind me was going to turn him into a drummer who might never sit down again—not comfortably, anyway.

"What I had to," he said.

I stared at him, at his brown, brown eyes, liked iced tea in the sunlight. "You didn't do this," I said, shaking my head.

"Well, not for real." He moved his lips so close to my ear I shivered. "But I might have kind of called in a bomb threat."

I pushed him hard, hard enough that he almost fell. "Are you fucking crazy?"

"Hey," the businessman behind me said, "the last thing we need is a riot."

His friend agreed with a more emphatic, *Mmm hmmm.*

I pulled Ben to the back of the line, away from everyone else. "You are," I said. "You're fucking crazy." I pushed him again.

Lisa Burstein

"Yes," he said, rubbing his chest where I'd hit him. "I told you, Cassie, I'm as fucked up as you are."

"This is beyond fucked up," I said, my words feeling like deflating balloons coming out of my mouth, shooting and flying around his head. "Why? Why would you do this?"

"For you," he said.

"What?" I asked.

"For you," he said again, titling his head to the side like he couldn't understand why I was confused.

"That makes no sense. I don't want this." I indicated the chaos around me, the contents of a whole airport spilled out onto the parking lot and held like prisoners.

"No," he said, "but I knew I'd regret it if I let you get on that plane. And I know you're more stubborn than anyone I've ever met." He paused. "So I got creative."

"Letting a skunk into the airport wouldn't have worked this time, huh?" I asked, not breaking his gaze.

"No." He smiled. "I needed something a little more dramatic."

"You could go to jail for this for a long, long time. Longer than for whatever you didn't do to get sent to Turning Pines." I was still talking so fast, as fast as the lights seemed to be spinning on the cop cars. I tried not to stare at them, tried not to think that everything good in my life ended with the color red.

"I just didn't get caught for any of the things I've done," he said, "and today won't change that. I had my brother call it in—he owes me."

There was so much noise around us. So much happening around us, but I could only hear him, only see him.

"I want to be with you," Ben said, grabbing my forearm. "Even if it's only for another couple of hours."

I let the words fill my ears, fill my chest. Let the warmth of his hand travel from my arm to my belly. It didn't seem real.

"What are you going to do, keep calling in bomb threats so I never can fly out of here?" I asked. It was totally crazy, but it was also totally, insanely romantic. I usually hated romantic, but maybe that was because romantic was perfumey flowers and sappy love songs and lame-ass teddy bears. It was never enough to put someone away for ten years.

It was never someone who was willing to put himself on the line to prove he was "unworthy" of me.

"If I have to," he said. "Or maybe I'll use the time I have left to convince you . . . or kiss you."

"You're wasting time, then," I said, my lips on his before the words were even out of my mouth. I kissed him once, gently on the lips, and pulled back like I needed to see him again to believe he was still there. There—like he always had been, and if I knew Ben, like he always would be.

He held his hand out, stretching his fingers in a way that let me know he was asking for so much more than just my hand, than just a kiss.

I knew I had to forgive myself. This was how to start. There was no better way than to do the one thing in this world that had the potential to make me happy.

I wasn't sure what choosing Ben would mean. I wasn't sure how long it would last. I wasn't sure if I would get hurt again, but for him I could try.

For me, I could try.

Lisa Burstein

I took his hand. He tapped his thumb ring against the top of mine with a beat that was in his head. We walked away from the airport, away from the parking lot. I didn't know where we were going. I didn't know how long we had, but I followed him.

He is the kind of boy who makes me feel, but he can also help me forget.

The forgiveness will come.

Acknowledgments

First, I want to thank the publishing gods who found their way to giving me their blessing on a second book.

Then of course there are all the people who made this possible:

My tireless, genius editor, Stacy Cantor Abrams, who takes my words, my vision, and gives me the tools to turn them into something amazing. She makes me look far more talented than I am.

My agent, Susan Finesman, who stands by me book after book, and who gave me some of the best advice I've ever gotten by reminding me that I can never know what the next day will bring, in life or in publishing.

My publicist, Heather Riccio, who is as much friend, psychologist, drill sergeant, and ninja as publicist. Her enthusiasm for my work is infectious.

Kari Bradley and Alycia Tornetta, whose editorial notes were spot on and who were the best extra sets of eyes I could have hoped for, for Cassie.

Liz Pelletier for her editorial wisdom, unwavering leadership, and the fact she admits that my work makes her cry.

My publisher-sisters at Entangled and in the Entangled Teen Mafia, some of the best women and writers I've ever met. I can't imagine this journey without you.

My Twitter and Facebook followers, who are always there to help me with a line or an idea, with a special shout-out to Jennifer Iacopelli who provided one of the main plot points in *Dear Cassie*.

The readers and bloggers who loved Cassie enough to think she deserved her own book and who have become my friends. Your support means everything.

Finally, to my family, for listening, letting me write, allowing me to be crazy, and keeping me sane.

Acknowledgments

Sometimes date is a four-letter word

**Experience where Cassie's story began
with _Pretty Amy_**

Amy is fine living in the shadows of beautiful Lila and uber-cool Cassie, because at least she's somewhat beautiful and uber-cool by association. But when their dates stand them up for prom, and the girls take matters into their own hands—earning them a night in jail outfitted in satin, stilettos, and Spanx—Amy discovers even a prom spent in handcuffs might be better than the humiliating "rehabilitation techniques" now filling up her summer. Worse, with Lila and Cassie parentally banned, Amy feels like she has nothing—like she is nothing.

Navigating unlikely alliances with her new coworker, two very different boys, and possibly even her parents, Amy struggles to decide if it's worth being a best friend when it makes you a public enemy. Bringing readers along on an often hilarious and heartwarming journey, Amy finds that maybe getting a life only happens once you think your life is over.

A Note from Lisa Burstein

As a thank-you to my awesome readers, I held a contest in honor of *Dear Cassie* being an epistolary novel, where entrants would write a diary entry in the voice of their favorite fictional character. The grand prize was one lucky entry being published in the back of the book. I chose four finalists and then people voted online for their favorites.

Read on for the the winning entry by Monica Fumarolo . . .

INSPIRED BY THE TV SHOW *DOCTOR WHO*

Amelia Pond was seven when a spaceship crashed in her yard and out climbed a time traveler: the Doctor. She was quickly taken with the man and crushed when he didn't return like he'd promised. In his absence, people called her crazy for always insisting her "imaginary friend" was real. Twelve years later, he came back, bringing along danger and adventure. But that was two years ago, and he'd since vanished as quickly as he'd appeared. Now, the night before her wedding, Amy thinks of the excitement she experienced with the Doctor, not sure she's really ready to settle down just yet.

*

People have said I'm mad for fourteen years, but I never really started believing it until now. Because now, right now, I should be excited. Ecstatic. Over the moon and completely happy because they say tomorrow is the biggest day of my life.

They would say that, though, because they also say I'm mad. That a man in a blue box didn't really fall out of the sky and into my life *twice,* save all of humanity, change everything, then disappear again. If meeting the Raggedy Doctor and helping him save the world weren't the biggest days of my life, then I really don't think a wedding can top that.

Even if it is my wedding. Even if it is to Rory.

Amelia Pond became Amy Pond, and now I'm about to become Mrs. Amy Williams. I think I had an easier time accepting the fact that the Doctor landed outside this very house in a time machine that looks like a police box.

And that's the thing that makes me start to believe that everyone else really was right about me all along. I mean, Rory really is *great.* He is a good guy and he loves me and he's all kinds of dependable and reliable and stable. He even put up with an entire childhood of my forcing him to play Raggedy Doctor with me, trying to bring my imaginary friend to life just to make me happy. If he was willing to do all that, even when we were just kids, then I know that he'll do just about anything for me.

I know that we'll have a very nice life together here in

A Note From Lisa Burstein

Ledworth, with him as a nurse in hospital and me doing . . .
something. I'm sure I'll find something . . .

Only that's not true. I'm *not* sure. Because as nice as Ledworth is, it's just Ledworth. Here I'm the crazy girl who was a kiss-o-gram and stayed up all night in the garden when she was a little girl, waiting for a time machine to take her away because an equally crazy man who ate fish fingers and custard promised he would come back.

He did come back, technically, I suppose. He came, the Atraxi left, and there's no longer an alien living in my house (I hope).

It was dangerous and insane.

It was brilliant.

And I want more of that. I want to have big adventures and do more impossible things and see more impossible places. I want to know who the Doctor is and why he came here and why he picked me and why he stopped and took the time for me and a crack in my wall.

I want to see more cracks in the universe, whatever that means. It sounds like something that only ever happens once in Ledworth if you're really lucky, and now that it has, how can I ever dream of something so big happening in my life again as long as I stay here?

When I say it like that, though, it sounds all wrong. It sounds like I don't even care about Rory, but I do. It's just . . . It's hard to say what it is exactly. I'm scared. I know I want to marry him. I do know that, but it's tomorrow. Tomorrow. It's really here. Years of dating, months of planning, and there's nothing left to do but wake up in the morning, put on that dress, and walk down the aisle. It's only a few hours away now.

A Note From Lisa Burstein

What I guess all of this comes down to, though, is a plea for more time. More time for something to happen. The first time the Doctor left, it was hard. I suddenly felt even more alone here than ever before, even more so than when I was just the Scottish girl trapped in an English town. I still refused to give up on him, though. I waited twelve years and then something amazing did happen. And now it's been another two and I think if I had more time, I could keep waiting if I knew for sure that it would mean incredible, impossible things were in store.

But wishing only does so much. It can't make time machines show up or adventures unfold, so it's probably just as well that I go to bed, because tomorrow it really is time to grow up.

Or maybe not. Because I just looked out the window, and you'll never guess what's in the garden. Or who.

Monica Fumarolo is a Chicago-area native, two-time University of Illinois at Urbana-Champaign graduate, librarian by day, and aspiring writer by night who is thrilled to see her writing in print for the first time.

A Note From Lisa Burstein